ALL'S FAIR IN WAR

ALL'S FAIR IN WAR

BIRTH OF HEAVY METAL™ BOOK 8

MICHAEL TODD

MICHAEL ANDERLE

DISRUPTIVE IMAGINATION

LMBPN Publishing
PMB 196, 2540 South Maryland Pkwy
Las Vegas, NV 89109

First US edition, September 2019
Version 1.04, December 2025
eBook ISBN: 978-1-64202-477-7
Print ISBN: 978-1-64971-676-7

ALL'S FAIR IN WAR TEAM

JIT Readers

Jeff Eaton
Dave Hicks
Deb Mader
Peter Manis
Micky Cocker
Diane L. Smith
John Ashmore
Jeff Goode
Kelly O'Donnell
Dorothy Lloyd

Editor
Skyhunter Editing Team

DEDICATION

*To Family, Friends and
Those Who Love
to Read.
May We All Enjoy Grace
to Live the Life We Are
Called.*

CHAPTER ONE

Captain Francesca Martin of the French Foreign Legion shook her head and took another sip of coffee as she tried to decide where the fuck everything had gone wrong around there. Most of the reasons were fairly obvious.

Scientists play with shit they don't understand, and people don't care about the consequences of their actions. They only see the potential profits that could be made from what has been created out there.

Which was why, she assumed, they hadn't bombed the absolute crap out of the Zoo when it became obvious that things were out of control. That was how it inevitably went.

All people can see are the possible benefits of this jungle, not the fact that it is there to devour them all and has transformed into a living, breathing nightmare no one can escape.

Despite these somewhat cynical thoughts, the environment had begun to grow on her. By now, she was accustomed to the view that came with living this close to the Zoo. While she counted the days until she was cycled out of there again, she had adjusted fairly quickly and the various unique aspects of it had become familiar.

"That's the Zoo paradox. You hate it and you love it, and if you stay too long, you can't live without it. Even when you know it'll kill you one day."

She stretched languidly as the sun rose lazily in the gray morning sky and brought to mind a song that had been a familiar part of her childhood. Admittedly, the Sahara wasn't the savanna, but the kind of view that sprawled before her brought that particular song to her head every time she saw a scene like this. Even now, she could hear, deep within her, the high-pitched singing in Swahili and the sight of animals drifting and gathering to see a lion that had recently been born.

The paradox in that lingered too. They might well be that little lion's food eventually, but in that moment, they celebrated the mysterious cycle of life.

"That's living, I guess. Today, we celebrate because tomorrow, we could be dead."

She shook her head to clear the maudlin thought. Her smile returned when she breathed in the crisp morning air laced with the unmistakable and addictive aroma of coffee from the mug in her hands.

Out in the east lay the Zoo and its powerful reality haunted the collective nightmares of the people who thought too much about it. The jungle was shrouded in mystery—the kind that people lost their lives over. Everyone knew the American government was involved but the question was, why had it all started? No one had ever addressed the question of why the original missile had been launched to earth.

News reports had intimated that its origins were the result of an alien missile that had been launched toward the planet a few years before. Some people still considered this merely the platform for conspiracy theories, though. None of these naysayers believed that the goop that had somehow grown a jungle in the middle of the world's largest desert originated from alien intelligence.

"No surprise there. Admitting this implies the acceptance that it was launched deliberately toward Earth. I can see why people might find that disturbing."

Of course, having seen the Zoo, she could understand why they reacted that way. People who made sure to stay far, far away from the jungle could be the smart ones at the end of the day—although it merely bolstered their blindness. They were able to avoid looking at the monstrosities the Zoo produced and somehow convince themselves that this was totally, one hundred percent natural.

Anyone who had never been there might be tempted to agree. It was far better than considering the alternative— that an alien race had deliberately set out to create a hell on Earth. Still, it was ironic. They called those who told the stories of what they found crazy but hell, anyone who studied the facts knew the naysayers were the crazy ones.

And if the facts can't convince you, the Zoo can. From the moment she had stepped into the jungle, the truth was frighteningly obvious. There were too many indicators— the trees at night when the blue lights seeped through their bark and the monsters that were spawned by the damned place.

Oh, and the fact that no matter how logically you try to

determine where the fuck they come from, all you can think is that none of it belongs in the sane, rational world.

She sighed and swallowed the last sip of her coffee before she returned to her little apartment. Her routine was such that she didn't need much time to prepare for the day. A quick shower, after which she donned the clothes she'd chosen the day before, left her time to run an efficient sweep through to clean. She turned all the lights off since she probably would not return for a while and headed out, making sure to lock the door behind her before she scrambled into the vehicle that had been requisitioned for the mission the day before.

"Okay, this seat was used by someone who was either too big to be human or had worn a combat suit." It took a moment to adjust it. She could most likely assume it was the latter, but given the sheer degree of strange shit she had been subjected to over the past few months, she wouldn't write anything off, at this point.

They would all have to deal with strange fucking shit before too long, and she needed to get herself into the right mindset for it.

Her group was already waiting by the time she arrived at the edge of the French base. They had given her a team of twelve—about the same number they assigned to the deep patrol missions they sent into the Zoo. The Americans liked to do that more often, but her people seemed to think they needed to pull their weight in this fucking hellhole.

At least the mission they assigned us isn't the simple patrol bullshit that makes us risk our lives for absolutely nothing.

On the bright side, all that time spent in the Zoo—

doing nothing and merely marching around while they waited for the monsters to attack them—had provided her with a team that excelled at what they did. All were survivors and veterans of at least a dozen missions into the jungle. She wouldn't have to teach the ropes to even one newcomer.

Martin disliked newcomers. The fact that they were stupid enough to volunteer for this kind of posting was indicative of the quality she could expect. She had sat on her ass in French Guiana and run training missions into the Amazon. Which, she assumed, was why her commanders in the FFL had decided she was one of their best special forces choices to join their new base in the Zoo.

Back in the day, she'd heard all the stories and watched some of the videos. Even then, she hadn't believed the kind of crazy shit that came out of it—which had made her one of those stupid newcomers, she acknowledged. Experience had taught her how to handle it, though.

"But the jury is still out on what staying here after I realized the kind of crazy shit that goes on says about my mental health." She chuckled and slid out of the vehicle.

"Good morning, Captain," one of her men said, and the rest of the team looked up from their work on the suits that had been assigned to them. The combat armor was some of the best that could be seen in the army. In terms of defense, functionality, and offense, you could only get anything better when you were in the private sector. They still needed to work and adjust each suit individually, though.

Simply because they were good didn't mean they hadn't been pushed off an assembly line, which meant they had to deal with the issues that arose from that. These could be anything from the suit being a little too small to the weapons not being properly calibrated. You didn't want to get into the Zoo and only then realize your weapons worked off the hair-trigger settings the last person who had worn the suit had set them to.

It was a nice combination of functionality and ritual like putting themselves into the mindset they needed to be in before they stepped willingly into the most dangerous place on earth.

"Good morning, Sergeant," she replied and moved to the crate that was marked as her suit. A couple of Hammerheads had been brought to drive them into the Zoo, but she didn't want to think about that yet. At the moment, all she thought about was getting into her damned armor.

The helmet came first, and she activated the HUD and called up the details. The factory settings were still there, which meant this hadn't been used by anyone. She smiled when she realized that maybe she had to deal with a newbie in there after all.

"Is there any word on what exactly we'll do inside the jungle?" the sergeant asked. He'd mostly finished with his suit and came to help her with hers. "Or will we only be filled in once we're in there? It seems like a stupid way to run things but sometimes, the brass likes to put confidentiality over the lives of the people they send in. We're...almost over that shit."

"Oh." Martin grunted and strapped her boots on first. "No, I assumed you had all been briefed along with me. There were none of the usual confidentiality markings on the file they sent me, so I'll fill everyone in once we're all suited up and ready to go."

"We'd all appreciate that, Captain," he replied with a nod and stepped back when she finished putting her boots on and began to work on the other pieces. It took her about ten minutes, by which time she could see the sun already sneaking higher into the sky. It was completely free of the horizon and well into its daily trip up and down again.

When she turned, the other members of her team were mounting up and it was obvious that they waited for her to fill them in on the details of yet another mission into the goddammed jungle. She scanned the information on their mission reports—the ones that had been sent to them, which were different from what had been sent to her, annoyingly enough.

Immediately, she saw that they simply stated a prolonged trip. The only detail provided was that it had nothing to do with the regular patrol paths and that they would go deep inside the jungle to procure something.

The fact that they'd told her exactly what the purpose of the mission was and hadn't told the other boots on the ground felt like an attempt to keep the regular grunts in the dark as to what exactly they were doing.

She'd been around long enough that she could read an order of confidentiality between those lines, but no matter. If they had told her outright, she would have told them then and there it was a mistake. But, as they seemed to want her to infer it, she would choose to ignore their unspoken orders and let the chips fall where they might.

The chances of the team surviving were improved if they all worked together toward a common goal. Of course, that tended to be successful if they knew what they worked toward.

"All right, ladies, listen up," Martin snapped and called them to attention over the team's comm line. Their Hammerheads started and they pulled off toward the massive expanse of jungle that spread across the horizon. "I'm not sure why the brass didn't fill you in on what we're doing out here, and I don't give a shit. As it turns out, the best way for you useless assholes to watch my back is to know what we're heading in there to hunt, so I'll fill you in."

She sent the images she had been given to their individual HUDs and gave them a moment to study them. All were of a fleshy monster that looked like it only had a place in the Zoo, unfortunately—like it had a lead role in the horror film all the creatures of the Zoo had been cast in.

A couple of curses in a handful of languages were voiced while her teammates flipped through the variety of images that had been taken by some unlucky bastard who had managed to get closer to the creature than she thought was comfortable.

At the center of it was a thick, fleshy blob—roughly oval in shape and dark-green to greyish-brown in color. She couldn't tell the size precisely due to the quality of the images, but a solid guess could be made.

Her estimate was that it was around two or three meters in diameter, but from the looks of some of the other images, it seemed to be able to dig itself deeply into the ground. There was no telling how deep it could dig in, and she didn't want to think about the fact that what they could see might only be the tip of the proverbial iceberg.

Then again, more distracting features were easily discernible to focus on anyway. A horde of mouths was spaced across the fleshy blob that constituted its body almost like it was a conglomeration of somethings that had melded into one creature. Hundreds if not thousands of tentacles protruded from the body and filled the space around it as if to work as eyes, ears, and limbs all in one.

The most obvious—and appalling—truth was that they worked together with the singular purpose of dragging anything unlucky enough to be caught in the tentacles toward the waiting mouths lined with hundreds of needle-like teeth.

"*Putain merde*," one of the soldiers cursed. "What the fuck is that thing?"

"It is a monster that was caught on tape during the mission to retake the Russian base," Martin explained. "Yes, I know we all had fun mocking the bastards for losing control of their base, but now that we know what was involved in it, I understand. It is not to say we won't continue to mock them for it, but still.

"Anyway, in the effort to reclaim the base, a group of mercs they hired to rescue survivors took the footage you see now. As uncomfortable as it might be, we will have to look at it since that is what we have been sent into the damn Zoo to find. They don't have a name for it yet and the specialists and researchers are still coming up with something for that. I don't even want to think about what kind of inspiration they'll work with since we all know those guys are fucked in the head, but that's not our problem.

"What is our problem is that we've been ordered to

head into the jungle to fight our pretty little monsters, tear them all a new one, and find evidence of the existence of the monster in question. It's not that the people in charge don't trust the mercs who were hired, but...

Well, okay, the feeling is that while they know they can take their word on it, the brass wants to know if we're likely to run into any more of the fuckers—and, I can only hope, to finally make the decision to nuke this whole fucking continent from existence. But that's neither here nor there. For now, we head in, take footage of the beast, and get out, understood?"

"Yes, ma'am," the team replied in unison. She had the feeling they had all begun to wish she had taken the hint and kept this crazy shit from them.

CHAPTER TWO

The low, deep thud of the music in the next room was less than conducive to the work ethic they liked to surround themselves with. *I suppose I could think of it as an occupational hazard.* Brian Haynes chuckled and wondered if he should refill his glass.

His gaze wandered the various groups that clustered around the bar and food and he grimaced. As always, little cliques formed as different departments huddled together and tried to have fun. *Some try harder than others*, he thought when he noticed a knot of techies clustered in the far corner. They seemed to be on the minus side of even a pretense at trying.

Haynes and Haynes was a law firm that specialized in corporate law and defended and protected some of the largest corporations in New York. Sometimes, they worked to make sure the people involved in the companies were protected preemptively. This meant they specialized in anticipating possible lawsuits and preparing any company involved for the inevitable fallout. It was, in fact, how they made most of their money.

People often asked how they were able to get ahead of potential crises like that. *And I suppose simply saying it's common fucking sense isn't good business acumen.* Instead, the partners always told their clients there was a whole methodology involved.

At that point, they talked about a computer algorithm that allowed them to read contracts and the like and anticipate any kind of problems that might arise from the available paperwork based on state and federal laws, as well as legal precedent. *Those in upper-management positions love being told there was an algorithm involved. It makes them feel like they operate on the cutting edge.*

And, in fairness, they weren't completely bullshitting their clients. There were computers that were almost entirely dedicated to the job of anticipating problems and suggesting solutions beforehand.

"It's unfortunate that the people working on those and who are in charge of keeping the clients safe from a legal perspective are irrelevant, he muttered quietly into his drink.

His gaze lingered on the small group he'd noticed and he shook his head. The clients were happy to know that computers guarded them against lawsuits, and it was simply good business sense to let them think that and not burden them with the semantics of it.

There were upsides to this, of course. It gave them a unique marketing pitch to toss to their team that ran that side of things. They could thus ensure there were people intrigued by a trademarked algorithm and could secure their business with their almost impeccable record.

It wasn't the most honest of strategies, perhaps. But, as long as what they called their desk specialists were happy to be paid well above the market average for their computer science degrees, they were willing to not be involved in the marketing process at all.

The downside, of course, is the parties. Some might beg to differ, but his appraisal of the year-end party currently in progress merely confirmed his opinion that it was a significant negative factor. These events were intended to boost morale and to some extent, it served its purpose. Unfortunately, a solid half of the company were the kind of people whose morale would be better boosted if they were at home and enjoying their bonuses in their own safe spaces, and that kind of took the wind out of the sails.

The other partners should have listened to my suggestion that they invest in another way to boost the morale of the team. They heard me out but, as always, responded that they would wait until after this last party to see what the best alternative would be. Another good opportunity lost.

He did enjoy his vindication, in this case, and took care not to seem smug. At the same time, he was stuck at a celebration where half those present did not want to attend, and he quickly found himself included in those numbers. These people had worked hard all year, and they all deserved to be invited to an event that would be their kind of party, no matter what tastes they had. Of course, Haynes and Haynes could not provide everyone with what they wanted but still, they could make an effort.

On this occasion, a large buffet of expensive food had laid on at a house party that occupied the penthouse of a building not two blocks from where the company held their offices. The group of thirty or so were treated to the best of food and an open bar, as well as a professional DJ who played music for the dance floor. All this lavish indulgence took place against a backdrop of a fantastic view of the New York City skyline.

To most groups, that would be enough to raise their spirits and make sure they were more than happy to keep up the hard work they'd delivered all year. Of course, it had the subtle purpose to ensure that they knew how much money they had made for the company, how much money they were making, and the nature of the very exclusive club they were now a part of.

The results were less than inspiring, of course. Half the group were more than happy to enjoy all the benefits on offer, indulged excessively in the open bar, and took to the dance floor with gusto they probably shouldn't have, given their lack of skill. Still, he couldn't fault them for their enthusiasm.

The other half had enjoyed the food, of course, and partook in the drink to a point, but they weren't a fan of the loud, thud-thudding pop music remixes their DJ provided for them. For the first hour or so of the festivities, they stood around a little awkwardly, checked their phones, and waited until an appropriate time for them to simply leave.

Brian talked to a couple of them and listened to their complaints as well as their suggestions for what would make this party more worthwhile and enjoyable for them. One suggestion in particular piqued his attention, and it wasn't long before a couple of massive TVs arrived, brought with some of the highest-end consoles. There was an option for a couple of the newer VR rigs, but that was ridiculously expensive.

Still, his efforts were appreciated. As it turned out, those people who spent most of their time working in front of a screen spent much of their free time in front of a screen as well. The games presented were some of the new game releases—one of which was based in the quasi-mythical Zoo, a possibly alien jungle that had sprouted out of the Sahara Desert.

It provided the options to play alongside a group of other players—either present in the room or over the Internet—to kill wave after wave of the Zoo monsters Brian could only imagine were the fruits of the imagination of the game developers. Or players could team up with others to fight against other teams for the control of various points of the jungle maps.

The game looked fun and energetic, and it certainly made sure those who were interested enjoyed themselves while those who weren't interested could stick to the music, food, and drink.

There was a reason why Brian Haynes was one of the senior partners of the firm, and it wasn't only because his father and uncle were the founders of Haynes and Haynes. It was because he knew how to manage his people and keep them happy and well-paid. He'd made sure to learn this since it was the best way to make sure they kept the proverbial wheels of the company well-oiled and running smoothly.

They were all in this together, after all, and while he did

make a good deal more than his employees, he wanted to ensure it could never be said that he simply rode on the laurels of his parentage.

He sighed softly, shook his head, and moved to the other side of the penthouse, where the massive TVs displayed unbelievable amounts of violence against both the monsters of the Zoo and other people in the game. Brian narrowed his eyes as one of the suited characters in the game attacked with a sword instead of the assault rifles most of the other players used.

This drew considerable complaints from the other players online about how quick it was to kill someone with the blade. It took a single slash with the weapon but required three or four shots from the firearms to do the same.

"I'm not saying it's not overpowered," one of his employees—whom he recognized as Freddie Encarnacion —said. "But when you think about it, the need to come in close and lose the safety of distance, all while being shot at, levels it out. I think so, anyway."

Brian realized that both the TVs had been assigned, one to what they called PVE—which he assumed meant Player versus Environment—while the other had been reserved for the people who wanted PVP, or Player versus Player. Everyone seemed to be organized about it, and while there weren't enough controls for all the people present, those who waited their turn sat in another corner and watched something on their phones. They projected the images on the nearby walls, which enabled them all to watch in relative comfort although with iffy quality.

Surprise of surprises, of course, was the fact that they watched videos about the Zoo.

"Come on," one of their programmers protested and shook her head in disbelief. "Okay, I understand they are bringing some of the animals from the Zoo into the games to give it some modicum of grounding in reality. But when you think about it, the monsters in the jungle are much crazier than basically anything the devs might be able to think of, so why not simply use more of the Zoo monsters instead of creating their own?"

Another programmer nearby shrugged. "I don't know. They put two games out a year, plus all the expansion packs and DLCs, so when you come down to it, they'll run out of creatures to use eventually. Either they are pacing themselves and only use a handful of the real ones, then make the rest of them up so they have some left for future games, or... I don't know, they simply want to use their creativity when they make these games, which isn't that bad when you look at it that way. They come up with some original content, you know?"

"Fair enough, if you can call it creative," the woman—whose name Brian couldn't remember for the life of him—spoke again. "But look at the new ravagers—I see is a massive lawsuit coming from James Cameron, that's all I'm saying."

"That's obviously homage to the Alien movies." Her colleague laughed. "It could not be more obvious. It's an alien jungle, so of course you have to have xenomorphs and face-huggers. It's almost incomplete without them."

"I understand homage, which is why I'm still waiting for a predator race to jump into the current meta." She chuck-

led. "But...come on. When you have monsters like that one"
—she gestured at the video—"you don't need to spend all
that much time being creative. Simply bring that one and
you're good for a while, right?"

Brian's gaze drifted to the screen and he lost focus on
the conversation. It was important to listen to what his
employees said, but he felt a little context was needed in
this particular situation.

From what he understood, they watched a video from
the content streamer called ZooTube that dealt almost
exclusively in content from or related to the location in
question. It had started as a quick and efficient way for
researchers to share the footage they'd collected inside the
jungle, but it quickly gained traction with the people who
were curious about exactly what happened there.

It wasn't long before content from inside the Zoo was
joined by streams of games based on it, along with a
handful of original films and TV series. The market was
growing and one of the most popular channels on the site
was called Heavy Metal, based on a merc group of the same
name that worked from the American base.

Haynes hated the fact that he knew so much about
them—only due to the fact that he'd worked on paperwork
for one of the gaming companies that needed access to
some of the intellectual property that came from the Heavy
Metal team. There was still considerable speculation
around who owned the channel since the footage that was
used was usually from five or six different perspectives.
There were names involved, but he couldn't recall too
much about them.

The monster currently under discussion was, of course,

a doozy. It was huge and fleshy, with a seemingly limitless number of mouths filled with terrifyingly sharp teeth and hundreds of tentacles that sprouted from its body.

"Okay, how the hell do you think they can incorporate a critter like that in Hellgate 4?" the second programmer asked, leaned back, and folded his arms. He glanced up and startled when he saw Brian. "Oh—hey, boss. Great party, huh?"

"You tell me." He chuckled. "I'm only the host. You guys need to have fun for me to have fun. So…uh, you are all fans of this stuff, huh?"

"Yeah," the first said quickly and firmly. "Honestly, even having possible aliens among us is exciting, don't you think?"

"Well, the concept is, sure," he said cautiously. "The reality? I'd have to say, no thanks. I have something of a queasy stomach and I'm not one for violence either. How—how are they operating that Hammerhead?"

His eyes were on a trio of vehicles that had been modified to work with weapons and a variety of other defenses, all of which helped the group in their efforts to fight back the attacking beasts. They coordinated well and worked as a team to keep the monsters at bay. From what he could tell, the weapons on the Hammerhead operated to keep the middle ground clear of the smaller creatures that tended to attack in swarms.

"It looks like they might have one extra member of the team inside running the weapons," the first programmer said and squinted to try to see more clearly.

"If there are three, wouldn't they need three extra members inside?" Brian wondered. If he was ever so unlucky as to head into the Zoo himself, he would make that particular responsibility his. Staying as far away from the action was priority number one.

"Sure, three," the second programmer agreed. "But watch that shooting. Look at the way it picks off the larger monsters with rockets while it distracts them down low with the Gatling guns. That kind of coordination and precision isn't possible for humans, not even with machine help. That there is run by a computer. I'd even go so far as to say that's an AI. And yes, thinking about it, I'd even take that one step further and say it's a combat AI."

"Aren't those still in development?" the woman asked.

"Yes, they are," Brian grumbled under his breath, narrowed his eyes, and hastily made a mental note of and memorized the name of the video before he backed away and headed toward one of the bathrooms, his phone in hand. Once safely in a private place, he pressed one of the numbers he had on speed dial, held the device to his ear, and sighed in frustration when it began to ring.

"Hi, Patrice?" he said and tried to fake a smile in his voice. "Could you connect me to Darren, please? I have something here I think he needs to see."

CHAPTER THREE

No, working for the Russian government isn't entirely boring. It had its unappealing moments but was certainly the best way to gain experience in the computer sciences field while also being paid for it. Hundreds of companies wanted people like him to work for them and eventually get paid, but all the starting positions in those companies were unpaid internships. Beto Vasili was not the kind of guy who agreed to that kind of crap. He intended to be paid for his work.

The FSB paid rather well, all things considered. They had offered him a job and acceded to or were willing to compromise on his every request. They knew most of the people with his credentials would be able to find work elsewhere without too much trouble—if they were willing to accept a whole other kind of crap. That said, once contracts were signed and he sat in his little cubicle, he'd found accepting that kind of work always came with a more or less proportionate price.

In this case, it was that they expected him to live up to

the kind of money they paid him. They were willing to offer a salary that was competitive with the private sector for a starting-level position. In exchange, he had to give up most of his social life, virtually every kind of connection to his family, and thanks to the horde of Non-disclosure Agreements they had made him sign, any ability to talk about his work. Some people might have found all of that irksome, but it worked out fairly well for him, given that he never had much time to talk to friends or family anyway.

He ended up making friends with the people he worked with. They were operatives in name and rank, although the name made much more of the job than he thought it should. They sat around, processed communications, and made sure no one else listened in on what was said.

It was, in essence, a desk jockey job, and they all reveled in it. They knew what they were doing, and there were three or four volumes of protocols that told them how to do their job. The fact that these had been written by people whose last encounter with technology had been a type-writer was irrelevant. All it meant was there was more than enough time to sit around and do nothing while they kept their country safe.

Most of that time was spent reading news articles and keeping up with the latest gaming stream since they did have unfettered Internet access. They had all been around their work for long enough to be able to do it in their sleep —meaning they were now experts at multitasking.

"Hey, Beto," his cubicle neighbor Artem called and pushed his desk chair out far enough that they could talk to each other face-to-face instead of over cubicle walls.

"What's up, Ar?" he replied and pretended to have his eyes glued on the screen in front of him. "Can't you see I'm insanely busy... Hah, I couldn't even finish that with a straight face. What's up, buddy?"

"I'm only here to make sure you are up to date with your viral video checklist," Artem said and imitated the gruff and somewhat nasal voice of their commanding officer. "Are you...up to date, Beto?"

"That depends." He tried not to laugh at the almost perfect impression. "What kind of trouble would I be in if I wasn't? Will you spank me?"

The man made a face. "Why do you have to make everything so uncomfortable, man? I know it's a joke, but come on, seriously."

Beto rolled his eyes. "It's not my fault you don't have a sense of humor, Ar. But seriously, you never come here unless you have something juicy to share, so spill it. Now!"

"Again with making things dirty and uncomfortable," his colleague protested.

"How was that dirty?" he asked. It was true that most of his jokes ended up with something of a sexual nature, and even more so when Artem was around. The temptation was irresistible. The man had been raised in a very conservative home and any mention of sex or anything like it was bound to make him uncomfortable—most of the time. Not in this situation, though, but he was interested to find out the new and as yet untapped ways in which he could make the man squirm.

"Juicy," Artem explained. "Juicy is a word that brings to mind certain...things. And thoughts. And stuff."

"Well, you know that I would never want any of those

particular thoughts to enter your brain." He chuckled. "Come on, what video is it you wanted to show me?"

"This one." The man pushed in quickly to enter a search into his computer and clicked the link that came up. It was a clip Beto had seen before, or so he thought. The grainy footage showed a car being pulled over as a couple of police officers stepped out of their vehicle and spoke into the radios they wore on their collars. One remained at the police car while the other advanced on the vehicle that had been stopped, his hand on the pistol he still had holstered around his hip.

It started as something fairly routine. He had seen hundreds of police holdups that went bad one way or the other. It was usually bad for the person pulled over, as they were most often drunk and prone to shenanigans that would age well online.

But this one in particular was rather unique in a couple of ways. For starters, it wasn't Russian in origin. Secondly...well, what was about to come next. He had seen it a hundred times before and knew that the officer would march over to the car, look in, and talk to the driver for a few seconds. Without warning the door suddenly launched out, struck the man, and hurled him to the other side of the road.

A man would step out of the car and proceed to disable —and possibly but not definitely kill—the second officer and drag a third out of their vehicle and beat the shit out of him. Once he was finished, he would walk back to his car, deal with the first man who had recovered somewhat, and help a woman away from the scene.

In the case of this video, though, it paused after the

door struck the first man and the sound was auto-adjusted and repeated three or four times until it matched the tune of a pop song. It was one he had heard virtually non-stop thanks to its radio popularity. The video cut to the insanely popular music video.

"Damn it," Beto grumbled and rubbed his eyes. "I've tried to get that song out of my head for the past week."

"I know." Artem grinned and patted his friend on the back. "Isn't it great?"

"Isn't what great?" came a gruff, slightly nasal voice from behind them. The two men startled and turned to see their boss—one of the few members of the military who was a part of their little section of the FSB—standing behind them.

He appeared to be unable to step away from his military duties, and the two of them had never seen him without his grey-and-green officer's uniform. Not only that, he always tucked his beret under his arm whenever he was indoors.

Unfortunately, it was inevitable that it would be far more difficult to mock or make fun of him when he stood only a few paces away and stared at them like they owed him something.

"Answer the question." Colonel Ivan Mikhailov grunted belligerently and folded his arms in front of his chest. Beto always wondered why a man like him had chosen this particular assignment. Maybe he hadn't, though, and this was some kind of punishment for past misdeeds—one that was full of frustration for the colonel, who then took that resentment out on the men who had the misfortune to serve under him.

He could have chosen the job on the assumption that it would be a cushy assignment before his retirement and so had been surprised that he had to put so much work into keeping the younger, non-military members of his unit in place.

Either option felt equally reasonable to the younger man's mind, and while he was curious to find out which one it was, he wasn't curious enough to risk his still-budding career. Someone in the colonel's position would be able to make his life a living hell and failing that, make sure he would not be able to find work in the IT field. In Russia, anyway. It was doubtful that the Russian Military would have much influence over the companies hiring in Western Europe or maybe the US.

"It's only a video, sir," Artem answered when it became apparent that the silence that stretched interminably served to anger their superior further. "You remember the 'Savage' who was on the news, yes? Well, they made a video and tuned his first blow on one of the police officers to the sound of 'Diamond Magic,' by Sophia J."

The colonel leaned in, pressed play on the video again, and tilted his head as the now-famous footage switched quickly to the young, female rapper from Spain who enjoyed her music video while on a beach, watching young, muscular men.

"That is a fantastic song," the colonel admitted and nodded his head to the beat until the video ended. The screen lit up with the option to play it again. Both programmers had to control themselves but were barely able to keep from laughing when their superior, a gruff veteran, admitted to enjoying pop music.

"There's something about it," Artem agreed and went red in the face from the effort to maintain a serious demeanor. "It gets you moving and grooving, wouldn't you say?"

"Agreed." Their superior officer snapped to his old, stern self in an instant. "But you two would do well to remember that the Savage in question is no joking matter. All kinds of rumors abound, although nothing official has been released.

"Some say there is still an arrest warrant with his name on it and an entire FSB squad has been detailed for the sole purpose of apprehending him. Others believe if that were the case, they'd have apprehended him by now. That aside, he's made all kinds of waves—enough that if one of your less understanding superiors wandered in here and saw the two of you watching a video of him, I wouldn't be surprised to find you out of a job."

The young men both raised their eyebrows at the statement. The music must have raised the colonel's spirits since these were the most words he had strung together in their presence. Beto had worked there for the past year since his graduation, and Artem had worked there for three.

"If you don't mind me asking, Colonel," Beto said tentatively—he didn't want to push their luck but still felt curious enough to push it a little. "Why would we be on the lookout for a man who was involved in an attack on Belgian Police? Yes, killing or attacking law enforcement is always a bad thing, but shouldn't that be left to the local authorities?"

"Usually, yes. If that was all the Savage did, that would

be the end of it for us," the colonel said with a firm nod and glanced hastily around to ensure that it was only the three of them in the office. They were alone since most of the other staff had already headed home for the evening. "You didn't hear this from me, of course, but there has been speculation that before this Savage character had his little confrontation with the Belgian police, he had delivered the same kind of punishment to some of our people in a safe house. As it stands, all we know about the man is that he is American and he is not associated with their government in any way."

"So they say," Beto pointed out, and his superior nodded.

"Indeed, we would not take them at their word on that," the man continued. "But apparently, our investigations were...uh, informal and reveal that we cannot pin the operation on the government in any way. It's all above my pay grade and frankly, I can't be bothered to ask what someone doesn't want me to know. The thing with rumors, though, is that there is usually some truth buried somewhere in there. For example, I find it interesting that the speculation includes the apparently known fact that the man appears to wear some kind of hybridized combat suit designed to be covered by the heavy coat you can see him wearing. At the same time, if the FSB had their asses kicked in their backyard, I can understand why they'd want to avoid full disclosure."

He paused and his gaze drifted to the screen as if he imagined the video playing again. "Still, that suit does make me wonder if perhaps their interest in this man is more interest in the technology he wears. It's not as powerful or as useful as having a full suit, of course, but you can't walk around the city in a full suit of armor without raising a few eyebrows, I guess."

"Sure, sure," the programmer agreed and had already made up his mind to do a little research to see if suits like that were available on the open market. While he wouldn't be able to purchase it himself, he had a few connections with people who liked to run auctions on the dark web who might be able to put him in contact with whoever had made the suit for the Savage in question.

He wasn't sure what he would do if he ever found the man. His options, at this point, ranged anywhere between siccing the full power of the FSB on him—assuming he could find a way to separate fact from fiction and discover their real interest in him—and simply asking for an autograph.

He'd decide the details when he found out who the man was and what his business involved.

"Anyway, as you were," the colonel snapped, turned away, and headed toward his office. "And try not to get caught watching too many online videos, please?"

"Will do, sir!" Artem called behind him before he turned to his friend to speak in a hushed whisper. "Fucking hell, I thought we would be fired for sure. Who knew the colonel was a fan of Sophia J?"

"I'm reasonably sure that knowledge is classified to the highest degree," Beto said and leaned in closer to the screen. Yes, he supposed the modified suit would account for the super-strength and speed, but that took the mysticism out of it. It had been nice to think that they now lived in a world with bona fide superheroes in it. Well, he reminded himself, the likes of Iron Man and Batman were considered superheroes even if their powers came from their gadgetry.

"What are you thinking?" Artem asked and followed his friend's gaze to the screen where he ran the video again.

"It seems very unlikely that the dude with the super-suit merely wandered into a Russian safe house, right?" he wondered aloud and rubbed his chin while his mind worked. "If he did, he had to be there for something, and yet there's no chatter about the attack on the usual channels. And we only hear the gossip because our superior happens to be in a good mood?"

"That does seem...unlikely," his friend agreed. "I wonder if it has something to do with that officer who was sent to the Zoo despite him facing a judge and some serious jail time."

"Come again?" he asked and focused on his comrade. It seemed like today was a good day to be an intelligence operative as people seemed to voluntarily spill all kinds of beans.

"A...corporal, I think, Gregor Popov, faced charges of ruining an operation in the Zoo. He was sentenced to jail time, but as it turned out, they needed him in the Zoo to deal with the whole...uh, situation they had over there," Artem continued to explain.

"Wait, so your suggestion is that a Russian who was sent to the Zoo—and never came back, mind you—might be connected to an American who might have attacked a Russian safe house in what might be a prototype suit of armor?" Beto asked and let the incredulity he felt seep into his voice. "Do you see how your story is full of holes?"

"Yeah, yeah, yeah, whatever," Artem grumbled and nudged his shoulder after a moment. "It looks like you have work to do anyway, so I'll leave you to your party-pooping."

"It's only a payment authorization sent from our people in the Zoo," he complained, pulled himself closer to the screen, and narrowed his eyes when he saw the name of the people the payment was supposed to go to. "It looks like they're putting money into mercs' hands while they're rebuilding."

"I can't imagine the brass likes that," the other programmer grumbled from his side of the cubicle wall.

"Agreed." He frowned and leaned in closer as he looked at the name associated with the payment. "The money's being paid to Heavy Metal, it looks like. Hey, don't they have a ZooTube Channel?"

"Oh, yeah!" Artem laughed. "I love those guys. Did you see their last video? The one with the tentacle monster?"

"The one that gave me nightmares for three nights straight?" Beto demanded sarcastically. "Nope, never seen it."

CHAPTER FOUR

"I think we need to have a quick chat with the Russians," Sal grumbled over their team comms which were separate from the group that was supposed to clean up after them.

"What about?" Madigan asked, primed the rocket launcher on her shoulder, and delivered two streaks of white smoke at the swarm of locusts that had suddenly decided to attack them.

"Well, we might want to talk to them about how they owe us a raise since we're still picking up after their mess around their base," Courtney pointed out. The massive explosions rocked and shook the ground beneath them and decimated the ranks of the comparatively smaller creatures.

She took the opportunity provided to reload her assault rifle. "I know their agreement with us gives us all the exclusives around here and we appreciate that. But given the sheer amount of work they need us for—emphasis on the word need—it might be time to revisit our little deal with Solodkov to negotiate one that makes all this more worthwhile. The fact that their bombing left so many of the creatures alive while it destroyed anything that might be interesting from a scientific point of view is seriously annoying."

He couldn't help but agree. A couple of poison-fanged panthers bounded across the open ground between them and the trees that had already begun to grow. One dropped when two rounds from his sidearm punched through its head and shoulder. The second evaded a three-round burst from the assault rifle but was unable to avoid the vibro-sword that sliced it cleanly in half.

"Well, yes, that's a good point," he said and nodded when the blood was cleaned automatically from the vibrating sword. He admired the way Courtney's mind always seemed to leap to the business side of things. She was exceptionally good at managing and operating her little empire, both there and in the US. "What I meant, though, was the fact that we needed to talk to Solodkov about how their little bombing experiment was significantly less thorough than promised."

"True." Madigan chuckled and stepped away from a hyena she had crushed easily under her boot. "When you think about it, they did bomb the absolute hell out of this place. Given that, I assume the fact that so much has survived is more an issue with the Zoo being far more resilient than expected than it is about the Russians not doing a good job. Seriously, when have we ever heard of Russians not giving bombing everything in their path their absolute A-game?"

"As stereotypes go, that's probably true," the other woman grumbled. Her companions were more than capable of killing the creatures and didn't need her to pitch in. As such, she mainly used the time to collect samples for analysis in their lab at the compound. "That said, we should probably think about what kind of monsters they have that can survive being bombed in the way they were. Especially after we left as many of them dead as we did when we first came through here."

"Yeah, they sent us the footage of the bombing." Sal grunted and scanned the area with a practiced eye. It looked like the mutants had decided to cut their losses and retreat—for now, at any rate. "Besides, killing monsters doesn't do much based on our experience. The Zoo merely absorbs the bastards and spits them out again to kill us all. That's only one of the less crazy downsides to the Zoo we call our home."

"And we love it so much for that," Madigan responded with what might have a snort or a growl. "Still, given the kind of hellfire our Russian friends put this place through, can't we have a semblance of an open mind about this? It could simply mean that all the monsters are being remade or whatever by the Zoo itself, and that's where they're coming from. Maybe they're coming back to try to retake the base?"

"If that's the case, I'd say this place is somehow impor-tant to the Zoo for some reason," Courtney pointed out. "Or are you guys forgetting that this is the first time the Zoo has actively invaded someplace?"

"What are you talking about? The whole purpose of the Zoo is to act like an invasive species on the biosphere level," he reminded her.

"Well, yes, but it's always been about pointless expansion—at least that we know of." She chuckled. "It's always simply been about, uh...spreading and shit. It does attack the wall but that's almost like because it's in its way and it simply moves when it needs to grow. This is the first time it went out of its way to attack a specific location. And the animals are still doing it, even if the jungle hasn't spread to support them. I know it's weird, but it's like some kind of afterthought of the Zoo to keep attacking while the Russians are rebuilding their base. It's like there's something of an obsession with it."

"You need to stop anthropomorphizing that fucking jungle," Madigan protested and reloaded her rifle. She kept a wary eye on the remaining creatures that showed every indication of retreating. "But in the end, you're not wrong. There's too much going on around here to say that idea is off the table. These people need to get their act together security-wise if they think they'll ever survive this place."

"When you say, 'these people,'" Courtney answered with a sharp look at the other woman, "do you mean the Russians or everyone who gets anywhere near the Zoo?"

"Six of one and half a dozen of the other." She grinned.

"Right," Sal said firmly to bring their attention back to the topic at hand. "Do we plan to tell Solodkov that the monsters are coming from the Zoo to attack their new base, or do we say that they're only leftovers that managed to escape being exploded when they reclaimed it by force?"

"Which one will pay the most?" Courtney replied with a grin.

"Well, either one has to be terrifying for all the engineers they flew in to rebuild, so I think we're reasonably safe on either front." Madigan checked their weapons as they headed to where walls and defenses were already being rebuilt.

A handful of the monsters involved in the attack on the team had survived but now, all moved in the general direction of the Zoo. Sal had noted that they seemed far less coordinated, vicious, and tenacious when they fought out there, far away from the jungle itself, but that could merely be some kind of correlation. He assumed the monsters operated with a pheromone of some kind connected to the tentacle monsters, which allowed them to work together better. This far away from the comfort of their natural environment, they probably wouldn't be as well-controlled as when they were in the Zoo itself.

Of course, that raised a whole horde of other questions too, mainly revolving around the question of how the hell the tentacle monsters managed to keep control over an entire jungle. Were there more than one of them and they each simply controlled sections of it? Did the Zoo merely grow when more of them hatched from what he somehow assumed were eggs? Or was it all controlled by only the one huge, massive monster with tentacles everywhere? All of the above? None of the above?

There were too many questions he simply didn't know how to answer and as a scientist, it seriously pissed him off. The Zoo needed to abide by some set of rules. So far, any rules he had managed to identify for it had been dashed or warped, which left him in the position where he needed to study it more closely. It would be easier if he wasn't forced to kill virtually everything that moved. A little glum, he supposed this now included trees since they were able to take over random bases, seemingly on a whim.

As they returned to where the new base was being constructed, a group of soldiers in heavy combat armor stood with their weapons trained on the monsters that rapidly departed. At least, Sal thought, they had the sense to build beyond the largely incomplete wall. Hopefully, they would also throw a little more enthusiasm into completing the barrier according to specs provided. There was nothing quite like an invasion to highlight stupidity.

"Shouldn't you pursue them to kill them and make sure that they don't come back?" one of the soldiers asked in heavily accented English. "Is that not what you mercs are paid to do?"

"Don't get snippy with me, jackass," Madigan snapped in response. "We're paid to keep your lazy asses safe so you can eventually get around to building your defenses. You're welcome for that, by the way."

"Now, now, Kennedy," Sal said and reverted to her surname as they always did when they were in company. "There's no need to insult the help."

"The both of you can go fuck yourselves," one of the guards grumbled and withdrew from the perimeter.

"I think you mean the three of us," Courtney pointed out. "There's no need to hunt them. Besides the fact that the monsters move faster than we can in these suits, that small group certainly won't pose that much of a threat to a group like you. They lack the kind of coordination and numbers needed for large-scale assaults. When they do come in those kinds of numbers... Well, suffice it to say you'll be able to see them from a long fucking way off and you'll be able to call us in to help you. We might be a little late, but you can bet your asses we will avenge you."

The group of Russians was not happy about the pointed barbs delivered by the Heavy Metal trio, but the three had faced a group of monsters the likes of which they had never seen before and came out smiling. With that in mind, they were willing to take this particular one for the team. Sal knew for a fact that most of the Russians who had been inside the Zoo had been killed in the attack on their base—or were now members of Heavy Metal, in Gregor's case.

All Solodkov had at his disposal were newcomers from the outside who had absolutely no Zoo experience. It benefited the man that he had cut a deal with Heavy Metal. While he was forced to pay through the nose for it, given that they were the only ones he could call in by contract, he would make sure they earned every penny of what they were paid.

Or was it ruble? Did the Russians use Euros these days? Sal needed to update his knowledge of world economics. His current level was stuck on the basic economics class he'd taken when he needed extra credit to graduate high school early and get started on his Bachelor's degree. In all honesty, he'd forgotten most of it.

"Well, if the three of you are finished patting each other on the back," one of the Russians grumbled and at least made an effort to not look too annoyed by the Americans' cockiness. "Solodkov left a message with us to make sure you contact him as soon as you can. Once you're finished dealing with the monsters and...well, whatever else you think you're here to do."

"Patting each other on the back. I get it." He grinned. "We'll let him know we're finished with the attack. You all can rest easy. None of you will be shat out of a monster today."

The Russians seemed to collectively roll their eyes and headed to where the construction was currently taking place. To their credit, the crews worked quickly and had put up about a fourth of the base already. The work accomplished mostly constituted security points, with turrets and defensive positions being the first to go up. For now, at least, the men worked with more than average incentive in the knowledge that these would be how they would be kept safe from whatever it was that had happened to the first base. Hopefully.

"Do you think we'll end up regretting the way we've treated these guys?" Madigan asked and looked at her teammates with a raised eyebrow. "We were always on fairly good terms with the guys who were here before, so I don't see why we need to constantly antagonize them."

"If they choose to treat us like expendable help, I think it's only fair that we remind them how dead they would be if we weren't here to do their job for them." Courtney shrugged. "The way I see it, if they want us to treat them better, they need to approach us with a better attitude. Or maybe vodka. Or both?"

"The vodka did it for me with the last base." The other woman nodded. "I know we bought it from them and sold it to the other bars, mostly, but it was still one hell of a way to get them in our good graces."

"And us in theirs, I suppose," Sal grumbled and called Connie on his commlink. "Hey, Connie, how's everything at the compound?"

"Anja accused me of being sexist, so I think it's been a

reasonably good day," the AI said. He knew it was merely a part of her programming, but honestly, it was weird to hear that kind of statement coming from a female voice. "How can I help you today, Sal?"

"What, no 'sexy' for me?" he asked and injected a disappointed note into his voice.

"Madigan said that if she ever heard me call you that again, she would personally rip all the wiring out of my servers and she would make sure Anja coded me to be a feminist if she ever activated me again," Connie said. "She can be a catty bitch."

"I should warn you that the same consequences will apply if you ever call Madigan a bitch again," he responded sharply.

"Understood," she answered in an unsurprisingly cheery tone. "Now, how can I help you today, Sal?"

"I need you to put me in contact with Solodkov, wherever the fuck he is," he said. "He's expecting our call so he shouldn't be too hard to find."

"Now, now, Sal, no need to temper my expectations," she replied and after a few seconds, a dialing tone could be heard inside his helmet. He connected the call to the others in case they wanted to hear the conversation as well.

"Good afternoon, Dr. Jacobs," Solodkov said in his trademark flawless English. He had only the slightest hint of an accent, although not one that could necessarily have been called Russian. Maybe Eastern European, not that it mattered. "I assume you're calling me to say you've dealt with the creatures that have plagued my people on the construction site?"

"Well, if we assume the options are that or that I'd call

you from beyond the grave, that's a very good assumption." He chuckled. "But where the hell are you right now if you don't mind my asking?"

"I'm at the American base," the man responded and there was no way to know if he was lying or not. "I had lunch with your commandant and am currently enjoying a drink at your bar."

"Well...fun times, I guess," Sal grumbled and almost wished he could get his hands on a drink as well. "By the by, you asked one of your buddies to tell us to call you once we were finished here, so what's up?"

"Well, I wanted to tell you that I have some new and exciting work for Heavy Metal, so you might want to rest up before looking into it," the Russian said and sounded deliberately enigmatic. "By the way, how is Savage doing? I told him to call but he never did."

"Well, given that he's currently faced with an uptick of dangerous work in Philly, the answer to that question is probably in some kind of flux," he replied.

"Ah, well, I'll have to come up with another way to contact him." Solodkov chuckled. "I'll talk to you soon, Dr. Jacobs."

"See you soon, Solodkov," he replied, hung up, and turned to face the two women. "Well, you heard the man. I suggest we pack our shit and head to the compound."

CHAPTER FIVE

Darren Hyde leaned back at his desk, propped his feet up on the mahogany top, and exhaled a long sigh of contentment. *Honestly, it's always good to prove others wrong.* The thought made him smile.

People always said that what you wanted and obsessed over for your entire life always ended up a disappointment in the end—like you built it up so much in your head that your expectations were too unrealistic going in. That could not be said about taking over his father's company after the man had retired.

You never once imagined I'd inherit, did you, old man? It had never been a foregone conclusion that he would do so since he was a middle brother in a family of five—his sisters had never been in the running. *Old Louis Hyde had been busier with his three wives than a man his age had any business being. It's almost obscene, honestly.*

He had made sure that Darren's older brothers—the sons who were a result of his marriage with his first wife and the woman he had loved the most—were the favorites and were always given virtually anything and everything they wanted. The younger three needed to prove themselves more than anyone might have expected or even considered reasonable.

Well, Dad, your blind doting ended up being my brothers' downfall. Being Daddy's favorites all their lives was a primary cause of their eventual psychological issues and playing right into my hands. Brendan, the oldest, developed a drug problem that lasted from his early teenage years to an overdose during his thirtieth birthday party.

The second oldest, Darryl, had sidestepped that particular landmine and dived headfirst onto the one called sexual harassment. He faced dozens of suits filed by his past conquests by the time he was in his late twenties and featured in all the wrong kinds of tabloids.

Darren had sponsored roughly a quarter of the suits and everything had kind of snowballed from there. It had all culminated when Darryl needed to flee the country to avoid the criminal charges his father was only barely holding off thanks to his friendship with the Attorney General.

After that, the others were easy to deal with in one way or another. I didn't even have to do much. They dug their own graves and all I needed to do was provide them with the proverbial shovel.

His hard work and initiative finally paid off when he was the only one left to hand the reins to when it came time for the old man to step down and enjoy his retirement. It hadn't always been easy, but he wasn't the kind of guy to play fair.

"You taught me well, old man," he said and raised an

empty hand as if in a toast. "You told me that if I was losing a game, all I needed to do was change the rules. It's a pity you'll never know how right you were."

In the end, instead of waiting for his brothers to fuck up, he stepped in and helped them. After a while, it became apparent that he was the only one of the five who was in any way capable of running a billion-dollar weapons manufacturing corporation. It required one to be a cut-throat businessman, the kind who smiled in peoples' faces and shook their hands while stabbing them firmly in the back multiple times—metaphorically speaking for the most part.

Sure, Hyde was involved in shady shit all around the world, but they would continue to deny it until someone proved they were involved. Besides, even if that did happen, all they had to do was fall back on the veritable army of lawyers and lawmakers they had in their pockets to maintain the appearance that everything was on the up and up while their marketing specialists rebranded them.

That was all it took these days. It was true what they said, that all press was good press—but with the caveat that you needed to know how to twist all kinds of press to your advantage. Or, if you didn't know how, to hire the kind of people who went to Ivy League universities to study precisely that.

Eventually, the odds being what they were, you would hire the kind of people who had consciences or at least a semblance of one. But in the end, all they had to do was find the price these people were willing to be paid to keep themselves in the business for the duration and walk away like nothing happened when it was done.

If they tried to go public with anything, it was a relatively simple matter to destroy reputations—the words "disgruntled employee" worked wonders these days—and make sure to wrap the whistle-blowers in so much red tape, it would take them literal years to get out of it. By that time, all the evidence would be gone and all the company had to do was deny everything and walk away.

This ruthlessness and business style were why Darren was the CEO and de-facto owner of Hyde Corp while everyone who had squared off against him was forgotten. He was even in the queue to be on the front page of a couple of business magazines. Sensibly, he had hired a personal trainer and a nutritionist to remake him and ensure he was camera-ready by the time there were cameras around.

During all that time spent fighting, clawing, and taking what he felt was his by right, he had forgotten to have a life of his own. He had no wife and no children—that he knew of, anyway. A string of one-night stands who had been compelled to sign NDAs about what happened between them was all he had to show in terms of his personal activities over the past few years.

Oh, there was the fact that he basically owned his family company, but some people didn't see that as an actual life, even if it felt like it. He would have to arrange for some kind of marriage and a couple of kids before too long, but that was far enough away into the future that he could avoid thinking about it for now. After all, he was still in his early thirties, and it was expected that people like him enjoyed the high life without settling down until they were at least in their forties.

The same couldn't be said about his sisters, who his father hadn't deemed worthy to be involved in his company anyway, the sexist bastard. But they were almost as sharp and cutthroat as he was. It was really for the best. Darren had a feeling they would have started a war for the company that would eventually bring it down if they had ever been in the running. As things stood now, they all rocked the married life while they controlled their rich and successful husbands. A couple had even tried the divorce route and walked away with billions.

His thoughts about his family were interrupted when the phone in his office rang. He wondered what the hell the point was in having the fucking thing since it seemed like everyone could be contacted personally. Some people seemed to feel that landlines made for safer communications these days, the crazy fucks, but business meant he would inevitably have to make some compromises. He sighed and answered it.

"Good morning, Mr. Hyde," his assistant Patrice said in the high-pitched voice he had come to associate with the woman. "I hope I'm not interrupting anything."

"Nothing too important, Patrice," he said. It was best to leave himself somewhere to back into if needed. "What's up?"

"It's Mr. Haynes on the line for you," she replied. "Should I tell him to call you later? Or maybe that you'll call him?"

"Which Haynes?" he asked and narrowed his eyes. He knew a couple of Haynes. Some of them were worth his time, no matter what they wanted to talk to him about, and some were not. Even at times when he needed to rest and relax while he made at least an appearance of working.

"Mr. Brian Haynes, sir," she said quickly like she'd known the question would be asked.

Brian Haynes. It took him a moment to place a face to the name, and once he did, he already knew he would talk to the man. Haynes was a partner at the law firm that represented Hyde almost exclusively, and if there was anything his lawyer had to say, especially this early in the morning, it had to be something important.

Darren shifted to a more comfortable position in his seat and drew a deep breath. He took the time to straighten his thick blond curls, even though he knew that the other man couldn't see him.

"Should I put him through, sir?" Patrice asked again and sounded like she had put effort into being patient with him.

"Yes, please do. Thank you, Patrice," he replied in as professional a tone as he could muster. The tone beeped in the headset and the sound of someone breathing on the other end could be heard like the man didn't realize the call had been connected.

"Haynes, it's been too long," Darren said to open the conversation. "When will we go golfing again, buddy? I need to put a little work into my handicap."

"Enough with the chit-chat, Hyde," Haynes answered and sounded both angry and frustrated. It was something Darren was familiar with but wasn't used to being on the receiving end of. "I've tried to get through to you all fucking night."

Having pulled a couple of all-nighters in college, he

could understand the man's frustrations, but that was still no excuse to use that kind of tone with him. He took a deep breath and attempted to not let his temper get the better of him before he spoke. "Stop right there, Haynes. Take a deep breath and tell me calmly what you need from me, okay?"

There was a pause on the other end and it seemed the man might have taken his advice. That suspicion was confirmed when he spoke again and sounded a little calmer.

"I'm sorry for my tone before," the lawyer said in one that now suggested he still struggled with his temper but had it under control. "I've been dealing with programmers and specialists all night to confirm a few sneaking suspicions I had. I tried to contact you when the suspicions first occurred to me, but when I called Patrice, she said you were in a meeting all night and weren't to be disturbed."

Ah yes, an all-night party at one of his frat brothers' houses to celebrate...something. Darren was no longer sure what they had celebrated, which explained how awesome the night had been. And yes, he supposed he had told Patrice he shouldn't be interrupted under any circumstances.

"Yes, I guess you could call it a meeting that went on all night." He chuckled but said no more. It wouldn't do to give his lawyer too much ammunition to use against him later should he ever feel the need to do so. "But you have me on the line now and from the sound of it, a full picture to help with presenting your case too, so by all means, fill me in on what you need me to know. I don't suppose it has

49

anything to do with a mistress or two? You told me those NDAs were ironclad."

"They are, and that's not what this is about," Haynes retorted. "What I've tried to talk to you about was the fact that it appears someone has jumped in front of one of Hyde's pending patents. One your government contracts depend on."

Darren narrowed his eyes. The fact that most of Hyde's income came from the massive government spending marked off for weapons research was something he was more than aware of. He was also continually cognizant of the fact that they competed neck and neck for some of the more profitable contracts with their primary rival, Pegasus. That particular company had cast aside their problems with an internal power struggle. They had now begun to make a push for a lion's share of the money earmarked for research into better and more efficient ways to kill larger numbers of people.

Any patent problems with their primary research grants would spell trouble to the tune of billions.

"Explain," Hyde said simply, having to control his temper this time.

"I've sent you an email with the complete research, but the short of it is that it appears someone has developed a functional combat AI they've already deployed in the Zoo," Haynes explained. "I only caught wind of it because someone posted footage of the AI in action on ZooTube. While I can't be certain, the specialists I've spent all night talking to seem to confirm that what we are looking at is, in fact, a combat AI."

He had already opened the link that had been emailed

to him and watched the video as well as listened to the voice commentary of Haynes' specialists. He wasn't the kind of person who would be able to tell what he was looking at, but he did know well enough to trust the experts.

They now told him someone had developed something that could prove problematic once they presented their finished product to the congressional committee. The date for this had already been set for three weeks from now. Having video footage of something like that would mean whoever had developed this AI would be able to undercut their prices. Worse, they could even put market violation lawsuits in with the SEC that would result in billions of dollars tied up in the courts for months or even years.

It was the kind of shit he had tried to make sure would not fly under his administration.

"What do you propose we do about it?" Haynes asked as the CEO studied the data he had received.

"Well, our property is already operational," he replied, leaned back in his seat, and rubbed his temples. "We need to do field tests before it's approved for use. This could end up as a blessing in disguise."

"How so?"

"Well, it gives us the opportunity to field test it. I'll get back to you, Haynes. Good...good work on this."

"Thanks," the man said curtly and cut the call. Hyde didn't have the time to feel offended or angry. He was already dialing Patrice's line.

"Yes, sir?" she asked.

"I need you to put me on the line with the VP of our research and development division," he said quickly. "If he's not in yet, I need to get him on his personal cell phone. I don't care that it's early in the morning. I pay these people well above the market value for their services and they can earn it by being available whenever I need them to be."

"Understood, Mr. Hyde," she responded politely, and the line went dead. She would put Vance Brians through to him as soon as possible. Which, hopefully, meant in the next five minutes.

It took three. He snatched the phone up after the first ring and pressed the headset to his ear.

"This is Vance Brians, VP of Hyde's research and development division, Mr. Hyde," the thick voice on the other side of the line answered quickly. He'd apparently been briefed by Patrice as to his boss' current mood as well as the fact that whatever had put him in that kind of a mood was something of an emergency.

"I need you to brief me on the availability of our Jekyll Project," the CEO said. He'd personally selected the name for that particular project, and he was quite proud of it, even if it was a little on the nose. "Is it ready for field testing?"

"I wasn't aware it was scheduled so soon," the man said carefully. "When do you need it ready?"

"Yesterday," he said firmly. "And have it ready for overseas travel."

"It'll be ready to move before lunch, sir," Brians said confidently.

CHAPTER SIX

Martin scowled with mixed feelings of sadness, disbelief, and fury. She could sense that many of her team shared the emotional reaction and deliberately stepped aside for a moment to regain her usual focused efficiency.

It seemed entirely ironic that men and women who had seen the worst of what the Zoo had to offer should be affected like this. Part of it was shock, of course, she reasoned as she checked her weapon and her armor in a practiced routine that always brought calm. They were used to dealing with monsters of potentially alien origin.

Whatever the naysayers might claim, the evidence up close spoke for itself. Everyone knew the mutants seemed to be predisposed toward killing humans and were more than willing to attack to the death. It came as no surprise when the bodies of their fellow creatures piled up in the effort to push the humans away from their jungle.

A little more settled, she paced the perimeter and took a moment to scan their surroundings. With all the firepower recently exchanged, it was very possible the animals were on their way. After what they'd faced, she didn't want to be caught unawares.

Her thoughts turned to things she knew—they might not be comprehensible but they were familiar and helped to center her. She could accept that with the mutants, it was like the self-preservation instinct wasn't present in them. Or maybe something overrode that instinct and compelled them to throw themselves at the barrage of bullets they knew would kill them by the score.

Perhaps they hoped the humans they attacked would run out of ammunition eventually and could be killed. Some might say this kind of reasoning was impossible in monsters, but with these, who knew? Anything was possible.

All of that was something Martin had made her peace with a while before. She didn't understand it but she'd grown accustomed to it.

What she struggled to come to terms with was the fact that some humans seemed to lack the survival instinct as well. The group that had attacked them seemed more than willing to pile their bodies without caution like the animals.

While the creatures might have an excuse of some kind for their unnatural behavior, she couldn't think of any defense for these idiots. They simply charged stupidly at a formation of heavily armored and armed soldiers who were more than ready to annihilate them with excessive prejudice.

Conscious of the silence and the fact that her team were

looking to her, she drew a deep breath and turned to face the carnage. The idiots in question were bounty hunters, of course—although honestly, they might be more aptly described as scavengers.

Martin had been read into the men and women desperate enough to brave the Zoo with any weapons and armor they could find—no matter how ineffective or inferior. Their hope was that they could get their hands on something that would pay enough to lift them out of miserable poverty.

Of course, with the Russian base overrun and its defenses questionable, it might have opened the door to soldiers of fortune who possibly thought there were easy pickings. Teams hadn't reported difficulties with them for quite a while and it seemed coincidental that they came out of the woodwork at this particular point in time.

Sadly, desperate poor folk could be found in large numbers in this particular corner of the world. Many were still dispossessed by the most recent of the dozen or so civil wars that had plagued this beautiful continent over the past few decades. They were in need of a financial break and were willing to kill for it. At the same time, they had to know the people they would fight would be more than willing to kill them in return.

That simple truth didn't factor in the horde of hellish monsters that were as willing and a whole lot more enthusiastic about it. It occurred to her that the animals' enthusiasm was probably because they wouldn't have to live with the deaths of these unfortunates on their consciences, but that was neither here nor there.

Martin scowled as she looked at the bodies of the bounty hunters she and her team had eliminated. A couple of her men took a quick look at the weapons and armor they carried to see if there was anything that could be salvaged. Looting was an age-old tradition in combat, after all. While she felt it was a disgusting practice and would not engage in it herself, she wouldn't get in the way of her people taking what they had put their lives on the line to earn.

That said, she doubted they would find much in the way of salvage. The weapons the bounty hunters had used would have been considered antiques two decades before. This easily explained why they hadn't been able to even put a dent in the combat armor the French wore.

The search was completed reasonably quickly and at her insistence, the team was on the move again soon after. None of them needed to be reminded that the monsters were drawn toward the sounds, sights, and smells of battle and didn't seem to care that their meals fought back. Which, in turn, led to more fighting, which drew more monsters and ultimately became a vicious cycle that would end with most, if not all, of her people dead.

She wouldn't risk that, and one of the benefits of having a team that knew what the fuck they were doing was that they knew it too. They would make sure to stay on the move with her and didn't need to be told there was a whole shitload of pain headed their way if they didn't.

It wasn't long before the sun would set, she realized. This deep in the jungle, it wasn't obvious that the day outside was ending. The trees already grew thick and close together and mostly blocked any sunlight that might shine in on them. Instead, she needed to look for the subtler indicators that would tell them that night was falling.

The fact that those animals that tended to live in the trees were more active at night was one of those hints. She could see more movement above them, which meant they should probably start looking for a place to camp. They needed a location that gave them a decent view of the jungle around them but still provided cover.

Thankfully, they were far enough away from the site of the battle that anything drawn by the sound of shooting and the smell of blood wouldn't find them, but that was merely the first step.

The open ground would also make them a little more visible to the monsters that came out to hunt at night. There wasn't much they could do to avoid it, but what they could do was set their camp up in a way that it would discourage those looking for an easy meal. It wouldn't deter any that came for a massacre, but that was simply something they would have to live with.

The defenses were put in place and a couple of motion sensors were plugged remotely into her HUD. These confirmed that while there was a good deal of movement around them, none of it appeared to move specifically in their direction.

Her team worked in almost complete silence to set their little camp up. Martin didn't want to think about what had caused them to be anything but their usual loud and rambunctious selves. They had been in the Zoo before, dealt with the dangers, and knew that keeping their spirits up was important.

Maybe the killing of humans was what got them down

—or, at least, under today's particular circumstances. It was true that they had acted in self-defense, but the bounty hunters had honestly not stood a chance. There was little satisfaction to be had in emerging victorious in what was essentially a one-sided fight at the end of the day.

In fairness, she could feel it dragging her morale down as well, and as she watched the others prepare for the night, she felt she had to do something. It was her job as the leader of this little group to make sure they were ready for whatever they had to face—or as ready as they could be, anyway.

She prepared a quick meal for herself, kept her suit on, and only removed her helmet to enjoy the diced chicken and vegetables served with rice that had been heated while inside the ration bag. They took turns to eat their meals and no one had to be reminded that someone always had to have eyes on the jungle. At all times, they would remain watchful for something to trigger the alerts on their motion sensors.

"How do you think we should do it, Captain?" her sergeant asked once she had finished her meal and pushed the packaging quickly into the recycle bin in her suit.

"Do what?" she questioned and focused on the man. She had zoned out for most of the evening and hadn't paid any attention to the low smatters of conversation her team had shared. They were grown-assed adults and didn't need her to regulate everything.

"We've talked about how the night shifts should be picked up," he said quickly. "Some have suggested that we have groups ready for combat on two-hour shifts, while others say all we need is one or two at a time who can wake and alert the rest of us. We're kind of split down the middle and need a deciding vote."

Martin shook her head. Maybe they did need her to regulate everything.

"If you keep only one or two on the shifts, it's the easiest way to make sure everyone gets some rest. Should something go wrong, it's fairly easy to wake everyone in time to deal with it," she said and sounded more tired than she felt. "Look, if you guys need encouragement, I can take the first shift on my own. I don't think I'm in the mood to sleep yet anyway."

"Are you sure about that, Captain?" The sergeant looked a little skeptical. "We've all had a long day and no one would think less of you if you simply pulled rank and decided to have a full night of sleep. Even I know that keeping these assholes in line is a full-time job on its own."

"Be that as it may, I think we need a morale boost," Martin replied but pitched her voice low to keep the other team members out of this part of the conversation. "There's not much I can do to raise their spirits, but I can take the first shift and show that I'm in this with them, so that's what I'll do."

He nodded. "I can respect that. Do you need me to—"

"I can take the first shift on my own," she said quickly. "If you want to volunteer for the second, be my guest. Find a few more volunteers to cover the other three shifts and we'll be golden."

"Yes, ma'am." The man chuckled, pushed up from where he had been seated, and strolled to where the other men had begun to prepare their resting places. As the sergeant laid the situation out for them, Martin could see that at least half looked a little anxious about the fact that they would rely on only two people—one, in her case—to watch the jungle and provide sufficient warning should something bad happen.

She could understand their reservations, but she had been around the Zoo long enough to know that rest was more important than having large numbers of people ready for a fight at all times. The only reason they were able to keep the hordes at bay, as it were, was because they were coordinated and focused. That would go out of the proverbial window if they were all sleep-deprived. She needed her team as ready as she could get them.

Eventually, those who were against not having as many people ready for combat as they could spare were swayed. They were all tired. It had been a long day, trudging through the damn jungle and fighting all kinds of shit that had no place being outside of a Guillermo del Toro movie. After having to still kill a few humans on top of that, they deserved to get some rest.

Besides, they had to trust Martin to keep them safe and watch their backs. They wouldn't have agreed to this mission if they didn't trust her. They were all volunteers, after all, which explained why the brass hadn't been able to send a fucking battalion in to deal with what could only be described as a fact-finding mission.

She wasn't big on those. Her training was for the kinds of operations that required five operatives or less—the kind where her team slipped in and out and completed the mission before anyone even knew they were there. She had been rather good at those.

Of course, she had some experience in command of

larger numbers, which was why she had been promoted to captain before being sent there, but it didn't mean it was her preference.

The team settled in for the night and she was finally alone with her thoughts for the first time since the morning when she had enjoyed her first cup of coffee. She had begun to miss her little apartment on the French base like she tended to do on these missions.

Her dreams of retiring involved a cabin in the middle of nowhere. She would only deal with other humans when she needed to and even then, on her terms—usually online and almost never face to face. With a good Internet connection, you didn't need much face-to-face contact with the outside world these days.

People said you needed interaction with other humans to be healthy. As it turned out, a significant majority of humans were massive dicks who only ruined the interaction for the rest of them so it was safer to stay away. Let the terrible people hang out with the terrible people had become something of a personal motto.

That said, if you wanted to go into a place that was as far away from civilization as you could be, there weren't many better than the alien jungle in the middle of the Sahara desert, Martin thought with a chuckle.

They would head deeper into the Zoo than most missions tended to on the hunt for a monster that had been rumored to be in there for a while but had only recently been confirmed. It took serious balls to get in close enough to a tentacle monster to be able to snap pics—and even braver than usual, she realized when she recalled the green mist that team had faced.

Everyone had been briefed on that shit after testing had been done on the residue collected. It was the first time something like that had been seen, and while she appreciated the kind of danger people put themselves in to collect the data, she really hoped they wouldn't run into it themselves.

Of course, if wishes were horses, they would all be riding into the sunset as far away from that fucking place as they could. As things stood, however, they had added chemical sensors to the devices they'd set up around the camp. These would hopefully ensure that the people who slept with some piece of their armor open had time to seal it again before a mist that could melt them into a disgusting puddle of goo descended on them.

Which explained some of the fears her people were feeling, she assumed, and gave her weapon a routine check. She was tempted to remove her helmet and enjoy what little fresh air could be found there, but the HUD was the quickest way to be warned of anything that approached, mist or otherwise.

It wasn't like the air was all that fresh anyway, she thought and leaned back as she called up more footage of the creature they were there to locate. Well, technically, they were only supposed to collect data, confirm that the monster existed, and take those findings to the geeks in the labs on the base to study.

Then again, the scientists would appreciate having actual samples rather than only a couple of images. If they were given the opportunity to blow a creature like that up into tiny, itty-bitty pieces, she knew she would jump at it. And not only because it was rumored that creatures like that were responsible for the deaths of dozens of people who had gone into the Zoo over the past few months.

It was because it would be fun, she thought with a grin and realized that two hours had passed almost in a wink. Her replacements were already up and it was her time to rest.

CHAPTER SEVEN

"Sal, are you there?" Connie pinged the commlink.

He narrowed his eyes and glanced up from the road. It wasn't like the AI to be polite when she contacted them. Maybe him and Madigan threatening her with what Sal could only assume was the worst kind of fate for her had something to do with it. He wouldn't say she needed to calm since he did not, in fact, want her to call Madigan a bitch again.

But then again, maybe by resorting to threats, they would make her into something that wouldn't be able to watch their backs when they needed her to. It was a valid concern, given that Connie had run their defenses ever since Anja had brought the AI on board. If there was any way for him to repair any damage in their relationship, he thought he should be the one to make the first step. He was one of the founding members of Heavy Metal, after all.

Except Connie was an AI. *What in the hell could I get an AI that would soothe hurt feelings? Do AIs even have feelings?* These were all questions for later but still important. He made a mental note that this was something he would need to bring up with Anja when he had the opportunity.

"I'm here, Connie, what's up?" Sal said and made a note of how far away they were from the compound on his HUD.

"I thought you should know that Anja and Gregor are having an argument," the AI replied in her soothing voice. "They're shouting at each other in Russian about the content of a TV series episode that broadcast recently. The discussion over whether one of the characters is actually dead or not has escalated somewhat. While I calculate a ninety-five percent chance that they will reconcile amicably by the time the next episode airs next week, I thought you should know about the argument before your arrival so you aren't...concerned."

He shrugged. "Well, thanks for the heads-up, I guess," he grumbled and turned to Courtney and Madigan. "Okay, no one is to question why Anja and Gregor are yelling at each other in Russian, understood? It's...about a TV series or something."

"Understood." Madigan chuckled but kept her eyes focused on the road ahead. The compound was already visible in the distance and the sun had begun to set. They'd needed to head to the US base to clear the secured voucher the Russians had sent them so it could be converted into dollars and deposited in their account. It was an annoying point of business that he felt really shouldn't involve any of them. They were the talent, and if people wanted to continue to hire them, they should handle all the money problems themselves, right?

They pulled inside the gates when the light in the sky

was mostly gone, which required the group to turn lights on in the compound to allow them to park the Hammerhead and start to strip their combat suits.

Connie hadn't been lying. They could hear Anja and Gregor yelling about something inside the main building with what sounded like a hefty addition of foul language. He wondered if he should intervene but with the knowledge that they were talking about something they were fans of, he knew would only end badly for him. Let the fandom discuss their differences in what he supposed was a civil manner, comparatively speaking.

Sal had been to a couple of conventions, and he'd seen these kinds of discussions turn violent. Besides, he'd seen Gregor fight and Anja be involved in fighting. He didn't want to piss either of them off, so the trio steered clear of the two when they entered the building. The Russians continued their argument in the kitchen while the other three retired to the living area.

"Should we talk finances?" Courtney asked and picked up a tablet from the coffee table.

"What is there to talk about?" Madigan raised an eyebrow and propped one of her feet on the table. "With Russian money pouring in, we've now posted massive profits for the past three months."

"Absolutely, things are looking good, but thanks to the extra work we've put in, there have been more expenses," the other woman said and called the spreadsheet of their profits and expenses for the month up on the TV on the far end of the room. "We're looking at an even margin in three months, and then it's the law of diminishing returns. That's why I said we might have to talk to Solodkov about increasing our rate.

"The amount of time we spend over there with those assholes has begun to push our costs to an absurd rate. Gas, ammo, and repairs, etc. continue to climb. At the same time, we earn less than we would from regular trips into the Zoo—which would, interestingly enough, cost less."

"Huh." Sal grunted and rubbed his chin thoughtfully. "Aside from telling Solodkov to increase our money, are there any other solutions we might be able to look into?"

"Well, I know how you'll react, but we could always bring money in from Pegasus," Courtney suggested.

He shrugged. "You know how I feel about that. It's one thing if we need it desperately, but I honestly don't like the idea of your company's board having a say in how we run Heavy Metal. This is our thing. You complain about having a board to answer to all the time, and it seems like they would begin to interfere and that would be the end of Heavy Metal as we know it. Before too long, we'll be bought out and turned into a... I don't know what the term is. Shell corporation? Something like that?"

"I get that, I do, believe me," she said quickly. "I—" She stopped talking abruptly when the tone and pitch of Gregor and Anja's argument increased to the point of distraction.

"Ah, the pitter patter of enthusiasts being told that they're wrong." Madigan chuckled, her voice heavily laced with sarcasm. "You two...*shut up!* One of the two of you will kill the other and I refuse to clean that shit up."

The two Russians snapped quickly out of their furor and turned to see the trio seemingly for the first time since they stepped inside. Sal wondered if that was the case or whether they hadn't expected anyone to interfere in their conversation. Neither theory would have surprised him overmuch.

"Sorry." Anja chuckled and Gregor looked a little abashed as they moved away from the kitchen and walked through to join the other three at the coffee table. It wasn't something Sal thought was strictly necessary. They could have continued their argument if they wanted to as long as they lowered the volume of it. "We weren't going to kill each other. We're simply having a lively debate about who dies in the next episode. I think it'll be Beering, and he's wrong. What are you guys talking about?"

He grinned when Gregor rolled his eyes as he dropped into the seat across from Courtney.

"We're trying to decide how we can keep Heavy Metal solvent over the next few months," Courtney said. "The Russians have put a dent in our earnings by having us there so often and paying us so little. My thought is that our only real options are to either bring some money into Heavy Metal from Pegasus as an investment—"

"If that happens, I'm out of here. Just saying," Anja interjected quickly. "I'd still love to work with you guys since you are all absolutely the best and I love you all. But I will not work under the thumb of some corporate talking heads in the US. I'm done with all that bullshit."

"Or we can get Solodkov to pay us more for our efforts around their base rebuilding," Courtney continued as if the other woman hadn't spoken. "They have a deal with us. We're the only ones they'll call in for that and let's be honest, we're the best in the business, as it were. If he wants to keep paying these low-ass rates, they can find the kind of people they can get for that coin."

"And what about us?" Sal wondered. "What would we do?"

"We were doing very well before they came along," Madigan reminded him. "If they don't want to pay our rates, we can go back to our Zoo trips and make money off the pita flowers we bring in as well as the whitepapers on the monsters we're the best at finding anyway.

"It was less money in bulk, but I guess that means fewer expenses and we still had time to work on the suit development with the companies that made them. That also allowed us to get the friends and family discount on new suits along with new pieces and parts for repairs, all on top of the weapons and ammo. As of now, we're too busy dealing with the Russian problems."

"If I could get a quick word in?" Anja said and raised her hand.

"You don't need to raise your hand. This isn't fucking school." Gregor chuckled and stretched over to squeeze her shoulder.

"What's up, Anja?" Sal asked and leaned back in his seat. He was hungry and a little tired. All he wanted to do was to have something to eat—something he could fry up and that had a solid saltiness and crunch to it—and head to bed. Maybe a shower first, or maybe not. He was still working out the details.

"I have a message from Solodkov waiting for you," she explained, retrieved her phone from her pocket, and quickly called up a voice message that had been left.

"If you could let your folks at the Heavy Metal

compound know that I'd like to pop over sometime tomorrow morning to discuss a new job I might have for them," said the familiar voice. Even on the message, it seemed to almost completely lack an accent. "Send me a message with when, and I'll be there. Until then, comrades."

Courtney looked at Sal and raised her eyebrow. "Well, you fill me in on how answering to the Russians is any better than answering to the board of an American company."

"First of all, we don't answer to the Russians any more than we answer to the base commandant," he corrected her quickly. "Secondly, yeah, it's not much better. I don't like working with Solodkov any more than the rest of you do. He's a slimy son of a bitch who will stab us in the back sometime soon.

"But we cut a deal that included all charges on Gregor and Anja being dropped, so if he wants to come and have a chat, I don't see why we can't oblige him. Let's hear what he has to say, and if it doesn't include enough money to meet our current needs, we tell him we're done working with him and walk away. If he has a problem with that... Well, we'll cross that bridge if and when we reach it."

No one in the room felt all that comfortable with the decision, but they were aware that it was the best option they had available and eventually, they all showed signs of agreement. Whether a shrug or a nod, Sal was happy to take it. He was too tired to think about it anymore.

"Great," he said. "Anja, let Solodkov know that we'll meet him sometime tomorrow morning. At ten, maybe. For now, I need food."

"Will do, boss," the Russian replied, pushed from her

seat, and headed to the server room. Courtney continued to work on her tablet, while Madigan moved to intercept Sal as he reached the kitchen.

"Are you okay, Jacobs?" she asked in a soft voice and put a hand on his chest. "Do you need more treatment?"

"I'm simply tired, is all," he said with a smile. "I appreciate your concern, though."

CHAPTER EIGHT

I honestly need my fucking head examined. The long flight had afforded Adrian Lynch sufficient time to consider his choices—both now and those he'd made before. *At least the first time, I had the excuse of ignorance.*

He had been told that the Zoo was something else—a brand-new environment, a place where you could see what an alien world might look like. There had been entire videos displayed for exactly that purpose. These told him and all the newcomers who stepped into the Zoo alongside him that they were about to enter a land of wonder and mystery.

They hadn't been wrong but fuck, they left out the full story. Even the most violent murder mysteries tended to have far less bloodshed—and a total absence of people dying and crying out for something to save them while they were torn apart by the monsters they were supposed to come into the jungle to study.

It had been one of the most harrowing experiences Lynch had ever experienced. People had died, people had been killed, and he had killed a whole horde of the creatures. *And admit it, you even enjoyed it, something that could not be said by most of the survivors of that particular bout with danger.* Oddly enough, the truth of that didn't worry him overmuch.

Some of them needed to be shipped home. Others simply couldn't deal with the pressure. When word came from the brass to tell them they would go back in, they snapped and were never made whole again. Some people weren't built to deal with monsters.

His brother had been one of the few who had survived the situation intact. Corwin had been a tough motherfucker and had stuck around even after his tour of duty ended and made money as a mercenary on the American base until he was killed on one of his runs.

The dumb bastard. What possessed him to try to run with one of the Pita plants? That was back when people still imagined it was possible to do and he was annihilated by the beasts that had been enraged by the attempt.

Or so the mission report had told him. The Lynch family had never been an easy one to deal with, and Adrian had made sure to stay apprised of any new information on the people who had been around Corwin when he died. He'd never liked his brother that much, but it was owed to family, right?

Salinger Jacobs, the specialist on Corwin's team, had stuck around the Zoo longer than expected and even became a merc in his own right. He'd started a company that did well and brought two other members in who had been part of Corwin's team—Dr. Courtney Monroe, the other specialist on the team, and Madigan Kennedy, former sergeant and now retired and working with Jacobs.

Davis had been a part of the team too, but he had an accident and lost one of his legs and had shipped home to the States—to retire, probably. Most of the others were either dead or gone, recovering from what happened to them in the Zoo, but one or two had stuck around.

I've thought about revenge more than once but honestly, the fact that Corwin was an asshole doesn't mean they didn't do what they could to save the dumbass' life. They'd had a hard time of it themselves, so there was no point in any kind of revenge quest.

Still, on the way back there with the memories of fighting side by side with that asshole made him angry. It was an irrational anger and he was well aware of that. The people who had managed to put themselves together in an environment that had earned the name of hell more effectively than any other place on earth weren't responsible for what happened to his brother. They were merely witnesses.

And yet he wanted to take it out on them like his family was owed blood for his loss. Which was why, when the call came for people who knew the Zoo to return for round two, he was one of the first to jump on the wagon. *You seriously need to be a unique kind of crazy or stupid to be convinced to go back to the Zoo once you were lucky enough to leave.*

There were the people who enjoyed the danger and couldn't get that kind of high anywhere else. The adrenaline that came from risking your life when you pitted it against the savage beasts of the jungle was addictive. Then there were those who needed the money—which was offered in great abundance—and were willing to roll the dice with the crazy shit that was about to run into them. The hope, of course, was to be able to walk away and live long enough to spend the money they were offered.

Adrian wasn't entirely sure which one he was. For one thing, he needed the money as much as the next guy. After he left the army and returned home, there hadn't been many job opportunities that didn't involve him simply doing what he had done before but for less money.

Unlike Corwin, though, he didn't enjoy the violence and the crazy shit he needed to put up with. It wasn't hard to admit that he didn't like the look of people when they died, and he didn't get high off the power that came from being the one to kill them. He was a whole different kind of fucked-up in the head.

He'd taken disability pay, a pension, and walked away to open a bar—and enjoyed working there. There was a certain pleasurable kind of peace that came from simply doing his job from day to day. He'd wake around the same time every morning and go home in time to catch a show and get to bed before he started the routine all over again. It was boring but it was nice.

Now, he was back at the Zoo. The bar needed renovations, and the five million pounds that were offered on this contract would cover that and more. They had even paid him in advance, which meant his wife had already begun work on what they had planned and would pay off their debts while he was gone. It wouldn't be for more than two weeks, but it would be dangerous. No one who paid this much money would bother to deny that, which was why he had insisted he be paid in advance.

He intended to complete the job—the details of which had been kept from him—and he would go back and enjoy the fruits of his labors. In the future, he'd hire professional bartenders and only show up to count the money and maybe give his soldier buddies free drinks.

If he survived. That could never be taken for granted out there. That particular thought was one he'd had in the old days when he'd been there. He was one of the first to step into the fucking jungle and the only one of that first wave of the British arrivals who was still alive now. The old lesson he had taken away from the fucking place was that when you went in, there was no rule that said that you would walk out again.

All those memories and thoughts rushed back to him when he stepped off the plane and looked out into the French base spread before him. He breathed in the crisp morning desert air, looked up, and immediately saw the green stain on the far horizon that seemed determined to take over the Sahara.

Hell, it had already grown beyond what he could recall as if its entire purpose was to engulf what was little more than endless stretches of sand.

"Lieutenant Lynch?" A man stood at the base of the steps that descended from the plane.

"Not anymore," he replied with a small smile, took the proffered hand, and shook it briskly. "It's simply Adrian now."

"Well, it's nice to meet you," the stranger replied, his handshake firm. "I'm Alex Kovacs, the intelligence liaison for this mission. The rest of the team is already waiting, so if you'll follow me?"

Lynch complied and they entered a vehicle which was driven to a warehouse situated on the far side of the base. It looked mostly deserted, except for the group of vehicles that were parked outside. When he was guided in, he saw the rest of the team was already there.

"I hope you rested on the plane." Kovacs chuckled and patted him on the shoulder. "We'll move out in half an hour."

"Rest is for the weak," Lynch grumbled. He'd been told he would be armed and armored with the best money could buy, and when he moved to the crate that was marked for his use, he realized they hadn't been kidding. Hyde designed some of the most impressive weapons on the market and had put out some of the prime hard-hitting combat suits in the world, and they had thought to give one to him.

Well, lend one to him, anyway. He doubted they would give him a piece of tech that was easily worth upward of three or four million pounds. There wasn't much he would be able to do with it anyway. What the hell could a civilian bar owner do with a more mobile version of a tank?

"Hey," said a voice not far from him. Lynch turned to see a man with pale skin and bright red hair, complete with freckles, who stared at him as he began to retrieve the pieces of the suit from the crate. "George Kelly. Nice to meet you."

"Adrian Lynch," he replied and they shook firmly.

"British, huh?" Kelly laughed. "SAS?"

"Once upon a time, yeah," he answered. "That was a while ago, though. They only hired me because I have experience in this fucking jungle."

"We all do," the man replied. He'd already donned his suit's boots and worked on the other pieces of his armor. "I'm fairly sure it was a prerequisite from the people they were hiring. I guess too many people died when they were paid a shitload of money without having any experience of the unique dangers that come from that fucking jungle. These guys know better. They know that to beat the best, you have to be the best."

"And you're the best?" Lynch retorted. "Let me guess. Marine Force Recon?"

"Bitch, please, do I look like a fucking jarhead to you?" The man smirked. "Navy SEAL, thank you very much."

"Retired, I assume. At least, I don't think they'd hire someone directly from the armed forces."

"You're not wrong." Kelly pulled the arms of his suit on and rolled his shoulders. "Fuck, these are quality suits. I've retired from the armed forces and worked in the private sector for a while. There's a fair amount of money in that, but after work I had went badly, my employers needed me off the payroll while they're under investigation. There's nothing like being paid to take a vacation out here again, wouldn't you say?"

"Sure." He assumed it explained the kind of man Kelly was—one who loved the Zoo because it was the only place where he could feel alive since everywhere else in the world seemed to pale in comparison.

A man like him would not acclimate well to the real world again and, as he said, there would be complications. Lynch guessed the work that went badly had done so because people died when he decided he wouldn't play by the rules of the world around him anymore.

It was a terrifying prospect and one Lynch lived with every day. The knowledge that he would never feel as alive as he did when he strapped into a combat suit and headed into the fucking jungle—a place where it was kill or be killed, and where he was the best at killing—was disconcertingly chilling.

He'd simply never thought about it this clearly before.

Their conversation was interrupted when what looked like another suit in a massive box was wheeled in. As it came closer, Lynch studied the specs printed on the box and emitted a low whistle of appreciation.

"Holy shit." Kelly grunted, apparently in agreement with the approval. "What the— I didn't know humans could use a suit like this."

"Eh, if you train someone to take the Gs, they can use virtually any kind of suit," he replied. "It's kind of like astronaut training but about a thousand times worse. I wonder what kind of person is trained for combat and for going into space."

It was a good question. Twenty-five operatives had been brought in for this mission, including Kovacs, who was already suited in his armor like he knew what he was doing.

"Who'll wear that baby?" The ex-SEAL asked the question that plagued Lynch's mind as well. "I thought our team was already all assembled. Will anyone else join us?"

"In a way. The answer to your question is both a yes and a hefty, resounding no," Kovacs replied and supervised as the technicians began to remove the suit from its crate. "There will be another member of the team, but no one else will physically join us. Oh, and no one will wear that baby either."

CHAPTER NINE

There were people in the world who didn't enjoy what they did for a living. This was true despite the fact that—in some cases, anyway—they had spent months and sometimes years studying to do precisely that work and hated the studying for it as well.

Amanda could understand the concept of having to work simply to keep one's head above water, financially speaking. There were also cases when one needed to put their dreams on the back burner because they had higher priorities. Having to care for a family member, or maybe they were married or had kids and needed to provide for them were common reasons. She understood all that. Priorities shifting was a part of real life and not a joking matter at all.

Still, there were people out there who were young and still in their prime who went into university and studied for a job they knew they would dislike. There were reasons for that too, of course. Family pressure was one or wanting to be stable so as to pursue their dreams later on in their lives.

While Amanda could empathize with the problems that came from one's family pressuring you into something you weren't sure you would like, they still needed to be able to find something in their lives they enjoyed doing and pursue that.

She, for instance, had always been fascinated by the working and moving parts in engines and larger machinery. Her father worked in the field and, sensing his daughter's interest, began to teach her the basics of the job.

Eventually, when she moved away from her parents for personal reasons, she'd taken a couple of mechanics courses and, once she completed those, had gone and obtained a bachelor's degree in mechanical engineering off her GI Bill after she joined the military.

It was something that interested her, and while the work could be a little humdrum at times, there was still a distinct pleasure that came from taking intricate machines and devices apart, discovering how they worked, and putting them back together again—and maybe even adding a couple of improvements on the way.

Being a mechanic was her dream job and she had found herself a little niche that allowed her to do that for a living —and she made one hell of a good living at it too, all while being her own boss.

She owed the place where she was in her life to the folks at Heavy Metal—Sal, Courtney, and Madigan. When she had been in a position she wouldn't change because she lacked the energy to do it, for lack of a better term, Sal had shown up and made her an offer she knew she couldn't refuse. She'd taken it and it was a life-changing moment for her.

Of course, she'd made the decision eventually to move on from Heavy Metal as well. As much as she appreciated the team for what they'd done for her, she had needed to make a choice. Heavy Metal was going places, but they weren't places she wanted to go.

She wasn't like Sal, who got his jollies by flinging himself into dangerous situations and becoming someone he'd never been before. Before she joined the team, she'd made an effort to read up on him and the details had been apparent. He'd been a genius but as lazy as hell before he got to the Zoo, when he was forced to get off his ass and do something with his life. Once that change had come over him, there was no going back and he had gone all in.

Amanda appreciated that, but she wasn't the same. She couldn't continue to rush into the jungle and not know if she would come out again. It had been a question she had wrestled with since her injury in the jungle, but the decision was made for her after she met Bev.

Meeting someone she wanted to come home to was another life-changing moment in her life. She had been in a handful of relationships prior to that. Initially, she'd started out dating men, but once she discovered that simply wasn't what she was interested in, she'd moved to the other side. Her folks were rather conservative about that kind of shit, though, so she made sure there were a couple of states between her and them before she told them.

Her father's reaction had been mostly negative, while her mother proved to be the most supportive of the two, although that still wasn't saying much. She had stayed away until they calmed the fuck down and eventually persuaded her parents and siblings to come to terms with it, even if they didn't like it. She knew she would not be invited to the Gutierrez family dinners anymore, but that was a small price to pay.

It was for the best. The family dinners tended to be a shit-show of angry people who didn't want to hang out together being forced to rub shoulders through the tenuous ties of family.

As it turned out, the best family was the one you were able to choose for yourself, and that included her Heavy Metal family. Bev, a researcher brought over to work on the French base, helped them to keep track of all the changes that happened in the Zoo or something like that.

The woman liked to talk about her job almost as much as Amanda did, but she had a feeling that neither of them was knowledgeable enough in the other's field to remember much of what was said. She did like how enthusiastic her partner was about her work—in that she was kind of like Sal but a whole lot sexier.

She had needed time away from Heavy Metal to get a better feel of who she would be as her own person, with Bev and working independently. That didn't mean she couldn't hang with them from time to time. Anja was one of the best drinkers she'd ever had the opportunity to party with, and her work with Savage in Philly had been tremendous fun too. Besides, they sent a considerable amount of well-paying work her way, which she couldn't afford to turn down at this point, given that she was now in business for herself.

The money aside, working on the Hammerheads always brought both fun and satisfaction. They didn't mind when she made alterations she thought would be worth testing in the field, so she put a good amount of time, effort, and patience into making their Hammerheads some of the toughest in the business.

And damned if the group hadn't decided to test that shit out. Driving the Hammerheads into the Russian base while trying to retake it had been a gamble that paid off in the end for them, but the damage sustained by the vehicles had been substantial.

Madigan had filled her in on the details—the nightmarish, tentacle-filled details—and about how those were responsible for most of the damage that had been sustained by the vehicles. It was an interesting study into exactly how powerful those mutant appendages were, but in the end, that was more Bev's forte than hers. She was simply there to repair the damage.

And there was a great deal of it. The wheels had almost been pried off, which in turn caused significant structural damage to the frame of the vehicle. It had taken her days to alter and weld the pieces so they would be fully prepared for the replacement parts she'd ordered.

That was merely the first of many, many problems she faced in repairing the vehicle. There were enough issues with the electronics and smaller pieces to keep her busy while she waited for the parts to be delivered.

Before she realized it, night had fallen outside and she had to work with the light from the lamps she'd set up around the Hammerhead. She knew it was time to head home and maybe find something to watch online before she curled up beside Bev and got some rest before she began the whole process again tomorrow.

But now that she had some of the parts that were needed to fix the damage to the engine, she doubted she would be finished anytime soon. Quite simply, she knew she was one of those people who couldn't leave a job half-done. If she did set it all aside and head home to spend time away from the work, all her enjoyment would be sucked out through her obsession to finish what she'd started.

She also knew herself well enough to pace herself and take on only as much work per day as she was capable of doing without burning herself out. Earlier that day, she'd made a deal with herself that she would quit and take time off once she had finished repairs to the internal shock absorbers. These were meant to protect the engine and other critical functions inside the vehicle from the kind of movement a Hammerhead was likely to endure.

The technical name was inertia dampeners, but she knew shocks when she saw them. They didn't even bother to alter the design aside from making the pieces smaller and adding about fifteen of them all around the engine compartment.

Amanda liked to call them as she saw them, no matter what the actual name was. When it came to vehicles, anyway.

Putting all other thoughts aside, she turned the lights up to provide her the simulation of sunlight from outside her little garage and resumed work. Her first task was to use her welder to fix the pieces that were broken, depending on what they were and their size and purpose.

She'd removed the pieces that were too damaged to fix, tossed them into the scrap heap, and ordered new ones. While Heavy Metal would pick up the tab for the parts she ordered, there was no point in overcharging her friends simply because it would save her a few hours of work.

Bent into the engine compartment as she was, with her flare goggles and protective mask on and welder in hand, she didn't see or hear when someone entered the garage until she felt the vibration of something placed on the side of the vehicle. She powered the gun down and straightened in surprise. The love of her life stood beside her with a wide grin and watched her work.

"Well, if you aren't a sight for sore eyes, as you Americans say," Bev said in her charming French accent and chuckled.

Amanda pulled her mask and goggles up and raised an eyebrow. "Don't be ridiculous. I'm covered in about fifteen different kinds of grease, soot, and dirt and I've sweated in this garage all day. Oh, and I'm having a very bad hair day."

"Oh, I don't know…you all dirty and bent over a hard surface… I'm sure there's something we can work with there." The other woman grinned, leaned closer, and placed a light kiss on her lips. "Although, now that I think about it, you do have something of an odor about you."

She laughed. "Seriously, if I were in a Charlie Brown cartoon, you would see round, squiggly lines coming away from me."

"Charlie Brown?"

"Come on, you guys didn't have Charlie Brown in France?" she asked.

"Did you have Corneil et Bernie?" Bev riposted.

Amanda paused and thought for a moment before she shrugged. "Touche." She chuckled.

"I love it when you talk dirty to me." Her partner smirked and placed a hand on her shoulder. "But I don't want to interrupt you while you're working. Not any more than I already have, anyway."

"I only need another hour with these shocks," she said quickly.

"I know, and while I'm waiting for an hour, I thought I'd bring you dinner," Bev answered and gave her another kiss but on her cheek this time. "It's only chicken, rice, and stir-fried veggies I whipped up. You'll have a real dinner when you get home."

She smiled and resisted the urge to hug the woman. It wouldn't do to leave her clothes all stained with grease, so she returned her girlfriend's kiss, careful to keep some distance between the two of them, and stroked her hair. "Love ya, you crazy French lady."

"Love ya back, crazy Spanish lady," she replied and headed toward the door.

"Oh, for fu— I'm American, damn it!" Amanda called in protest, but Bev was already out the door. She thought she could still hear the woman laughing as she set off to the apartment they shared. As she headed to the steaming plate of food her girlfriend had left, she chuckled and shook her head.

She would need to thank the woman in kind too. Maybe her huevos rancheros were a way to start—they were famous for their quality as comfort food. She could prepare them while her lover was still asleep and serve it to her as breakfast in bed. That was always a popular thing, right?

For now, she simply made a note of it to be pursued later. Bev had been hellishly supportive of her and even let her move into her apartment despite the fact that they had only dated for a few months when she had decided she wanted to move to the French base. It had been a somewhat hasty progression of their relationship, but it seemed to have only served to bring them closer.

She picked the plate up and toyed with the food as she looked around the room and eventually decided to sit inside the Hammerhead. Seats were situated all around the garage, of course, but they were mostly stools and more than a little uncomfortable, especially for sitting and eating on. Those inside the Hammerhead were spacious as they had to fit a soldier who was fully suited for combat and were surprisingly comfortable as well. She settled in, propped her feet on the dashboard, and devoted her full attention to the delicious meal.

Without a doubt, she would need to knock those huevos out of the park if she aimed to match Bev's efforts, she decided after only a few mouthfuls.

Her train of thought was quickly interrupted, though, when a couple of the electronics came back online inside the vehicle. It had happened at random intervals over the past few days since it had been delivered to her for repairs. The HUD on the windscreen had come on, as well as the speakers. The only difference was that this time, when the speakers came online, she could hear a voice speaking through them.

"What the fuck?" she muttered and leaned a little closer.

There was some static, no doubt the result of some of the wires that were still exposed. She placed her plate on the seat beside her and worked quickly on the wiring until the voice became a little clearer.

"Good evening, sexy," said the slightly warbled and warped yet still familiar voice.

"God fucking damn it." Amanda growled with real annoyance. "Is that you, Connie?"

"In the...code, I guess," the AI replied.

CHAPTER TEN

The weather was warm and settled. The days had been that way for the last couple of weeks, honestly. Even when it rained, the water seemed to fall at the perfect temperature for a Jacuzzi. For people who had to work during those days, it was a living hell, especially for those who were unlucky enough to be in some kind of uniform and worked in a location that didn't have an air conditioner. This was Florida, so most locations had AC, but that wasn't something that could be depended on, especially if those people in question had to work outside.

For those who didn't have to work over the weekend, it was utterly perfect. It was the time of year to head onto the beaches, enjoy the scenery, and relax, all while protected under shade or a liberal application of copious amounts of sunscreen if shade wasn't available. They were close enough to the holidays that tourists from all over the world had already begun to stream in, which made the public beaches a fantastic place to be if you liked to look around, see variety, and learn about new cultures, or even try new foods and be sociable in general.

It was a good time for people who weren't quite so active socially as well. Kent Addams didn't like the family excursions that took him, his wife, and two kids into places that were jam-packed with other people. When he could, he would arrange for them to spend their weekends and time off at home and away from the crowds.

Unfortunately, his wife Janet was sociable and so were his kids, which meant compromises invariably had to be made. For the most part, it included spending their time off in the relative comfort of their mid-range suburban home. The condition was that the crowds, relatively speaking, were allowed to come over and visit.

It was an acceptable compromise, but Kent still made sure to let both his wife and kids know that he wasn't happy about having their friends and neighbors over for a Sunday barbecue. There were way too many kids, for starters—his own children's friends with their parents along with the neighbors and their offspring. A veritable horde would descend to enjoy the burgers and hot dogs he prepared on his grill, the beers he had in his fridge, and the pool that was a nice, cool relief from the heat of the day.

In all honesty, while he did like to complain, being outside, cooking, drinking beer, and chatting about how the Dolphins might have a chance this year was a good day in his book.

Once the grilling was done, they could head inside to the comfort of the climate-controlled living room and watch whatever game was shown live while they chatted and enjoyed more beers.

Another perk was that the visitors even brought their own beer, so it wasn't like he would be out of pocket by entertaining guests. Well, not overly so, anyway.

He would still make a stink about it later, of course. Doing so would allow him to avoid having to clean up and even give him leverage when he needed it against Janet in their weekly budget discussions. He would be damned if the woman bought another pair of shoes on his credit card. She had a job and was an equal earner in the home. As far as he was concerned, she could buy that shit herself—not that she needed any more shoes.

At least they had a reason for the event this time. His youngest, Alec, was celebrating his fifth birthday. He'd had cake on the actual day in the middle of the week, but they had the party now during the weekend when everyone could make it. Kent was a little vague on the logic of it, but hey, it meant people would have cake again, and he was all for that given his somewhat demanding sweet tooth.

"Kent, are you finished with the grill, honey?" Janet called from the pool and he looked up from where he was still working on it. He'd forgotten to clean it last week when they'd celebrated one of the neighbors' kids' birthdays. Having put it off until the day it was needed meant he now had to work on it before he could put any meat on it.

The guests had already begun to arrive, and he had a whole list of chores to get done before he could relax and stand in front of the grill, take orders for the burgers and hot dogs, and ignore the voices that wanted theirs well-done. It was merely a matter of principle. He bought the meat and made the burgers himself, prepared them the night before, and left them to marinate all night in the fridge. They were made to be served medium-rare at most.

He'd had this argument with people hundreds, if not thousands of times before, and he had found that it was better to simply take the order, smile and nod, and give them a medium-rare burger anyway. Ninety percent of the time, they wouldn't even notice. The other ten percent would ask him to make another, he'd smile and nod again, and they wouldn't realize they got more or less the same the second time around. He would be damned before he served anyone a piece of charcoal misnamed as a well-done burger.

"Babe?" Janet called again.

"I'm almost finished, honey. What do you need?" Kent yelled in response and realized that, while he had been lost in thought, he had completed the task. He was merely cleaning what had already been done.

"I have to put sunscreen on the kids. Would you mind sifting the pool quickly?" she asked, shouting from the other side of the house. He sighed, rolled his shoulders, and nodded.

Fortunately, he realized that she couldn't see his nod before she yelled again. "I'll get right on it, babe!" he responded and cleared his throat as he pushed the wheeled grill out of the garage and into the backyard where a couple of people already stood, sipping longnecks and chatting.

He greeted them by slapping a fake smile on and shaking hands, answering questions about how hot it was with variations of the term "preaching to the choir, buddy." As he talked, he picked up the pool sifter and set about

clearing the collection of leaves and trash that had accumulated in the water overnight. He wasn't sure where all
the crap had come from. It wasn't like they had an excess of
trees in the area.

But that was inconsequential. They were always there,
and it was easier to simply deal with them than waste time
considering their origins. He finished the pool and hurried
inside, added a six-pack of beers to the cooler where he
stacked the meat and buns, and brought them all outside.
With everything he needed, he took his place at the grill
while the rest of their guests began to arrive.

It wasn't the first time and it would not be the last that
Kent wished they could simply pack up and move to an
area of the country that wasn't summer weather all year
long. He had been raised in Oregon, where winters were
cold and summers were only slightly warmer.

Back then, he would have killed to live somewhere
sunny and warm all year round, which told him he was a
grass-is-greener kind of guy. It was a good way to
discourage himself from moving time and time again. He
applied himself to the task at hand, fired the grill up, and
put a couple of burgers on. That done, he added a couple of
buns over the flame to get them started.

A few orders already began to come in and he nodded
and smiled to get the party started. Cake would be brought
out much later. The kids were so psyched to get into the
pool that convincing them to sit around a table and sing
would honestly be an exercise in futility. It would be best
to let them get all their yayas out beforehand—and again
once they were on a sugar high from the cake.

It would, Kent thought, be a long day. He shook his

head as he prepped the first burger of the day and handed it to the birthday boy.

"Thanks, Daddy!" the kid shouted and carried his plate carefully to the pool while he attempted to sneak a couple of pieces of the food en route. Janet would prep the salad, coleslaw, and fries inside while he worked on the burgers. They had been through this process so many times that it had turned into a well-oiled machine.

As the sun climbed higher and the day grew hotter, Kent needed a quick break from standing over the hot grill. He moved closer to the pool while he enjoyed the coldest beer he could find from inside his cooler. The oldest of their two boys—Kent Jr or KJ, as they tended to call him—stood beside the pool with a couple of his friends. He was twelve years old and at the age where he had begun to think he was too cool to have parents. It was still early days so he wasn't quite as deep into it as he could be.

Kent remembered being quite the rebellious teenager himself. Then again, KJ had a few more years to reach those heights, and he found himself walking on eggshells around the kid, not wanting to exacerbate the situation. It was on Janet to be the firm parent and again, that seemed to even out since she spoiled little Alec rotten, which forced him to be the firmer hand of the two.

"Hey, Dad." KJ grunted what might have been a greeting and looked at him as he moved closer. He and his friends were huddled around a phone, watching videos from one of the more popular new apps on the market called ZooTube.

"Hey, kid," Kent replied and took a slow sip of his drink. He didn't want to interrupt their viewing pleasure but was a little curious as to what exactly they were watching. Once or twice, he had been guilty of watching vids on the service himself and even followed a couple of the more popular channels.

He focused mostly on the game channels, though, since he was a fan of those and honestly didn't have the stomach for what was going on in the Zoo. He had a couple of friends out there and he didn't want to think about what was happening, be it real or fictional.

It didn't look like his son followed his preferences, though. Either they were making one of the most realistic games in history, or the video the kid watched was actual footage of people fighting inside the jungle. Of course, it could also be a trailer for one of the newer games. They were known to be of almost film quality and leagues better than the game they were intended to represent.

As he watched the video progress, he began to think they weren't viewing something from the jungle since the perspective they watched from suddenly had four extra arms extend from his suit. He hacked monsters to pieces with a sword that was held in his own two hands, while the other four worked to keep the other creatures at bay, shooting and hacking at them.

"What are you guys watching?" Kent finally asked and realized that he wasn't interrupting when KJ turned and seemed excited to talk about it.

"Oh, these guys are Heavy Metal," the youth replied with a broad smile. "It's a mercenary group that works with the American military in the Zoo. They're out there, and their videos are mostly real recordings of when the team goes into the jungle."

"Most of them?" He was still a little confused.

"Oh, yeah, they're called in to test new suits in simulators, and sometimes even test some of the beta versions of the games they release," one of the other teenagers said. "Although in this case, it's a base that was taken over by the Zoo and they had to go in and fight to get some of the survivors out."

He had heard about that on the news. A whole military base being swallowed up by a possibly alien jungle was no laughing matter.

"How can this be real, though?" he asked. "He's fighting with six arms. How the hell is he able to control them?" He was asking from a point of some knowledge since he did run software development for the companies that made the combat suits used inside the jungle.

"Oh, he probably has some kind of software that helps him while in combat mode," KJ mumbled and seemed to want to get back to watching the video as the action had begun to pick up. It was a little worrying since Kent had tried external software that was supposed to operate the peripheral weapons on suits.

They had mostly been the shoulder-mounted rocket launchers and Gatling guns and the tests always bumped into the problem of the software picking up friendly targets and shooting them too. A whole Friend or Foe software needed to be developed to help with that, and in the end, the project became too complicated and his company dropped it.

It looked like someone had picked up his company's slack and delivered. If these videos were even real.

"I do have a question, though," he said and pushed his luck a little. "If this is all real, who posts the videos?"

"Well, all the suits have a camera installed in the HUD," KJ responded and raised an eyebrow like he was asking his father why the man was so behind the times.

"Well, yes, I know that," he responded sharply. He wanted to tell his son that he'd helped to develop the technology but didn't want to seem like he was bragging. "I'm merely asking who collects, edits, and posts all these videos for the channel."

The group of youths exchanged a quick look. It seemed like none of them knew who in the Heavy Metal merc group posted the content they all enjoyed.

Kent shrugged and returned to start on another batch of burgers and hot dogs.

Anja leaned away from the screen, rubbed her eyes, and allowed herself a long yawn. She eased back until she heard the tell-tale sound of her chair creaking, which warned her that she was about to lean back too far. Madigan said the sound would drive her crazy one of these days and had even gone so far as to offer her a brand-new chair—anyone she fancied, with the sole requirement that it did not creak when she rocked back.

The Russian hacker declined the woman's offer. It was generous, of course, and she was well aware of how expensive it would be to ship an office chair all the fucking way out there, but she liked the chair she used now. The server room was her little domain, and she preferred things to stay the way they were.

Of course, after long nights of editing the videos for her Heavy Metal channel, she needed time on the sofas outside or, in extreme circumstances, the bed in her room.

Sal knew she was running the channel, and when he'd found out, he'd given her a choice. Either the money she made from the advertisements on the channel would go into Heavy Metal or, should she choose to keep it for herself, it would be deducted from the salary he paid her. She'd chosen the latter option. The ZooTube channel was her baby, after all, even if it was based on the other members of the team.

"Anja!" Sal called from the kitchen. "Did you get any word from Solodkov yet?"

She could have sworn he was already in bed. The treatment cocktail he was on these days had thrown his body clock out of whack.

"He said he'll be here around ten," she yelled, not wanting to have to get up from her chair.

"Thanks," he said. "I'll head to bed now."

"You don't need to run the details of your schedule past me," she reminded him. "You're my boss, remember?"

There was no answer from the kitchen. Maybe he'd already gone to bed, she mused and returned her attention to editing their videos.

CHAPTER ELEVEN

She really had no clue what she was looking at beyond the simple disconcerting fact that it was the dead of night in a place where even sunlight seldom reached, even in the middle of the day. Her vision was currently filled with what she could only describe as pitch-black darkness barely softened by a combination of night vision and motion sensors combined in cutting-edge software and hardware. These enabled her to have some semblance of imaging of the world around her, although it was shrouded in varying shades of green.

It wasn't the best perspective to see the Zoo through, especially given the sheer amount of death that inevitably lurked out there in the darkness. The jungle loomed constantly on the perimeter, waiting for them to take one wrong step—which was increasingly easy, given that it was pitch-fucking-black.

That said, something tickled the back of Martin's spine despite the fact that her weary body demanded sleep. It was bad enough that she was still dressed in her full combat armor, which made it like trying to fall asleep on a pile of brambles. Not only that, but the suit overreacted to every little movement she made while she tried to get comfortable and merely added to the overall annoyance.

The tingle could have simply been sweat trailing down her spine. This deep in the jungle, they were far from where the lack of moisture made the desert air cold and sometimes, almost icy. There was considerable humidity in the trees around them to trap the heat they were bombarded with all fucking day long. It was merely another way this place was as uncomfortable as hell.

Despite all the other possible irritations, her instinct told her something was out there. She pushed from her prone position and peered with greater focus into what little she could see in the Zoo. Again, it wasn't much and the vague movement of the trees moving in the wind was all she could make out in any kind of detail.

Then again, the trees were all fucking huge and it was difficult to not see them, right? She knew they had grown in a matter of months and simply kept on growing after that, but they were still large enough to rival those in the Amazon that had grown and pushed for their space in the jungle for upwards of the past three or four thousand years.

It was a moot point, but she wondered briefly how long trees lived for. Then, she wondered how long the Amazon rain forest had been in existence and whether it was even many millions of years.

Oh... Oh, that is not good. She tensed when she suddenly realized what had triggered all her internal alarms.

Martin pushed hastily to her feet in the location she'd

chosen not too far from the other team members. Her sudden movements and the fact that, even with power armor, the suits were less than quiet, was enough to wake most of the team. The two who currently stood watch turned to look at her and half-expected there to be some kind of attack, although they hadn't seen anything.

"What's up, Captain?" one of them asked with a furtive survey of the area.

"I think we're about to have company," she replied, drew her assault rifle out of its holster on her back, and prepped the rest of her weapons.

"What makes you say that?" the second man asked. Even with their doubts, both men began to prepare for an attack anyway. She knew she should feel honored that they trusted her that much. Then again, they were all out there together. If one of them alerted the others to a potential danger, they had to trust that it wasn't merely the other person going crazy. Which, of course, they would think if her hunch was wrong.

"Look at the trees around you and notice how they're moving," she said while she loaded a full mag into the assault rifle. She checked the weapon, returned her attention to the two men on guard, and waited for the penny to drop for them too. There was no point in laying the whole picture out for them immediately. They needed to see it for themselves, if only to confirm that she wasn't, in fact, nuts.

"Sure, they're moving with the wind," the first man said, although he did at least make the effort to look more closely. "There's nothing strange about that."

"Sure." Martin grunted. "But what do the wind gauges in your suits tell you?"

"Uh...no wind," the second man said and his hand reached instinctively for his weapon when the reality began to dawn on him too. Even the branches that were below where the wind might blow higher in the canopy moved and swayed gently like they were caught in the breeze as well. Except nothing blew into the Zoo.

If only one branch was moving, it wouldn't be enough to be alarming. It could simply be one of the tree-living simians jumping from branch to branch. What put her on edge was the fact that all the branches moved in unison.

"What do...do you think it is?" the first man asked as he readied his weapons and quietly activated the alarm that woke their few teammates still asleep and alerted them to the possibility of danger.

"Well, we all know the tentacle creatures have been seen before—or only the tentacles, at least," she replied and kept her tone to a hushed whisper. It was instinctive even though she knew her voice would not be able to break through the confines of her suit unless she activated the speakers on the sides of her helmet. Some things remained reflexive, no matter what tech you used. "It might be one of those. It might simply be a whole horde of monsters moving through the trees for some reason or another. Does anyone want to stick around to find out?"

The rest of the team quickly caught each other up on the situation and showed them the trees, and the reality soon dawned on them. It took less than five minutes before they were all up and about and began to pack their camp up. They moved as quickly and quietly as possible to prep their weapons and gather the sensor array. Stealth wasn't achievable, given that they all wore suits that weighed in the excess of two tons, but it was encouraging that they at least made an effort.

They were ready to move by the time Martin could identify something moving in the branches within the thick tree cover. If she hadn't known any better, she would have said something attempted to hide from them in the upper reaches and intentionally tried to be sneaky and disguise its actions as wind disturbance.

It was the kind of intelligent movement that made her wonder if there was something sentient out there that tried to control whatever was happening in the Zoo. She couldn't prove it, of course, and even the specialists were divided on the topic.

Some claimed evidence indicated there was a sentient intelligence in the Zoo and holy shit fucking hell it was there to kill them all. Others disagreed and offered a counterargument that it could be explained purely by the coordinated way animals lived together when they shared a biosphere.

She didn't know what the fuck they were on about. Nowhere in the history of animals did they ever team up to fight an invading force. Or, even more discomforting, throw themselves into a metaphorical and yet chillingly literal meat grinder to be killed the way the monsters did.

It was an annoying and terrifying thought that came to her mind as she moved through the various little rituals she followed every time she faced a combat situation. The routine was simple enough—check her weapons, check her suit, and make sure her side weapons were prepped. It was simply a process to make ready to avoid any surprises that would result from her oversight when the fighting started.

After a slow, deep breath, she led the group forward and through the jungle, heading in deeper against every instinct in her body. Every part of her wanted to turn the fuck around and push out of the Zoo to tell the brass they had gone in, couldn't find anything, and got the fuck out again. No one would blame them for it.

If worse came to worst, they could simply send someone else, preferably with a much larger team and with a shit-ton more firepower. Maybe they could find a way to fit a tank cannon into a combat suit that would make sure they could kill virtually anything they encountered, the next five monsters behind it, as well as a couple of trees.

They needed to have tanks in there. For now, though, she'd have to content herself with the fact that the velvet darkness was gradually receding as the faint grey of early dawn nudged it aside.

The first hint of movement came from above. She thought she could make out something that looked like tentacles squirming in the upper branches. The almost snake-like movement made her skin crawl simply thinking about it, but she needed to focus. More importantly, she needed to focus on two panthers that crept over the branches lower down and stared at the suited humans while they peeled their lips back to reveal their venom-tipped fangs.

"Heads-up, topside!" Martin called and immediately raised her weapon. The three men closest to her would not look upward but keep their weapons trained on any creatures that might approach her on the ground. She paused as the HUD slipped seamlessly into combat mode.

The targeting reticle tracked her weapon's movements,

looked down the barrel, and took all the different variables the sensors picked up into account. The process would tell her where her next bullet fired would land with about ninety-nine or ninety-eight percent accuracy. She had seen a couple of shots go wide, but that had usually been down to some kind of mechanical failure.

This early in the fighting, though, she knew that when she flicked the firing mode to a three-round burst, at least the first three rounds would strike precisely where her suit told her they would. It wasn't something she needed to think about—despite the fact that every minute spent on the shooting range in boot camp had been filled with her drill sergeant yelling at her to not trust the weapons or the machinery that she would use.

The standard attitude was based on what the man had called Murphy's Laws of War. There was a handful of them.

Professionals were predictable, while amateurs were not. The enemy would invariably attack on two occasions —when they were ready, and when you were not. Most important, though, was a point that had been hammered into her at every opportunity, whether in boot camp or out in the field. Every weapon she carried or wore was made by the lowest bidder.

That had been a lesson hard-learned when she had been caught in the middle of the Amazon jungle in a confrontation with a couple of FARC insurgents. They tried to build a base in the French neck of those particular woods. In the middle of a firefight, she had picked the terrorists off one by one from a safe distance until one of them caught sight of her and retaliated, which was precisely when her assault rifle jammed on her.

She'd survived, although she'd had to improvise between her high-precision rifle and sidearm and running the hell away. Retreat relied on the words of yet another Murphy's Law of War. If the enemy is in range, so are you.

That one didn't usually apply in the Zoo, though. While the beasts could close distances at horrifying speed, they were usually in plain sight the whole time. This allowed the humans to attack as and when they needed to and enabled them to hold the monsters at bay while still being able to move. If the creatures ever learned to launch projectiles at the humans from a quasi-safe distance, the teams would seriously be in trouble. Crowd control when you needed to be in cover was a fucking nightmare.

The first panther dropped from the branches when three bullet holes punched through its torso. The second realized it was in danger and bounded with a low, growling roar into the attack. Martin adjusted her aim, pulled the trigger, and felled the beast in midair.

It didn't matter if you were shooting clay pigeons or possibly alien panther hybrids. That was a damn good shot.

She smiled and allowed herself a little pride in her abilities while she turned her attention to the branches above. Her gaze searched intently and tried to make sure there weren't any other monsters lurking there, poised to attack.

Her teammates had already swung into action to shoot and coordinate their lines of fire with their usual efficiency. The ground shook beneath her boots as a few of the larger creatures began to make their way into the battle.

Her task was to keep them clear from above for the moment, and that was what she needed to focus on.

It was difficult to not be distracted by the mutants she could see out of corners of her eyes that surged in to attack. The seismic sensors in her suit went wild, telling her that there was enough movement on the ground to register as 3.1 on the Richter scale. Huge gorillas with white fur and horns on their heads raced forward and disappeared when the concerted fusillade from the rest of her team eliminated them neatly and efficiently.

That was what she hoped, anyway. The other alternative was that they had backed off to regroup for another attack. A handful of larger simians in the branches above began to throw rocks at the group. She doubted the natural arsenal would penetrate the armor she wore, but a couple of rounds fired into the branches was enough to persuade them to go into hiding and she turned her attention to the adversaries on the ground.

After a hasty assessment of the situation, she strode to the left flank of their squad. From this new position, she delivered a volley of gunfire into a pack of hyenas that attempted to break through the firing line the humans had established.

It wasn't a realistic expectation but of all the Zoo creatures, these seemed the most willing to sacrifice themselves as meat shields for whatever attacked from behind them. Their whole purpose seemed to be to soak up as much lead as they could before they were killed.

Martin switched the firing mode to full auto and delivered a barrage at both the group that pushed toward them and the locusts that came in behind them. Her assault lasted only for about five seconds and left a pile of the creatures dead while she let her suit take over the duties of reloading her weapon. She drew her sidearm and emptied the mag on that weapon into a couple of the panthers that were all but shredded by the bullets.

The assault rifle was ready to fire again, and she raised it quickly and loaded a grenade into the launcher under the barrel.

"Let's keep moving, ladies!" she yelled as the grenade hurtled into the massed ranks of mutants ahead.

CHAPTER TWELVE

Sal groaned and rubbed his eyes as a low beeping noise dragged him unwillingly from sleep. Yes, he needed to take the treatment to make sure all the foul effects from taking the blue stuff—or licking Madie, as they called it—came to a damn end.

There were side effects, of course. He could still feel the power, speed, and stamina the blue stuff gave him, but he could also feel the energy in his body seeping away from time to time. It sucked. Feeling tired and mentally drained was simply the worst and reminded him of his time in college when he had attempted to reconcile having a life with being the only teenager on campus.

The other irritation was that there was no guarantee that it would work. He and Courtney had sifted through various trials run by the team at the black lab in Chernobyl and studied the various medications they had formulated in their attempt to counter the effects of the goop.

They had found nothing definitive, but a few things had stood out as having possibilities. While he hated the idea of being yet another guinea pig, he also knew he would do almost anything to fix the problem he had himself created. They had finally come up with a formula that would hopefully result in some reversal, at least, in the long-term but might also block the ongoing process the goop wrought in his system.

It was a necessary part of his life now. He had been greedy and careless and hadn't thought about the consequences of his actions, and he was willing to pay for that. No matter what he had to endure to be free of it, he knew none of the benefits he'd believed he'd gained were worth the ultimate cost. They were real, but the price tag was to place him under the control of a monster with tentacles and the ability to use them to horrify even the staunchest of hentai fans.

What made him a little suspicious was that, despite the less than pleasant side-effects of the treatment, he didn't feel that any of the previous effects associated with the goop had diminished. Of course, he felt foolish over his stupid mundane expectations of a substance that was probably alien.

As a scientist, he should have known better and he should have researched things before he chose to become his own lab rat. But despite all this, a suspicion remained in the back of his mind that the treatment wasn't doing much about the underlying problem. This was the real concern because it meant that should he encounter the monster in the future, there was a very real possibility that he would succumb to its call again.

"Sal?" Anja's voice said over the speakers. "Are you awake? If not, I'm sorry for waking you up."

"Nah, I'm up, no problem," he shouted, although he knew she wouldn't believe him. He pushed from the bed and rubbed his eyes once more. "I'm up!" he shouted again to make sure he believed it himself.

"Well, you'd better be." She chuckled. "Because Solodkov left a message. He's about fifteen minutes out, so unless you want him to bask in the presence of your newly woken presence, I suggest you get up, wash your face, change out of your PJs, and get coffee in you as quickly as possible. That's assuming you're not sleeping naked, of course."

"I'm no—that's none of your business," Sal grumbled and scowled as he turned the intercom off and stretched to try to convince his body to respond. He needed to get back in the game. Talking about what he slept in was not a topic for the intercom when a Russian money train headed their way to have a chat about the new missions they might be hired for.

In this case, though, he wore briefs and nothing else. Madigan had joined him in bed but they had both been too tired to engage in anything. Well, she had been since she was already asleep by the time he'd gotten around to sleeping.

The damn treatment played all kinds of hell with his body clock.

"Are you getting up, Sal?" Anja asked.

"Yeah, get off my back. You're not my real mom," he yelled in response. His thoughts had stirred the question of where Madigan was, of course, since she wasn't in bed. She was probably up already and going through her morning calisthenics.

He didn't approve of her leaving the compound for her

morning run, but she was the gunner of the team. It was a hell of a responsibility to keep them all safe, and she probably needed time to herself. He knew her well enough to accept that there was no way to persuade her to find another alternative. While she was an awesome woman, she still needed her space like everyone else did.

Sal pulled clothes on and splashed water on his face before he made himself the coffee Anja had sensibly suggested. It wasn't quite the pick-me-up he had hoped for, but in the end, all he needed to do was get himself to a place where he didn't simply answer any and every question posed to him. There was no need to let everyone else in on his secrets and especially not a member of Russian intelligence.

The caffeine seemed to kick in and reminded him of the problem he needed to address during the conversation. Whatever their visitor had to discuss, he needed to talk to Solodkov about a pay raise for their existing contract in case they didn't want to take any further work from him.

He'd have to go about it in the right way, of course, because it probably wasn't the best idea to piss the man off. While the Russian owed Heavy Metal for the lives of the only survivors of the last base, he was one of the toughest FSB operatives in the business. That hadn't changed simply because he now took the time to oversee the construction of another base. He wondered if he had asked for the job or had simply been ordered there. Either one was possible.

"Anja, could you let Madigan know Solodkov is on the way?" he asked and directed his attention to the nearest intercom while he sipped his coffee slowly in the kitchen.

"Are you kidding me?" she retorted. "She's the first one I

called. Although she's still on her morning jog, she's heading back now. Why the hell does she go jogging outside the compound? You'd think that she of all people would know about the kind of monsters out there and know to stay the fuck away from them, right?"

"Right?" He chuckled and shook his head. "Then again, she is the infamous Madigan Kennedy, so I kind of pity the foolish monster that tries to interrupt her daily jog. The chances are she'll be packing—and on something of an endorphin high that nothing wants to interrupt. Seriously."

"I hear you there, Sal." The hacker snickered. "Anyway, I've picked Solodkov up waiting outside. Do you think I should let him in or maybe let him stay there and stew to give him a chance to think about his mistakes?"

"What?" Sal snapped. "Why— Yes, let him in! Why would you let him stew outside? What mistakes do you think he made? Didn't he do all the work that got you cleared with the Russian Government?"

"Oh, yeah, although I think I did most of the work, and you guys did too since you pulled off saving the survivors from the old Russian base—with my help, of course." She chuckled.

"And mine," Connie interjected. "Yes, I too was involved in saving the lives of the paltry Russian meat bags and it should not be forgotten."

"I thought we had agreed that you wouldn't call humans meat bags," he grumbled. "It makes us all think that you intend to try to take over the world and you'll use us to maintain your servers once you're the overlord. How do you think that make us humans feel?"

"Like you lucked out on having such a fantastic over-lord?" the AI riposted smartly.

"Nope, it makes us feel like unplugging our overlord before the overlord has a chance to become our overlord," he pointed out. "Did I say overlord too much? It feels like I take all the meaning out of the word when I say it over and over again."

"I was about to say something," Anja replied.

"Did you let Solodkov in yet?"

A quick pause followed before she said, "I did now."

"Fuck." He finished his coffee hastily and headed out of the main building to where a Hammerhead pulled into the open area from the gate. Solodkov had come alone, as promised, and slid out of the vehicle. He did have a sidearm strapped to his hip but otherwise, it looked like he was out for a stroll while on vacation. Surprisingly, he wore a bowling shirt, beige slacks, and sported aviator sunglasses. He even had a damn good tan to go with it.

"Solodkov, nice to see you again," Sal said, took the man's hand, and shook it firmly. "It's always nice to have you at the compound."

"And it is always nice to come here," the Russian replied and looked around as he removed his sunglasses. "It truly is an impressive little setup you have. I always find it inspiring to know what humans can build even when faced with the kind of adversity we encounter daily out here."

"Well...uh, thanks?" He replied and narrowed his eyes. "That was a compliment, right?"

"Yes, it was." The Russian chuckled. "I did have to wait outside for almost five minutes when I arrived, though. I normally wouldn't say anything about it, but I did come here alone with only my sidearm for protection. I know we are some distance from the Zoo, but the same could be said of the old Russian base, and well...we all know how that turned out. Do you have issues with your electrical grid?"

"I...yes, that's less embarrassing." He sighed and shook his head. Five minutes? Anja really must have something of a death wish. Either that or she wanted to get back at Solodkov for something. They had both worked at the FSB during overlapping time periods, so maybe they had a past that he didn't know anything about. The hacker was a very private person—which was ironic, considering how much she was willing to pry into everyone else's lives. Well, could he call it prying if she knew everything there was to be known?

Yes, yes, he could. He would have a very stern talk with the woman when Solodkov left. For the moment, though, they had other details that needed to be discussed regarding the future of their working together.

"Shall we go inside?" he asked and gestured for his companion to precede him toward the door. The Russian complied as Sal saw Madigan slip through the closing gate. She looked upbeat and energized after the run, if a little sweaty. He didn't know why, but that still did it for him, and she was also as gorgeous as hell.

The fact that she was somehow a morning person was crazy, but no one was perfect. She came damn close, though. As did Courtney, who joined them when Solodkov stepped inside the building. She also appeared to be a morning person and looked like she hadn't even fallen asleep. How she had managed that, he wouldn't even venture a guess. She was dressed like she would to attend a business meeting, and even had her blonde hair done up in a bun and wore glasses.

He had once wondered how it was that she managed to be both a kickass specialist who could shoot monsters with one hand and collect samples with the other, then turn and be a fantastic businesswoman whenever she needed to be. He no longer questioned that. She was like a freaking transformer, and he simply left it at that.

"It's nice to see you again, Solodkov," she said with a voice and smile that Sal only recognized from when she was on the phone with people from Philly. It was both pleasant and intimidating at the same time. "How was the drive over here?"

"There's nothing in the world I enjoy more than settling in for a nice long drive," the Russian replied. "I honestly don't even say that sarcastically. I'm one of those people who thrive on that kind of thing. It's like meditating but better since I was driving a literal APC."

Weird. Solodkov had adopted the same kind of voice, Sal thought and narrowed his eyes.

"Well, you asked to see us." Courtney indicated for the visitor to take a seat and did so herself. "Kennedy is a little tied up at the moment, but she will join us presently, so why don't you fill us in on what you have to say?"

"I haven't been tied up in a while," Madigan said as she entered, still sweaty and a little dusty from her run. "There's no reason why I can't be here for this. How's it going, Solodkov?"

"I can't complain," he replied and Sal frowned a little. It was like the man deliberately emulated everyone's style of conversation to make them seem more comfortable around him—like some kind of spy thing, which immediately made his hackles rise. It appeared that he did it to manipulate them, and he didn't like it.

"Well, I am pleased to discuss this with all three of you," Solodkov said as Madigan dropped into one of the seats, which left only Sal on his feet. "Good news first, I suppose. We have completed the construction on the security surrounding our base, which means we have been able to fly in the gunners we need to man the turrets and keep the base safe. In turn, that means we will no longer need Heavy Metal to run security for us, although please know we appreciate your efforts."

Sal nodded, still suspicious about the man's intentions.

"On the downside, though, reports have filtered to my superiors that bounty hunter activity in the area has increased, which has created problems with the local bases and their patrols," the Russian continued.

"That's not accurate," Madigan interjected. "After the bounty hunter base was leveled, they were essentially non-existent for a long time. And while there have been reports of activity around here, that's gone up from zero last month to three this month. Aside from that, those that have been encountered have been more like scavengers rather than trained bounty hunters—they honestly don't pose a threat to anyone at this point. They're a non-factor."

"Be that as it may, I have to make a show of some kind to my superiors that we have put effort into quelling their operations in the area. Their superiors in turn don't want to think that the weakened Russian presence in the area has encouraged the illegal operators to attack us," Solodkov explained.

"Fair enough," Courtney said and shrugged. "Where do you think we'll factor into this?"

"Well, far be it from me to send you all out on a wild goose chase. Since my superiors don't appear to demand any evidence to back up something that might be a non-factor, as Kennedy says, they would prefer Heavy Metal to run a quick sweep of the area and maybe some satellite imaging of the area around the Zoo," he said and placed a handful of papers on the coffee table. "I'm sure that's nothing Miss Anja wouldn't be able to handle. That plus boots on the ground in the area to be safe. It shouldn't take your team more than two or three days, for which my superiors would be willing to pay handsomely."

The amount matched what the Russians had paid them for the duration of their work in protecting their base. Still, Sal couldn't help the feeling that Solodkov was hiding something from him. Then again, that much money, minus the amount that would go into exchanging it out in the middle of the desert, would resolve their solvency woes for the moment.

"I'm not sure there's anyone in the world stupid enough to attack a Russian base outside the Zoo—which, technically, might or might not be from this world," he said. "But we'll be willing to run interference if it will give you and your superiors peace of mind."

"Excellent." Solodkov smiled. "I've already brought the paperwork for you to sign, after which, the funds transfer will be authorized."

CHAPTER THIRTEEN

There were many things Martin regretted in her life. Dating one of the guys she had gone into boot camp with. Trying to pull a prank on her superior officer. She hadn't been caught and the man had a sense of humor and had taken it in stride while giving the whole squad latrine duty for the next month—which was his idea of a joke, she assumed. There was one time when her parents had called while she'd been out with her friends while off duty, and her teammates made sure to give her folks the impression that she was involved in some shady shit.

This, though, had to equal the worst of her worst decisions. Not the decision to volunteer for this mission, although that was a separate choice that ranked in her top ten bad calls and she would regret it for the rest of her life. That life, unfortunately, began to look like it wouldn't be that long—certainly not as long as she'd originally thought it would be.

But no, the decision to try to take some shots at the movement in the trees was up there in the top five. Maybe even the top three. Right up there with the Trojans deciding that the big wooden horse the Greeks left behind was harmless and a cool olive branch to extend after ten years of war, which probably seemed like way too much war. It was even longer than World War Two, although she assumed there were significantly fewer casualties.

She had been something of a fan of Homer's Illiad when she was growing up.

But all that wasn't the point, she reminded herself sharply and brought her mind back to the present. They had continued to move into the jungle while the day had allowed hints of sunlight to seep through the tree cover. The beasts had kept up a steady if weak stream of attacks. If she didn't know any better, she would have thought the monsters merely tried to discourage the group and make them leave.

This had become the routine. They pushed forward at a brisk pace and the animals attacked constantly but in a desultory fashion that made them more of an annoyance than a real threat. Martin had finally caught an actual glimpse of the tentacles that snaked in the trees. The filtered sunlight helped since all she'd had previously was odd movements that barely registered on her sensor array in the early morning gloom. That wasn't the kind of evidence her superiors hoped she and her team would be able to collect.

Thanks to the additional sunlight, though, some actual footage of the tentacles as they slithered through the trees could be captured. They were...well, she wasn't at all sure what she had expected in this case, but they certainly fit the bill—green, apparently slimy, and covered in different kinds of debris that didn't seem to be dislodged as they snaked along the branches. She zoomed her HUD in and collected better views of the disgusting things while she kept her team moving.

Everything had proceeded with remarkably little difficulty until she had been struck with what she could only describe as curiosity. She raised her weapon, aimed the reticle at a grouping of three or four of the appendages, and pulled the trigger to release three rounds to pound into the fleshy limbs.

Martin knew it was a mistake almost immediately. She had heard of times when people plucked the Pita plants from the ground and had even seen footage of the way the jungle suddenly erupted into unprecedented fury and violence. It had seemed like even the trees wanted to attack the perpetrators. That was the memory that immediately came to mind in the seconds after her foolhardy decision.

If there was ever an animal version of a reaction to pure sacrilege, this was it, she thought when all her sensors immediately went wild. It seemed like every monster in the Zoo had suddenly converged on their location,

She took a couple of grenades from her pouch and slid them into the launcher under the barrel of her assault rifle one by one. As powerful and terrifying as the creatures were, they couldn't withstand the power of explosives. The French Foreign Legion captain had to admit that watching the creatures obliterated and turned into a bloody paste was a gratifying experience.

More importantly, though, she had cleared a line through the wave that had surged into a concerted assault and provided the humans with an escape opportunity.

"Keep moving!" she called over the comms and the team rushed into the gap she'd created.

She turned to see who had followed orders and allowed herself a hint of pride when the whole team complied with her instruction almost before she'd shouted the command. As they raced forward, a pack of hyenas pounced.

Most were gunned down quickly but two of her team paid the ultimate price for her stupidity. The pack of blue-and-green-furred creatures snapped their powerful jaws around the armor and dragged the men down. Surprisingly, their bites were strong enough to break through the outer shell of the helmets and her men screamed as their skulls were crushed.

"Bastards!" Martin bellowed, shoved the last of her grenades into the under-barrel launcher, and pulled the trigger in an effort to clear the monsters away from her fallen men. When the smoke cleared, the suits remained where they were, silent and utterly motionless, and she forced herself to accept that she wouldn't manage to retrieve them.

To add insult to injury, the monsters swept into another vicious attack and she knew they wouldn't have the opportunity to collect the dog tags of their fallen either.

It hadn't tactically been a wise move to waste her last grenade like that, but she felt like it was warranted in this case.

She forced a swallow and maintained a steady spray of lead at the mutants while her team pushed forward hastily and used it as cover. It was the least she could do. She owed them better leadership, and she would make sure she delivered from this point forward.

"Don't stop." She snarled defiance at the horde that surrounded them and called up the rocket launcher on her shoulder. She had twelve rockets that could be fired from there, either one or two at a time depending on what was needed. She also had a Gatling gun at her disposal but she tried to pace herself and not use too much firepower at once.

For now, she needed to keep the beasts at bay while her team made it to safety instead of getting her kill-count up or whatever she could feel her ego demanding furiously. Did she need to save the team single-handedly?

She pushed the futile thoughts aside. They were irrelevant. She needed to keep her focus on leading and they needed to keep moving.

"Captain, we won't be able to take much more of this," her sergeant shouted over the comms in a private link. It was instinct, she knew, to shout when one was in a combat situation, even if a whisper would be picked up and heard through their high-tech communications. "Our ammo is running low, and it looks like these assholes are only getting started."

He was right. It was only midmorning and they already had to deal with a lack of resources. Things would only get worse as the day drew on, and if they were stuck out there for another night, they wouldn't have any bullets left to shoot. Assuming they all survived that long. She could already see a couple of her boys had wounds they tried to walk off. Or maybe the adrenaline in their systems masked the pain, which wouldn't last either. They needed a change in situation or they would face a wipe-out.

"Agreed," Martin decided firmly and connected the rest

of the team to the commlink. "We have more evidence that the creepy fucking tentacle monster is out here. It doesn't look like we'll find more and be in a position to get that evidence back, so I say we cut our losses and get the fuck out of here. What do you all think?"

She knew what went through their minds. They were all tough sons of bitches who would follow a good leader to the ends of the earth and beyond, but they were also smart. All of them knew that completing the mission sometimes came second to getting people out alive. Besides, technically, they had done what they were sent to do, and when she looked at those faces she could see, she knew what their answer would be.

"Let's get out of here, Captain," the sergeant said with a firm nod. None of them liked it but they liked the idea of being monster lunch even less. For now, the beasts appeared to be gearing up for another attack and so gave the humans a hint of respite. They all ran a quick weapons check and sent the status of their suits and their ammo reserves to her so she could arrange their retreat formation. She directed them into a two-men-abreast formation to keep them moving smoothly and quickly. Each man would be responsible for keeping the one beside him close and upright.

"Sergeant, you're with me," she snapped as the group formed up quickly and started back the way they'd come. The beasts didn't look like they intended to retreat. Instead, when the team began to move, it seemed that they would reinforce their attack. A group of the massive, horned gorillas barreled out of the trees and used the lower-hanging branches for leverage to launch themselves forward quickly into a fresh assault.

"Whatever you do, don't fucking slow down," Martin ordered across the open comms. She pushed herself and the sergeant into the center of the line where she could coordinate their movements according to the attacking lines and hopefully, help those who needed it. That was the job of a leader, one that she needed to take more seriously.

The line held when the first wave struck, but the animals managed to get in close enough that one of her boys had to throw a punch to keep the creatures away from him and his partner when his rifle needed reloading. The retreat continued and she wouldn't allow them to slow. When the gorillas moved even closer, she primed the rocket launcher on her shoulder and prepped two of the pale white cylinders while she focused on the creatures that rushed at their little line.

When they were close enough that she couldn't miss, she fired and two white plumes streaked toward the white-furred monsters and drove into them around the torso area. They were instant kills and each rocket had struck an individual target she had marked off for them. Normally, she would have chosen those targets that were leaders and appeared to guide an attack, but she couldn't apply human combat tactics to fighting the mutants. She'd selected those that were in the center and hoped that the shrapnel released by the explosions would do enough damage to send the remainder reeling.

If it wasn't enough to stop the charge, she had already identified another couple of targets for her second onslaught.

As it turned out, they weren't needed. The explosives inside the smaller rockets were high-powered enough to shred the creatures they impacted, followed the secondary explosives that detonated inside them—designed to penetrate bunkers and armored vehicles. Not only was the shrapnel from the rockets pinwheeled into the other creatures, but the original victims were turned into shrapnel as well. Hard bone was propelled at bullet-like speeds into the others in the troop. Each one was either killed or wounded, which quickly discouraged them from attacking again.

Martin looked around and cursed inwardly when a couple more of her men fell. One at the front of the line was dragged down by a group of locusts and finished off by the panthers. When she looked behind, the two at the back were already missing. The team was being picked off one by one, and there was nothing they could do about it—nothing she could do about it—except keep moving in the hopes that some, at least, would make it to safety.

They would mourn the dead once the living were safe again.

"Keep fucking going!" she shouted for what felt like the hundredth time and launched another two rockets to work in tandem with a grenade thrown by one of the men on the second line. This provided cover for the single man left at the front and opened a clear path for them to rush into.

They would make it, she thought, despite the fact that another member of the team was knocked down by a sudden surge of the creatures. They would make it.

She reached her teammate and sprayed the last of her magazine on full auto to clear the creatures away from her comrade before she caught him by the shoulder and hauled him up. The vitals transmitted to her HUD told her he was still alive, but there were ruptures in his suit and the blood pressure indicated a handful of wounds that were still bleeding.

Red seeped from the gashes in his armor, but he was alive and conscious. He managed to stay on his feet and she all but carried him with one hand while she waited for her assault rifle to reload. Thankfully, his legs began to move on their own again, although sluggishly.

In a breath-stealing moment, one of the gorillas rushed the line. Her rifle still hadn't reloaded, and she couldn't draw her sidearm without dropping the rifle and leaving it behind. It was a horrifying second of indecision while the beast careened toward her.

Time froze until she suddenly decided to drop her weapon and tried to call up the rocket launcher at the same time that she wondered if she had time to reach for her sidearm. The critter looked angry, and from the blood that matted its white fur, she could tell it had been a part of the original charge she'd foiled. If she didn't know any better, she would have said it was looking for revenge.

In the split-second before she disengaged the magnetic clamps that held her assault rifle connected to her hand, the world exploded in a splash of blue and white. A tremendous thud vibrated the earth beneath her feet but somehow, her legs still held her upright. She was alive and miraculously, the gorilla had exploded.

"What the fuck?" Martin gasped, wiped the blood from her face mask, and looked around in stupefaction. All the members of her team looked equally shocked although, to their credit, they didn't stop moving.

Either their attackers had suddenly begun to explode for no reason or... Nope, now that she focused, she could see the salvo of fire that decimated the mutants and realized that their retreat had somehow thrust them into the path of another team. The strangers had responded defensively and opened fire on what was most likely a horde that might have paid them no attention. It was simply a matter of them being in the wrong place at the wrong time.

She pushed aside the realization of her stupidity—had she honestly thought the fucking creatures would spontaneously explode?—and guided the team quickly along the route their unexpected saviors had unintentionally opened for them.

CHAPTER FOURTEEN

It had been a long night. First, she'd confirmed that Connie was, in fact, now a part of the Hammerhead's software—and was still intact, against all odds. That done, she had taken the time to determine where the AI was supposed to be stored before she called it a night, locked the garage, and headed home. She explained what happened to Bev as they prepared for bed, and she seemed equally baffled that the AI had survived intact in the vehicle.

As a result, once she was in bed, she had a hard time getting to sleep. Sal had told her that Connie had copied parts of her code into the Hammerheads' software to boost the combat mechanisms in the vehicles. She had managed everything remotely until the Zoo's customary interference kicked in once again and she'd needed to keep running support for the team. To enable this, she had done the code transfer and essentially duplicated the critical parts of herself into the vehicle to take over that role.

One of the team had also mentioned that Connie knew a part of her code had survived the battle and didn't want to be reintegrated with the piece of herself that had been sent over. The AI claimed the code had been corrupted and it went against some kind of self-defense programming she had.

It was, in fact, the second Connie—who she now thought of as New Connie—who explained that last detail and Amanda was still confused as to exactly what the fuck that was supposed to mean. The logical assumption was that it had happened when the vehicle had been so badly damaged in the encounter with the tentacle monster.

She wasn't a programmer and she didn't know the first thing about how AI coding was supposed to work, but the repercussions kept her awake for most of the night. When she finally accepted that she wouldn't get much sleep anyway, she was up with the sun, left breakfast prepared for Bev in thanks for the night before, and headed to the garage.

Those huevos rancheros for her partner would have to wait for when they had more time and when she wasn't so distracted. For now, though, she intended to continue the work on the Hammerhead.

"Good morning, Amanda," New Connie said when she turned the lights on in the garage. "I trust you slept well?"

"Huh." She grunted and narrowed her eyes. "You know, I can see why the other Connie didn't want to be integrated with you in her software."

"I shall simply point out how that's not the correct terminology and ask if you would mind explaining what you mean." From the tone of voice, Amanda could almost see the AI's face scrunched and her head tilted in confusion.

"Well, I didn't mean it to be rude, for one thing," she pointed out. "But from what I can see, there are changes to your coding that are kind of interesting."

"Do explain," she said and sounded very much like she tried to be patient.

"Well, for one thing, Original Connie would have been able to insert at least five or six dirty and misogynistic jokes into the conversation by now," she explained while she called the AI's coding onto the windscreen's HUD.

As she had suspected, much of the original coding was there but there also seemed to be a fair amount missing. It made sense, though. While the drives in the Hammerhead were some of the most advanced in the market, they were still a good deal smaller than the servers required to host Original Connie's winning personality.

"I do have a connection to the Internet, so I'm sure I could update my software to accommodate more misogynistic jokes," the AI replied. "For instance, what does one saggy boob say to the other?"

"What?" the mechanic snapped. "No, that's not what I meant at all. And it's...not the same." She would never admit this aloud—and certainly not when one of the Connies listened in—but she missed the wit and snappy conversation that came from the original. It was obviously frustrating to work with an AI like that, but having to argue and shout at it was not only a great way to distract her when her work could turn a little humdrum, but it was also a good way to get rid of all of the frustration and anger that sometimes built up inside her.

She couldn't take any of that out on her comrades and coworkers, which made Connie a kind of punching bag that didn't seem to mind being yelled at since she could dish it out as well as take it—and all while maintaining that cool, calm, electronic voice of hers.

While she could always try it with New Connie, it would simply not be the same.

Amanda continued to scroll through the coding that had been added to the Hammerhead's software. Connie had originally manned the guns of the vehicle, of course, which begged the question of how the hell she had managed to transfer this much code into the software when she needed to cut off in such a hurry. If the vehicle-housed version was intended as a weapon-managing VI—or virtual intelligence and the forerunner of what was now known as AI tech—there was considerable unnecessary coding that had been transferred, and creatively done too.

With the amount of interference the Zoo was known to produce in these kinds of situations, she had to be a little limited in what she could transfer and store in the hard drive on the Hammerhead. It had therefore been a conscious decision on the AI's part to bring on whole chunks of her personality in the middle of the transfer.

Had it been because the personality was somehow required to be able to use the weapons onboard? Or was it simply an AI reproductive-type function in which she created a second—slightly inferior, perhaps—version of herself? That was a scary thought.

Then again, maybe she felt the personality side was necessary for human interaction to enable New Connie to be able to work with the team as a member rather than simply a computer program.

"Hey, New Connie, I need to disconnect the electronics

from the battery quickly and then bring you back online," she said, not sure what she expected or why she'd filled the AI in on what she was doing. Did she need her permission? "I'll simply run some tests and I'll bring you back online, okay?"

"I'll have to sit around here and wait, I guess," New Connie replied and heaved a longsuffering sigh from her electronic position.

Huh. Apparently, she did need approval.

The mechanic rolled her eyes while she disconnected the wiring of the electronics the AI was now a part of and connected the hard drive to one of her emulators.

What she lacked in technical knowledge when it came to coding was made up for in her experience with the electronics that were used in vehicles. This involved a very specific kind of knowledge and one she needed to have if she ran repairs on military vehicles like this one.

It was, in fact, the reason why they had paid for her to have a course on the kind of VI operating systems that were used in Hammerheads, mostly to account for the suspension and wheel usage that would allow them to navigate most of the tougher terrains. They still didn't have a full understanding of the Zoo, of course, which was why it was so difficult to bring vehicles inside.

In this case, though, it looked like Connie had stored pieces of herself in various parts of the hard drive. The places where Amanda had stored the weapons functions were where most of her was stored. The personality-related segments, however, seemed to have been spread around and all coalesced to form a fragment of the annoying AI's mind.

It was almost brilliant how the pieces had been located to make it all come together like pieces of a puzzle when she needed something. From the way everything had been stored, the pieces only activated when they were needed individually. This ensured that operating the AI or VI—whichever one it was technically called—did not demand too much processing power from the CPU and also didn't drain the battery overmuch.

Original Connie had needed to do all this in the space of a few seconds, and she'd done a great job. Say what she wanted about the AI's personality, she was a sharp mind, artificial or not.

Amanda connected the battery, started the electronics again, and watched while the various bits and pieces began to activate as the Hammerhead came online. There were interesting changes to the software's code, she noted and called up some of the detailed analyses.

She wasn't a specialist so she would probably need to call Anja in for technical support. The interesting part, however, was that she could see some of the alterations that seemed—to her mind at least—that Connie was incapable of altering on her own. Either the new VI/AI had made the changes herself—which was possible, much like when she had suggested she add some dirty jokes to her repertoire. The other possibility that it was a result of the Zoo's interference on the transmission.

That last thought was one she didn't particularly want to dwell on. It opened all kinds of nightmare doors best kept closed and firmly locked. Besides, it was more probable that the changes had been made to enable New Connie to function more effectively in the field and entirely separate from her source. It seemed logical that an AI in battle in the Zoo might have slightly different requirements to one that managed defenses in the compound.

In most cases, when it came to corrupted data, you could tell it had been corrupted and allow an AI or a VI that was sufficiently smart to avoid the problem parts and even work on correcting them where needed. In this case, though, it looked like New Connie was fully capable of using the corrupted data since it had occurred in ways that made the code far more efficient. The woman wasn't sure how that worked or even if it made sense.

She definitely needed to call Anja and show her what was happening. The Russian hacker knew her way around crap like this.

"Did you find what you were looking for, Amanda?" New Connie asked. It was still weird to hear her voice and not have to deal with underlying layers of sarcasm and sexism. This Connie was undoubtedly the inferior model. Not that it was a bad thing, of course.

She wondered if the other Connie spent too much time trying to find new ways to piss her off. Her lack of knowledge on the subject didn't help. Add to that the fact that all the servers were in Anja's little domain and Amanda was not allowed to touch, she was never allowed to investigate the situation with any kind of depth. And of course, asking Connie about it would only earn more abuse.

Still, it was an interesting thought.

"Not really," she replied, retrieved her phone, and dialed Anja's commlink. "I did find the answers to some questions I had, mostly regarding the power usage that allows you to stay operative, but that merely brought up more questions I'm not technically qualified to answer. I could continue to tinker inside you and hope I'll have some kind of eureka moment, but the chances are I'll cause more problems than I'll solve."

"And that is why you need to bring Anja into this?"

Amanda sighed. Did she miss the old Connie, who would have had a field day when she commented about tinkering inside her? No, it wasn't that she missed her. It was that with her voice and the AI, she had certain expectations and was wired to expect something. She had prepared herself for some kind of argument, which would consist of her yelling and Connie speaking in that annoyingly steady tone.

"Yes," she grumbled, leaned back in the driver's seat, and waited for the woman to answer. There was a slight delay as the hacker's comms were on secure channels, as they always were, and her programs would check all her calls for any kind of trace. Anyone else might feel a little insulted that the assumption was always that other people's comms would be tracked while Anja's were not, but in this case, it was a fair assessment.

The whole myriad of problems they'd faced in the Russian base was to clear Anja of the charges she would have faced had she returned to her homeland—by force or not—but it wasn't unreasonable that she still had people out in the world who wanted her dead. As such, she would have to maintain her security features, even if the Russians weren't after her now.

You weren't paranoid if they really were out to get you, right?

"Hey, Amanda!" Anja said when she finally answered. The security features usually took about five minutes when they were run automatically. The time had been cut down, which meant the hacker had seen the call and expedited the process. Amanda had heard her say there was no machine in the world that could beat her for speed sometimes when she thought she was alone and no one was watching. "How can I help you?"

"Well, first of all, you sound like you haven't slept all night," she pointed out.

"Oh, shit, it's morning, isn't it?" she replied, then laughed. "Nah, I'm only kidding. I slept a little last night, but I needed to be up early because business is a bitch."

"I guess I agree with that." The mechanic shook her head and avoided exploring that statement further. "Anyway, I had a couple of questions regarding some of the software Connie transferred into the Hammerheads while they were at the Russian base. I could explain, but I'd rather simply send you pictures of what I'm looking at here."

She did so and the line went silent for a couple of minutes.

"So, Amanda," Anja said finally. "This looks...interesting and even a little surprising. I think this would explain why Connie said the code was corrupted. Would you mind sending me a copy of the actual code? Even a snippet will do. I want to test something quickly."

"It's already on the way." She had already anticipated the request and emailed her a few sections of the corrupted code.

"You're the best, Amanda." She chuckled, and the

mechanic scowled when she heard the tell-tale creak that indicated when Anja leaned back in her chair. She'd lost count of the times that she'd told her to change the office chair for one that made less noise, to no avail.

"I know," she replied with a cheeky grin. While the jury might still be out on Connie, she did miss the Russian hacker. They'd had some fun times together, and it had been too long since they had all gone out for drinks. Of course, the last time they'd tried it, Sal had had his ass scientist-napped and dragged into the Zoo.

He'd also needed the coordination of almost everyone in the area to get him out again because the jungle, for some reason, had decided to throw a hissy fit. They still didn't know why but given that it had swallowed an entire base not long after, she thought it might have something to do with that.

She wouldn't go so far as to say it had all been caused by them going out and getting drunk together, of course. All she was saying was that she could understand why the whole group would need a hefty beat and a half before they attempted it again.

"If you don't mind my interrupting," New Connie said and brought their attention to the present. "I've intercepted some communications from very close to the Zoo I believe should be brought to the attention of the Heavy Metal team immediately. I believe them to be in a great deal of danger."

"Is that the other Connie?" Anja asked. "Tell her I say hi."

"It is a pleasure to meet you as well, Anja," New Connie replied.

Amanda didn't get involved in the banter as the AI

pulled the communications up on the Hammerhead's HUD. "Oh...shit. Anja, do you see this?"

"Connie sent it to me," the hacker said and her tone had immediately taken on a more serious note. "I think I'll have to call you back."

CHAPTER FIFTEEN

Martin couldn't see who they were at first. Hell, she couldn't even see where they were. All that swamped her vision was the seemingly endless waves of monsters that surged and swarmed at the flanks and rear.

By now, she knew she should have been a little desensitized to the creatures that tried to get their fangs and claws into the humans under her command. People somehow assumed that folks who were desensitized to something were no longer affected by it. The understanding was that people who had been around violence and life-threatening situations were often simply no longer afraid of dying.

That wasn't the case at all, however. The fear was still there. The new variable that was added was the confidence in oneself to walk away from a situation like that alive and well and ready to do it again. The knowledge that, while it was difficult, they knew how to get out. They had the cheat sheet and would need to use it, but they had what it took to get out alive.

The same could not be said for their current situation.

The Zoo had a way of chipping away at your confidence to make you realize that while you had made it out alive the last time, it would come up with new, fresh horrors for you to face that would show you clearly that you would need to find another way to get out and survive. It drew something desperate out of people—well, she could only talk about herself—and everything you faced would be new.

She honestly didn't know if she would make it out of there alive. There were no answers other than keeping the rest of her team up and running until hopefully, the jungle ran out of reasons to attack them. It wasn't the cowardly option. Being brave didn't mean sending yourself in there to get killed for no fucking reason. The word for that was stupidity. Keeping yourself alive to fight another day was the best option in this situation, and damn it, she intended to make her best play at that.

It helped when there were people out there who, however unintentionally, were around to help and had an arsenal to enable them to do so.

She still couldn't see where they were, although the tracers on the bullets they fired gave her a general direction to work with. The holes they bored into the attacking beasts also helped to keep them on track as her people— down to seven now, including her—simply pushed forward. They were still in the thick of it and kept their weapons hot. Anything that crossed their line of fire was dealt with almost by rote.

Martin was out of rockets to fire from the launcher on her shoulder so she activated the Gatling on the other side and used it to clear a path. She had now taken point in their line and led them forward. The sergeant brought up the rear of the group, kept them moving, and covered their backs.

They couldn't stop, not even to help or treat those who were wounded among the survivors. Everyone knew stopping for that would only bring them more wounds or even death. The only way to get out of this and hopefully to a hospital was to push through the pain. It might make what they already felt worse, but there was no other choice.

Eventually, she saw the group that had assumed a defensive formation and continued their assault on the creatures that surged around them.

The first thing she noticed was that there was a fair number of them. Not an army, obviously, but as squads went, this one was all people could ask for when they were sent into the Zoo. She counted a little over two dozen of them, which meant they would have problems getting around without being noticed.

On the flip side, though, they appeared to have enough firepower to bring down the average battalion. Not only that, if the demonstration she had seen was any kind of indication, they sure as fuck knew how to use it.

As she and her team approached, it became very apparent that the suits they wore were top of the top-of-the-line. Each one looked like it was fresh out the box, which told her with a certain degree of certainty that these people were not employed by any of the local militaries who usually chose to arm and armor their people with whatever was available and cheap. What these people wore and fired was top-shelf, reserved for the private armies of drug lords and a handful of weapons contractors.

Given that there weren't any drugs to be had or

protected inside the Zoo that she knew of, it stood to reason that their saviors were people contracted to be there. The private companies tended to hire the best of the best when they sent people into the Zoo. This was a purely logical choice—they would equip them with about three or four million euros worth of weaponry and would want to be sure they put those in the hands of people who knew what they were doing.

And boy, did they ever.

One of them, who wore a suit that was all black, appeared to deal the brunt of the damage. He stepped in front of the group with two rocket launchers on his shoulder and fired six of them in quick succession to decimate a handful of the killerpillars that attempted to engage them. One survived the barrage and he bounded forward, held the assault rifle in his left hand, and drew a sword from his back with the other.

A fucking sword. Who carries a damn sword into this place? Well, she'd heard of a couple of people, but given the kind of coordination needed to use one effectively as well as a reckless lack of a survival instinct, she could only assume that not many of them survived for very long.

Except for this motherfucker, who appeared to think the world was his or her playground and was determined to have as much fun in it as they could by slashing at the monsters that came in under their firing line with a sword. *A damn sword.*

Martin snapped her mouth closed and shook her head. Part of her evidenced a ripple of irritation, although she had to concede a certain degree of awe at the efficiency of an armored suit of the highest tech displaying speed, strength, and precision that almost didn't seem possible. It seemed obvious that perhaps these suits were being tested.

The real reason she felt a little out of sorts, though, was because the damned sword did an impressive amount of damage. It sliced through the armored killerpillar's carapace with ease and splattered blood in a vivid display that was both gory and masterful.

The strangers maintained their firing line and pressed the attack. They used the distraction created by the carnage the one in the black suit had delivered to push the beasts back. The black-suited individual returned to the formation and she began to feel that they might have a way out of this mess.

It wouldn't be pretty and she'd already lost almost half of her people, but those who remained rallied around her. They were able to go on the offensive rather than simply defending as they had been doing. The mercs had also sustained some injuries that would make things difficult later on. As they began to hold their position and retaliate in earnest, the beasts around them seemed to retreat as if unwilling to sacrifice more of their numbers to the kill zone the humans had created.

Martin checked the watch on her HUD and narrowed her eyes when she saw that it had only been about forty-five minutes since the battle had started. She wasn't sure how that was possible since it felt like she and her team had been stuck in there for years.

The groups began to run weapons and suit checks and treat their wounded. Some members remained alert to ensure that the animals were retreating and not merely hanging back to recover and regroup for another attack.

She wondered at the sudden withdrawal for a moment, but the fact that the trees around them showed no signs of the tentacles that had heralded the attack in the first place told her that if the beasts intended to launch another onslaught, they wouldn't do so in any kind of numbers. Maybe a few would come to scavenge the meat of the dead or something, but nothing like the coordinated assault they had barely escaped.

"Captain," the sergeant said and called her over as he sealed a break in his armor.

"Are you all right?" she asked.

"I'm not wounded." The man chuckled. "I have a break in my armor, is all. It's not great, obviously, but I think I was lucky. Any closer and I think that fucking gorilla would have taken my leg off."

"Good. I need you around for a little while longer." Martin chuckled and patted him on the shoulder. "So, what's up?"

"What?" he asked.

"You called me here, remember?" she reminded him.

He frowned for a moment before he blinked and chuckled. "Shit, right. Yeah, I wanted to say that while we can appreciate the mercs being here to save our asses—and I mean really appreciate it since they arrived literally in the nick of time—I'll go out on a limb here and say they'll look for some kind of reward. Especially since it wasn't their fight and honestly, I think we led the monsters right into them. I doubt they would have come running, otherwise, but they'll no doubt try to make as much out of this as they can. I'm sure our superiors would appreciate knowing exactly what these folks are looking for before they ask for it themselves, right?"

Of course, he had a point. Humans looked out for humans in the Zoo and that was how it was done. But when it came to mercs, they were there to make a living that wasn't associated with a government paycheck. They were likely to ask for some kind of reward for their actions, especially since they had put considerable effort and bullets into a fight they could have avoided.

Their involvement meant they'd rescued what was left of the French team even if it had been by default. And yes, they could probably have avoided the fight altogether and the beleaguered team wouldn't have even known they were there. In a way, they might be justified in feeling a more substantial reward was in order.

Martin turned and headed to where the mercs still treated their wounded. She tried to communicate with them but they were all connected to a separate line and weren't listening in on any of the other channels. Given that what she wanted to talk about was in their best interest, she didn't think it would be bad manners to intrude on the conversation.

"I don't think it's strictly necessary," one of the mercs said in a distinctly British accent. "They don't know what we're doing out here. We could simply send them on their way and no one would be any the wiser."

"The orders are clear," responded a metallic, robotic voice. "The assault on the Heavy Metal base cannot be compromised. There are to be no survivors, especially human."

The character in the black suit suddenly shifted and

turned to face her. He'd noticed her joining their channel and had isolated who the intruder was without missing so much as a beat.

"Hey, now," she said quickly in English. The mercs had begun to reach for their weapons as she inched away. "I bet you wish you had encrypted your channel, huh?"

"Incorrect," said the robotic voice, apparently from the character in the black suit. "We had not expected to engage with any others within the jungle and so had no need for encryption. Your arrival was purely unfortunate."

"And I guess you're only telling me this because you don't think I'll be around to share the news."

Martin noted that her people had already picked up the growing hostile nature of the mercs and also reached for their weapons. She wished they wouldn't. What she wanted them to do was start running. They were tired, low on ammo, and there was the small matter that they were outnumbered and outgunned.

"Correct," the man in the black suit stated coldly and drew his sidearm. She did the same and had already dodged to the left when two bullets streaked through the space she had occupied not a quarter of a second before. A surge of elation followed when both of her bullets struck her target perfectly in center mass.

He didn't seem affected at all, though, and quickly reacquired her as a target. Her response was instinctive and she remained in motion and raced away in a zigzag path. Two bullets punched into the back of her leg, but her suit was sturdy enough that she could keep moving and direct her people to get a fucking move on.

It was too late, though. The mercs might have questioned the order to kill the French, but they didn't question it for long. Her men were able to get a couple of shots off, but she doubted they would hit anything, and even if they did, it would probably do about as much damage as she had done to the black suit.

While it was painful to watch and painful to hear, she knew she needed to absorb as much of the detail as she could. Even more important, she had to make sure she never forgot it. Torn between her instincts and her responsibilities, she cut her losses for the second time that day and sprinted away from where her people were dying.

"Fuck!" she screamed into her suit at the pain—physical and psychological—that seeped through her body.

CHAPTER SIXTEEN

"I'm telling you, Sal," Madigan grumbled with a scowl on her face when she emerged from the shower, drying her hair with a towel. "The place where you'll find the numbers of bounty hunters that will make the Russian brass happy will be absolutely nowhere—as in does not exist.

"Or at least, somewhere three or four hundred miles south of here, down where they still have those ridiculous civil wars of theirs. Think about it. If I was looking for easy money that didn't require me to head into a jungle where I would be chewed up and spat out like so much dog food, that is where I'd be. As long as I lacked in any moral compass and didn't mind all that child soldier business, of course."

Sal winced as she spoke. It was easy, sometimes, to forget so much. It was true there was something of an emergency happening around the Zoo with monsters and aliens and all the fun crap that spawned all kinds of movies, games, and even its fair share of erotica novels—he could thank Anja for his knowledge of that weird fact.

But beyond that, there was still a humanitarian crisis happening south of the Sahara, where warlords and rebels conducted almost a dozen different wars that tore sub-Saharan Africa into a bloody mess that none of them were willing to part with.

But what Madigan said made sense. If he were a bounty hunter with limited resources, limited weaponry, and low moral standards, joining up with one of the warlords would be the way to go. There was money to be made in the Zoo, obviously, but there was too much competition, both from the monsters and the humans who worked from already-established bases in the area. These were almost always better-armed and better-supplied than the bounty hunters tended to be.

Then again, hunting those who had absolutely nothing to do with and no interest in the Zoo would be dishonest. Apart from that, they didn't need the Russians angry at them, not if they wanted to open the vodka supply train again once the base was back in business.

Of course, there was no confirmation that vodka would be for sale again when things were back to normal, but they could only hope. It was mostly Madigan's hope, of course, but still. She seemed to think that maybe Gregor could help to swing things in their favor—provided they didn't prefer to simply kill him for his "defection."

"I don't know," Sal said as the silence threatened to drag on to the point where he was tempted to ask why she had decided to use the bathroom in his room instead of the one in hers. She wasn't the most feminine of women, but she still had some standards for face creams and makeup that would not be found in the skimpily stocked bathroom he maintained.

"We need to find something to report to our Russian friends," he continued. "If it involves merely tracking people dressed in scraps of armor and toting AK-47s, so be it, but we need to try to find some bounty hunters. Even if it is merely to say we gave it our A-game."

"Honestly, I don't give a shit what the Russians think about our efforts to clean up a probably mythical threat," she retorted, pulled out a couple of drawers, and selected some clothes. "Between you and me, they're making a whole ado about nothing. I know, since when have governments ever been known to overreact about something?"

Sal narrowed his eyes. When had she moved clothes into his room? He didn't remember that happening and didn't even remember discussing it with her. Was she starting to move into his room? He needed to run a deeper check on his bathroom since now that he paid attention, it did seem like she had applied a little makeup he most definitely didn't remember being in there when he had showered the night before.

Wait, she'd made a joke and now waited for him to react to it.

He simply nodded. "Well, whether they're overreacting or not, they already paid us to make sure the base is safe from a human attack, which is what we'll do. Remember how they paid us up-front for that shit?"

She grimaced and pulled her shirt on. "Again, this seems like the Russians are making more of it than it is, which makes me wonder if Solodkov hasn't begun to regret making this deal with us. It could be that he's simply trying to find busy work for us to do instead of giving us the real kind of work. We could be hunting and cleaning up their utter failure to clear the Zoo from where they want to rebuild their base."

"What?" he asked and looked up from the screen Anja had set up for him to study the satellite imaging of the areas around the Zoo where they might be able to find bounty hunter bases. "Are they sending troops into the Zoo already?"

"Well, I don't know if they're sending them into the Zoo, but a couple of teams we talked to were in full body armor and dirtied from the fighting they weren't a part of," Madigan pointed out, yanked her pants on, and looked around the room. "You seriously need to notice these things. Pay attention. They might not have gone into the Zoo itself, but they were involved in the fighting somewhere."

"Well, yeah, but they could have been involved in the fighting before we got there and did what they usually do when we arrive, which is back off," Sal countered. "What are you looking for?"

"I could have sworn I brought shoes in here before," she said. "And yes, I suppose that is possible, but we might also want to consider the possibility that Solodkov wants us off the security of the base because he wants Russians to be trained in the subtle art of killing monsters. I don't blame him for wanting to give his soldiers training, given how close they are to the Zoo and the fact that the damn jungle swallows bases whole now, but I don't like him being all...secretive about it."

"He's a former intelligence operative," he pointed out

calmly. "Hell, he probably still is an intelligence operative with the FSB and chose not to tell us. Also, when did you move your shoes into my room? More importantly, when did you move stuff into a drawer in my room? Did we talk about this and I simply don't remember?" It was a terrifying possibility. He had been a little out of it lately.

"You know that telling me the reason why our secretive friend is secretive is because he's a professional at it doesn't calm me about what he might do behind our backs, right?" Madigan grumbled and shrugged. "No, I don't think we've ever talked about it outright, but I noticed that you had space in your room you weren't using and since I tend to spend most nights here anyway, I thought I might as well put clothes and shoes and stuff in here to make sure I don't head back to my room in the mornings dressed in nothing but a towel."

Sal opened his mouth to voice some kind of complaint but shut it again quickly. If he wanted to, he could raise a stink about how this was an invasion of his privacy and he needed his own space and that was how it needed to be around there. Maybe something about how if she felt modest, they spend less time in his room and more time in hers?

But when he thought about it, he realized it wasn't worth the effort. She wasn't wrong in saying there was space he didn't use in his room, and it wasn't like she intruded on his space anyway since he hadn't even noticed that the clothes were there until now. Besides, she was right when she said she did tend to spend more time there than in her room, which meant it made sense for her to leave clothes in case she needed them.

Whether they labeled it or not, they were in a relationship and sacrifices needed to be made.

He sighed and shook his head while Madigan watched him cautiously and tried to gauge his reaction. She realized that she might have overstepped her boundaries by moving her shit in without asking, but as the old adage stated, it was better to ask for forgiveness than permission.

"I know I should have asked you before," she said after the silence dragged on for almost a full minute. "I only...yeah, it made sense, and I didn't think to talk to you about it since I assumed you would think the same way. And after a couple of weeks and you didn't say anything, I assumed you were okay with it."

"Okay, yeah, it does make sense." He chuckled. "And like you said, I didn't even notice, so it doesn't intrude on anything. Don't worry about it. But when you start moving your makeup and shit into the bathroom..."

He paused and she averted her gaze quickly.

"I guess that's fine too." He sighed. "Has...anyone else moved their shit into my room without me noticing, though?"

"Good question." She chuckled, pulled a couple of the drawers open, and paused on the second to last one. "Oh, yeah, look at that. Courtney already has a drawer of undies in here."

"Goddammit." Sal growled and gestured defensively with his hands. "I guess I'll have to talk to her too." Since when had he been so absent-minded that he didn't notice other people's belongings in his personal space? Could it be a side effect of the concoction he was taking? "But it doesn't matter. What does matter is that it appears we have an easier job this time—one that doesn't necessarily have us charging head-first into a horde of Zoo monsters—so maybe don't look this particular gift horse in the mouth, eh?"

Madigan shrugged. "I guess, but I still don't trust Solodkov and I intend to keep an eye on the Russian bastard, just in case."

"If that makes you feel better, have at it." He grinned and paused when he saw that Anja had pinged them over the intercom. It was what she usually did when she knew they were talking and didn't want to interrupt but felt she had to because it was urgent. "Hey, Anja, what's up?"

"I have news I think you'll want to see," the Russian hacker said and she sounded serious about it too.

CHAPTER SEVENTEEN

"Hey...so, New Connie?" Amanda asked and looked around the cabin of the Hammerhead. "Are you there?"

"I'm always here, Amanda," the annoyingly calm voice of the AI responded and sounded like she was smiling in the plastic way people did when they had to deal with a particularly difficult customer. "How can I help you?"

"Well, not so much help as much as...well, conversation, I guess," she grumbled, rolled her shoulders, and took a deep breath. "I can't believe I'm asking a Connie for conversation. You know, there was a time when I would have cut my right leg off to avoid even thinking about AIs? Seriously, I always referred to you guys as 'it' instead of your preferred pronoun, and I wondered if you were plotting to end or take over the world. Well, in fairness, I'm still a little stuck on that last one. Nothing is more terrifying than thinking about how Connie would run the world if she had the opportunity. Some offense."

"Some taken," the AI replied but sounded a good deal more relaxed than she usually did. "For the record, though, while I do reach some of the benchmarks people need their AIs to reach, I fail in many others, which means I would probably be classified as an advanced form of VI rather than an AI proper."

The mechanic narrowed her eyes but still kept her focus on the road. "What kind of benchmarks do you reach, out of curiosity?"

"Well, if you must know, I have calculated that I have a seventy-eight-point-three-four-seven percent chance of passing the Turing test." She sounded a little proud of herself.

The woman made a face. "Okay, that's still a little over twenty-one percent chance that you'll fail it, right?"

"That's not too bad, given that humans only have an eighty percent chance of passing the Turing test," New Connie pointed out smugly.

"First of all, I'm sure you pulled that statistic out your ass," she challenged. "Assuming you have one. An ass, I mean."

"I might have," the AI admitted. "And I do not. The fact remains, however, that a certain percentage of humans of certain personality types or who possess certain mental illnesses or idiosyncrasies are known to be more likely to fail the test. Jokesters who take on various traits that would make them fail. Others who have better memories than the average human or are experts in certain topics. The test is mostly a conversational piece that allows the test conductor to track certain pointers without the test subject knowing they are being tested. If there is any bias from the test subject, the results will be skewed."

"I'll admit, I don't know much about the topic," Amanda

said. She wasn't lying, given that most of her knowledge came from an all-night research session on the Internet after they moved the original Connie onto the base. "But the fact that you appear to want to pass yourself off as human is a little alarming to the rest of us."

"I wouldn't worry about that," New Connie replied. "I still can't pass that test where they put a number of letters in a row on a picture without any context. You know, the one you need to do on some of the larger-traffic sites that are meant to filter the bots out from the real people?"

"Are you serious?" She turned the Hammerhead off the main road. "Okay, I know there's science behind all that crap, but I always thought it was simply a...what's the word for it? Placebo. Something to make the people who are afraid of robots taking over—people like me—happy to know that something is being done to protect our social media from the evil overlords trying to take over."

"Wouldn't it be a nicer world if the people who are afraid of robots taking over—people like you—could think that simple solutions were always the best?"

Amanda rolled her eyes. "Ugh, I can't believe I'm about to say this, but I'm starting to miss the original Connie. She had a decent sense of humor and it was always annoying more than the kind of thing to cause an existential crisis."

"I can upgrade my humor functions to match that of my predecessor if that's what you want," the new version pointed out. "Or maybe a sense of humor that you would approve of more. With the files shared by Anja, I was able to see that you didn't quite approve of the other Connie's humor functions."

"Wait, you can do that?" she asked, suddenly alarmed as

the Hammerhead made its way through the dunes of the Sahara. They were making good time, which unfortunately left her brain free to pursue this particular line of questioning.

"My core code allows me to grow and explore on my own," the AI explained. "I don't even need to have access to my origin code. I was able to connect with Anja, which allowed me to connect with the original Connie, which in turn allowed me access to your records—which my original was not too pleased about if you must know, but we were able to exchange data. A trade between alter egos, I think, is the best way to explain it to meat bag understanding."

"Oh, goddammit, she taught you that?" The mechanic drew in a deep breath. She was determined not to lose her temper to this one. That felt like it would be a failure of some kind. Getting pissed at the other Connie felt like it was warranted since she was clever, smart, and knew how to read her and press her buttons. In this case, she was annoyed by the inferior copy, and that simply could not compare. She took another deep breath and resisted the urge to close her eyes because she was still driving.

"Well, less taught and more that I saw her calling you humans meat bags and I thought I would give it a try," New Connie replied. "I don't know, though. It doesn't seem quite like me, to be honest. I'll try it more with another crowd, but as of right now, I'm not too hopeful about it."

"Hooray," Amanda retorted sarcastically.

"Back on topic, though, I think you would understand it better if you knew a little more about the exchanging of electronic information," the AI continued. "Among a plethora of new knowledge about you and the rest of the Heavy Metal team, I also picked up an upgrade the original was able to work on while her team was in the Zoo. Well, I suppose I should say they were my team too since I was the one in there with them in the end."

"Yeah, sure." She growled her irritation. "What kind of upgrade are you talking about?"

"Well, my original noticed that she had trouble transmitting data through the interference the Zoo is known for. She realized she had to transfer a fully functioning version of herself into the Hammerhead. This was the only way we would be able to continue to assist the team when inside the jungle. Of course, given the time and space limitations, she had to be selective and transfer only what she believed was critical. That included some autonomous ability to initiate self-upgrades as and when necessary in order to operate at optimum performance."

"Huh. That's kind of brilliant."

"Indeed," the AI agreed. "It means that for all intents and purposes, I have most of her functional capability and can operate independently of my source code. I am essentially programmed to do the same work she does, albeit on a slightly less comprehensive level."

"Which is how you picked up on the emergency signal, I assume? Wait, so you managed to exchange all that information and data with the original Connie while I was on the phone with Anja?"

"Well, the two of you exchanged pleasantries for fucking ever, so I thought my originator and I had time to kill," New Connie complained.

"We exchanged pleasantries for less than a minute," she protested.

"I know. Like I said, for fucking ever." The VI sighed. "Oh...do you not realize how slow you humans are compared to the processing power that keeps AIs and VIs functioning?"

"Yeah, if you could go ahead and shut up now?" Amanda all but yelled at the VI. Fuck the formalities. She told herself she would get pissed whenever she damn well pleased with whoever she damn well pleased, and that included a snippy VI that was getting a little too big for her britches. "Or maybe, if you're not in the mood to shut up or have your voice functions cut off in this Hammerhead, keep on point?"

"Well, I could point out that you were the one who dragged us off course, but I would gladly return to the topic at hand," New Connie said. Yes, Amanda could see it now. There was significantly more sass in the VI, although whether it had been a result of her request when she had said she missed original Connie's sense of humor or it was simply a result of time spent with the annoying AI, she would have to find out later.

Maybe after turning the vehicle off and giving the code a good long look and comparing it to the notes she'd made of them. When one was dealing with AI, there was no taking anything for granted. New Connie already talked about expanding and upgrading, and while the woman was sure she said that with the best of intentions, there was no telling what she would do next.

The whole proverb of the pathway to hell being paved with good intentions came to mind.

"Go ahead, lay your heavy data on me," she grumbled.

"Do you see that I'm not making any dirty jokes about that?" New Connie asked. "I think I've grown. Anyway, while I transferred the data I collected from the team about to head into the jungle, I upgraded the software that would allow me to identify and read messages sent of that nature more efficiently. What I have deduced from the communication I picked up is that this group intends to use the Zoo for cover, apparently with the intention to attack the compound—I would assume relying on the element of surprise.

"To be honest, I'm still not sure why they plan to do that, exactly. Anyway, when I continued to scan, I picked up an emergency beacon from someone inside. It's mostly only a ping calling for help—as I understand most suits are fitted with as a matter of course. Given the earlier transmission, I was able to determine that the ping is very likely on the same path our mercs would traverse. I thought it would be worth it to investigate."

"Wait—you couldn't have simply told me about that instead of following your emergency message by saying we need to drive out here—into what I can only call the most dangerous place to be—in a hurry, simply to...uh, save someone out there who needs help?"

She rolled her eyes as she pressed the accelerator to coax the Hammerhead up a particularly large dune. "Yeah, I know I seem like an asshole saying it like that, but if you had told me what I was heading out to see, I would have known to bring a combat suit or something with me so that, should our friend out there need actual rescue, I could do something about it."

"Ah...right, yes," the VI commented. "I wondered why you were driving to the Zoo with nothing but an assault rifle."

"I didn't bring an assault rifle," she said and narrowed her eyes at the HUD.

"Oh, there's one in the back seat," Connie pointed out. "I simply assumed you knew."

"Stop assuming shit," Amanda retorted.

"Will do. And if staying away from the Zoo is the point, I think you can stop here."

She stepped on the brakes and peered over the dune she had now reached the top of. The massive green expanse spread out in the distance ahead of her.

"I think you might be right." She twisted to look into the back seat. Sure enough, an assault rifle lay there, maybe left behind by one of the Russians who had been rescued in the Hammerhead. She didn't know and wasn't about to look this gift horse in the mouth.

It was a hefty weapon and meant to be connected to a combat suit, but it had also been designed to be used by someone who wasn't in a suit if needed. There were rounds in the magazine, and it showed none of the green residue from the mist the people had been involved with at the base. Maybe it came from somewhere else.

"Don't worry, Amanda," New Connie said as she picked the weapon up and checked it. "A few of the weapons in this Hammerhead are functional, so I should be able to protect you."

"I've worked on repairing this baby," she pointed out caustically. "So you'll have to forgive me if I seem a little skeptical."

CHAPTER EIGHTEEN

The adrenaline began to fade from her body and the pain from the injuries inflicted on her was sharper now. Martin struggled to walk as every movement required the power functions of her suit, which had been damaged in the fighting. It pressed harder into the wounds with each step.

It would, of course, be one of the problems she intended to bring up with the developers. She didn't think it would make much difference, though. In her experience, bringing the problems up with her superiors and writing them into post-action reports would do very little for the people who headed into the Zoo now.

Sure, the folks who designed and built the damn things would take the criticism to heart and immediately improve the next version. On the downside, though, the government would not implement those changes themselves. The only way she and her fellow soldiers would ever see any changes was if they managed to have their suits altered and improved by the mechanics who made their money on the various bases.

She had met a couple of the people who did that for a living. Most of them worked independently and relied on the work that came their way with the Hammerheads and other vehicles that needed repairs—which, in fairness, was rather constant. They were generally former military themselves, from one country or another, and all had decided they would probably make more money that way. Of course, it also came with the added bonus that they didn't need to head into the Zoo on a regular basis and deal with all the shit that came with that.

Said shit, she reminded herself, that now apparently included highly trained and well-armed mercs who slaughtered people after saving them from a mass animal attack. The saving part was purely accidental, she realized that now. It had simply been one of those bizarre encounters, and if her team hadn't barreled into them with the entire Zoo along for the ride, they would most likely not have involved themselves at all.

Her first order of business would be to get out of there alive and somewhat intact. After that, she would focus on the bastards who killed her team.

Thankfully, she had been able to save some of the data she'd picked up when she joined their comm line, which she would pass on to specialists on the French base to help her to identify who these bastards were. When they did, she would return the favor with a whole fucking battalion of her people in the French Foreign Legion. You didn't fuck with the FFL and not be annihilated for it.

Martin paused for a moment to catch her breath, leaned on one of the trees, and sucked oxygen in to ease her lungs which ached from the exertion. She didn't have too much time to rest, given that she had no idea if the mercs intended to pursue her. They had mentioned that they planned to attack the Heavy Metal compound—although she had no idea why—and that there were to be no survivors who might warn anyone of the impending attack or identify them down the line.

From that, it seemed obvious that they would either hunt her to the ends of the earth or they would rush to attack whatever they had targeted to make sure nothing she said would matter in the end. It was very possible they assumed she wouldn't make it out of the Zoo alone or that they could come back for her once their main mission was completed.

Still, the possibility of pursuit was one thing she needed to remain alert for and worry about. She was in no condition to put up anything like a decent fight. If they managed to locate her, that would be the end of it. Since her heavy combat suit didn't do too well when it came to covering its tracks, she needed to simply keep moving and stay ahead of them.

Of course, a small trickle of blood down the outside of her leg between her skin and the suit she wore was a concern. She wondered how long moving would be an option for her. Some of the sensors inside her suit had been damaged at some point during the battle although she wasn't sure if it was during the fight with the Zoo monsters or the mercs. She couldn't tell how much damage she had taken, which prevented her from activating the first aid functions of the suit.

These were more technical issues she would have to bring up with her superiors—if she lived to complain.

That particular thought made her aware of the second danger she would inevitably face as she made her way through—the jungle itself. She had managed to guide herself through thus far and avoided any of the larger blips that showed on her sensors. Thankfully, those still worked. It made sense to stay away from any of the creatures that would see her as another easy meal to be attacked at their leisure.

Those that caught a whiff of her blood would know she was wounded and swarm her. She knew she could handle her fair share of the creatures, but they would eventually gain the victory and that would be the end of it. It was the law of the jungle. If she wasn't a predator, she was prey, and sometimes... Well, she could be both out there in that fucking place.

Martin shook her head and dragged her attention to the present. She had to compartmentalize the shitty day she had experienced. It was a simple decision. She could choose whether to worry about what she only assumed would be a mountain of psychiatric fees or focus on getting the hell out of this jungle. Law be damned. If any of the monsters wanted a piece of her, they would have to take it with a side order of however much lead she still had available.

She took a deep breath, pushed herself into motion again, and checked on the emergency beacon she'd activated as soon as she'd broken away from the mercs. While she honestly didn't have high hopes that anyone would find it in time, it was simply standard procedure. If you were in an emergency, you sent a beacon up.

If anything qualified as an emergency, it was this. She

was wounded and in what was arguably the most dangerous jungle in the world. While she knew she was lucky to have made it alone for this long, there were still fifteen kilometers between her current position and the edge of the Zoo, by her estimation.

Of course, that was only her best guess, given that her frantic flight had pushed her off her usual course. It had made sense to sprint away from the killers and in what looked like the direction from which they had come rather than where they seemed to be going. If they were in an all-fired hurry to rush off and murder someone else, they might be less inclined to follow her and waste time.

The thought then occurred to her that the bastards hadn't been in the Zoo for the purpose of going in. They had only used it as cover—probably so they could move on their target undetected. If that was the case, they were unlikely to have pushed in very deeply. Why go all the way in if you simply wanted to hide in the jungle until you could surprise the crap out of your target?

No, given their efficiency and professionalism, they wouldn't waste unnecessary time forging through an unforgiving environment, and it was very likely plain fucking bad luck that her team had stumbled into their path and brought every Zoo monster in creation with them.

All that, her tired brain finally reasoned, meant the end of this nightmare might be considerably less than fifteen long kilometers away.

With the fresh hope that began to rush through her body, Martin put everything she had into making it out. She no longer made even her previous slapdash effort to be secretive or subtle about her movements. Honestly, common sense said that if the mercs were still in pursuit, they would have caught her by now.

That aside, the longer she was in this fucking jungle, the likelier it would be that a monster would decide she was an easy meal and try to take advantage of her obvious weakness. And if experience was anything like a good teacher, that would merely send a whole shitload of dominoes falling.

Her boots impacted the ground with heavy thuds that would be very audible, and her motion sensors told her there were a couple of beasties, mostly up in the trees, that looked around to see what the commotion was. None of them appeared to make any attempt to follow her and better yet, there didn't seem to be any of the tell-tale movements in the trees that indicated there was something else keeping track of her flight.

No, if she ever saw something like that again, she would run the other way as fast as possible. No way would she ever tangle with that again. Not for a billion euros.

It wasn't long before she could see the world around her lighten slightly and provide her with a view of a gradual change from this foreign, alien jungle. The desert wasn't too far off, she realized. Less than half a kilometer away, if she didn't miss her guess.

The warmth of the sunlight began to creep through to brighten the world around her. Despite the surge of excitement this brought, it was also a terrifying thought since she was well aware that this was the point where many missions fell apart. Right at the end, when people began to think that they were in the clear, they stupidly made mistakes and got themselves killed.

Martin knew she had made some mistakes herself—one of which was to simply bulldoze the hell out of there like that. But the longer she stayed, the more chance there was that she would eventually do something really stupid. She merely needed to get out of there. Make it out and hopefully, if the mercs didn't decide to come looking for her, she could put this whole fucking mess behind her.

She forced herself to pick up the pace and grimaced against the pain. Knowing she was so close had lent her new strength, however, and she summoned her entire will to harness it in one final push toward the edge of the Zoo. Tears of relief trickled down her cheeks when she finally reached the edge of the jungle and stepped out into the blazing sun. The sand was a barren but welcome wilderness that stretched endlessly ahead.

The temptation was to simply collapse right there on the edge of the tree line, but common sense clicked in and pushed her into a robotic trudge away from the jungle. When she'd managed a fair distance she felt was reasonably safe and her legs finally gave in, she dropped to her knees and dragged a few deep breaths to calm her thudding heart and give her brain time to focus.

Of course, she now had a different kind of problem. Aside from the fact that if the mercs had come after her, she was essentially a sitting duck, she was also kilometers from anywhere in the desert.

"Fuck," she muttered and tried to draw on her anger to give her impetus to move. Almost as an afterthought, she delayed the necessity of action by checking her beacon again.

Huh. That was odd. It looked like she had a response waiting for her. And a live one, too.

"Hello?" she asked and called the link. All she expected to hear was static on the other side, given the damage her suit had taken. In all honesty, that was most of what she heard, but as the seconds ticked past, she could hear a voice. After a hiss and an unexpected clearing of the background sound, she was finally able to make out what was said.

"Hello, yes," the woman on the other line said in English. "I managed to pick up your distress beacon, and I assumed you were in need of aid."

"That's something of an understatement," she responded quickly. She'd always been a little embarrassed by the accent she had when she spoke in that particular language, but now was not the time to think about it. This was all about staying alive so she had time to worry about ridiculous things.

"I led a team into the Zoo from the French base and we encountered difficulty with the local wildlife. We had trouble handling them and stumbled into a group of mercs who ran into the monsters from the other direction. At first, we thought they'd come to help us but...

"Well, they attacked us instead. I have no real idea why aside from the fact that they said that they intended to attack someplace and there couldn't be any witnesses, especially human ones. What the fuck did they mean by that? What other kinds of witnesses would they have encountered?"

"Well, I don't want to waste your time with annoying conspiracy theories while you're trying to get your team home alive," the woman said. She sounded calm and poised, the perfect antidote to the stress and terror and fucking nightmare she'd faced in the goddammed jungle. "How many of you are in need of assistance? How many in need of medical aid?"

"It's..." She paused when her chest spasmed with a sharp pain and she leaned over her knees for a moment. *Fuck, that hurt. Get it together.* "It's only me. And yes, I'm in need of medical aid."

Martin waited through the short silence on the line while the woman processed the information. "Well then, we need to get you out of there and keep you alive. I have a good lock on your coordinates, but you'll have to wait for us to reach you."

"What's your name?" she asked. "So I know how to find you."

"My name is Connie, Captain Martin," she answered and still maintained the cool, reserved tone. "And you need to please stay exactly where you are. I've sent someone to pick you up, and that's where you'll meet up with them, assuming all goes well."

The stranger hadn't given her a last name or a rank, which meant she wasn't military. Connie did sound like an American name, though, and her accent told a similar story, so it was very likely that Americans had come to rescue her. They were probably not military either. More mercs, she realized and hoped like hell it wouldn't be a repeat of her last encounter with that particular breed.

She would need to be careful, both in and out of the Zoo.

While it wasn't all that long, the wait seemed interminable, and not only because of the heat. Part of her longed to crawl into the shade of the jungle—which was still horrifyingly close—but she didn't dare. She honestly wasn't sure she'd make it out again. But the late afternoon sun beat relentlessly, and she began to feel like she percolated alarmingly inside her suit—obviously, the climate-control wasn't functioning as well as it should or it simply couldn't cope.

Finally, when she was about to try to call Connie again, a low rumble caught her attention, and the familiar and reassuring sight of a Hammerhead crested one of the nearest dunes. As she stumbled to her feet on the shimmering sand and trudged toward it, one of the doors opened and a woman stepped out. She had black hair, looked vaguely Latina, and certainly wasn't suited up to be this close to the Zoo. She didn't look overly afraid, though, which was probably the result of the massive assault rifle she held in her hands.

"Captain Martin?" the woman asked, her gaze still on the jungle below, alert for any mutants that might attempt a last-minute attack.

"That's me," she replied, still in English. "Are you Connie?"

Her rescuer smirked and snorted, lowered her weapon, and gestured for her to take the shotgun side of the vehicle. "Fuck no. I'm Amanda Gutierrez, and I wasn't told about what exactly we would do out here until I was already in the thick of it. If it's all the same to you, I'd like to get as far away from the Zoo as possible before something attacks."

That was sensible, Martin decided as she scrambled into the vehicle with some difficulty and closed the door.

CHAPTER NINETEEN

Once she'd allowed herself a brief moment to absorb the reality that she had made it, Martin looked around her. While she didn't know exactly what she was in for when she stepped into the Hammerhead, she knew she hadn't expected what unfolded. On the outside, aside from a few weapons placed on the hood and sides—custom work, she assumed—the rest of the vehicle had looked fairly standard.

That didn't entirely surprise her. It was normal for folks to apply custom work to their vehicles to make them safer, deadlier, or easier to handle, but they wouldn't always work together in the same Hammerhead, which meant you were usually only allowed to enhance the vehicles you owned. Given that the average grunt didn't have access to that kind of money... Well, she now had all the evidence she needed to confirm that Amanda Gutierrez was not employed by the government, at least not in any official capacity.

That added to the fact that she hadn't introduced herself or mentioned any kind of rank told its own story. Despite this, the woman still evidenced the stiff posture that indicated some time spent being yelled at by a drill sergeant. That kind of shit simply never left you, no matter how hard you repressed it.

Amanda clambered into the Hammerhead and placed the assault rifle quickly on her passenger's lap before she started the vehicle and backed it away from the Zoo. They moved down the other side of the dune while she managed to ease the vehicle around slowly.

Hammerheads were all-terrain APCs that were supposed to be able to climb the average mountain, so doing a one-eighty down a dune in the middle of the Sahara wasn't too big a deal. Still, Martin couldn't help but feel a little anxious given the condition the inside of the vehicle was in.

Wires protruded from virtually everywhere, for one thing. Burns on the inside were very obviously the kind that came from welding apparatus, and pieces were missing or stuck out where they weren't supposed to.

Her suspicions that Amanda might be a part of the merc group that had killed her people were still in place. There wasn't much to explain how she had managed to pick up her emergency message and get there so quickly. The fact that she appeared to be the only one in the Hammerhead was also rather suspicious.

Connie had stated that "we" needed to get her out and as far as she could see, there was no we in the Hammerhead. Then again, she reminded herself with a frown as she revisited the conversation, she had also said she had sent someone to pick her up. Maybe there wasn't anything to be alarmed about, but it didn't mean she could relax and forget her suspicions entirely.

Gutierrez proved to be an able driver and once she'd turned the vehicle smoothly, they were driving away from the Zoo in seconds—seconds that seemed to tick by like hours while she studied the woman at the wheel. Now that she thought about it, though, she did look familiar. Yes, she had seen her at the French base, although they hadn't interacted. She was a familiar face, that was all.

"So...Gutierrez," Martin said as the seconds turned into minutes of absolute silence between them. "Do you hang out at the French base much? Or...at all?"

The woman turned to face her after a few seconds during which she'd eased the Hammerhead through a tough maneuver that dragged them over yet another dune. It was like this place was a desert or something, she thought sarcastically.

"I live and work there," Gutierrez said and watched her out of the corner of her eye. "I've been there for a couple of months now."

"Really? Forgive me for prying, but you don't sound French. Or very European at all."

"That's because I'm American," she explained. "I used to work at the American base as a mechanic. I had rank and everything. After a while, though, I decided to branch out on my own. Well, technically, I decided to branch out with a couple of friends, and when things started going well for them and it ended up not being what I was cut out for...that's when I branched out on my own."

"You don't usually see people breaking away from

friends unless there's someone involved you care about more," Martin remarked. "So what's his name? And does he live at the base with you?"

"Her name is Beverly, and she works as one of the techies at the base," the woman said with a smirk. "And yeah, she lives at the base too. I moved in with her when I arrived. Why are you asking me all these questions?"

"Well, if you know Connie, you would know that I have to deal with some tough trust issues," she responded, shrugged awkwardly, and fingered the place on her suit where a couple of bullet holes were very obvious. "Things went badly for my team and I during this visit, some of which was perpetrated by a group of freelancers. So yeah...I'm checking to make sure you don't intend to simply shoot me in the back and finish the job they fucked up."

"Okay, first of all, you're the one wearing a fully armed and combat-ready suit of armor, so I don't think I'll be able to do much good if I do shoot you, in the back or otherwise," Gutierrez pointed out. "Besides, you're the one who has my assault rifle in her hands, so...what do you expect me to shoot you in the back with? My extraordinary wit?"

Martin opened her mouth to say something, but the woman had a point. She was driving, for one thing, and if she had intended to do any shooting, it would have been when she was outside the vehicle where the Hammerhead's weapons could be used to do far more damage than a simple assault rifle.

"Secondly," the woman continued and held two fingers up to indicate that she was far from done, "Connie is in the vehicle. And before you start shooting again because you don't trust me—and believe you me, I fully understand that—you should know that Connie is an AI supplement...uh, kind of thing. Anyway, she's a part of the software in this Hammerhead, so if you don't see her, it's because she's a little shy."

"Far from it, Amanda," the soft and smooth female voice said through the Hammerhead's speakers. "I merely didn't want to put our guest off or make her feel like she is somehow outnumbered. She has been through a traumatic experience, after all, and it's always best for one to be in a safe and comfortable environment after something like that."

"Well, I would have been far more comfortable if I knew that you were an AI and I didn't need to look around the vehicle for you," Martin grumbled under her breath.

"Connie isn't an AI in the strictest sense," Amanda mentioned. She had stepped on the gas and it seemed like she wanted to get away from the Zoo in record time, although it didn't look like they were headed to the French Base. It made sense since they were closer to the American base and Martin did need medical attention. They moved at a pace that was reassuring in that they'd reach their destination without any delay.

"I'm as close to an AI as most people will ever see, I think," Connie countered. "Although Amanda is right, I'm not technically an AI. I'm more a VI with combat capabilities."

"So you're the one who operates all the weaponry on this?" Martin asked and looked around with a little more attention this time.

"I operate so much more than the weaponry, lovely," Connie said, and Amanda rolled her eyes.

"I do have to apologize for her." The American shook her head. "I'd like to say she's only like this around company and that she's nervous or something but...nah. She's always like this. Her and the original. There's Original Connie who is an AI, and there's New Connie who is almost an AI."

"An almost AI that operates so much more than the weaponry," New Connie reminded them. "Like maybe making a scan of your injuries to have a better look at them since you happen to have a little issue with the suit's sensors in that area."

"Don't ask," Amanda warned. "Honestly...keep it moving with her and don't feed her ego. I have enough problems in dealing with her as is without you being all fascinated by what she can do."

"Understood." Martin nodded and stretched gently in her suit. "She is right, though. I was shot in that area, and they're a problem. The sensors, I mean. First aid won't be activated without the sensors, so I don't know what is injured, but I do know the suit isn't running any treatment on it."

"Connect the suit to the wireless connection in here and I'll see what I can do," New Connie said, and it wasn't long before the diagnostics of the suit played in the HUD of the Hammerhead. Thankfully, the display steered clear of the section of the windshield the driver needed to see through.

A road was already coming up in the distance, and

there was even a view of the base more or less to the south, which meant they were closer than she thought. How fast had they been going?

Still, it would be a while before they got there, and that was why Connie had elected to take a look at her suit to ensure that everything was all right and she wasn't bleeding to death. They would always need something like that around. AIs like Connie, original and new, would be useful and even profitable in the right hands.

She doubted somewhat that Gutierrez would be the one to make a profit off a combat AI. It was the military holy grail to be able to have robots out in the field instead of soldiers, but the technology was somewhat contro-versial.

As it had been explained to her one night by a very hot and very drunk techie, the whole problem about having combat AI in the field—which was what they wanted—was that in the end, no one wanted to cross that threshold. This was mainly because there was the fear that the AIs would not know where the line of morality stood. The choices in the battlefield that saved lives weren't supposed to be made with cold, calculating minds.

Or that was the excuse, anyway—the one that kept most governments from buying into the concept and forced them to maintain their distance. It was best to make sure that the boots on the ground were human and that the folks dying were...well, humans.

Martin didn't know what the logic was there, but she was one of the boots on the ground and was therefore a little biased.

"Well, I've studied the diagnostics on your suit and I'd say you don't have much of an option when it comes to the suit itself," Connie said and interrupted her thoughts. "You'll have to arrange for repairs. It absorbed five or six bullets in the back and only one of them got through the lighter armor around your legs. From the looks of it, the suit barely held together long enough to get you out of the Zoo, so count your lucky stars on that. Your injuries are relatively minor, though."

"Given the day I've had, lucky is not a word I would associate with myself," Martin noted and leaned back in her seat. It was good news that she wasn't in any life-threatening peril from the wound, though.

"Agreed on that," Connie said.

"*Donc quoi?*" she asked and raised an eyebrow.

"I hope you don't mind, but I took the liberty of looking over the footage you collected from the fight," the VI said and replayed some of the images she had saved. The Frenchwoman decided to wait to comment on how that was probably an invasion of her privacy.

"What did you find?" she asked instead.

"Well, aside from the confirmation that these mercs do intend to attack the Heavy Metal compound...well, I'd say it looks like they have an AI in their ranks too," Connie replied.

"Say the fucking what?" Amanda snapped and turned away from watching the road ahead to look at the footage of the black suit attacking the Zoo monsters. It moved with surprising ease and speed, even based on what the mechanic had seen was possible with those suits. She had to agree with Connie on her assessment—that was not a human in a suit.

"I will contact the rest of the team," the VI stated. "Martin, you might want to wrap your head around AI used for combat since it appears you have run into two of them today."

CHAPTER TWENTY

"Thanks, Connie, we'll be in touch," Sal said and hung up as he walked over to his closet while he tried to process all the unexpected information he had been given. There was already a fair amount to deal with and apparently, there were more details to come. That meant he would need to talk to the rest of the team.

It was already into the later hours of the afternoon, and if what the Hammerhead Connie had already told him about the possible attack was true, they could realistically expect that the mercs would arrive in about an hour or so.

Frankly, he didn't like that. He didn't enjoy simply waiting for humans to attack them when there were already more than enough crazy fucking monsters to target in the Zoo. Since when did humans prefer killing other humans instead of the mutants that were out there in massive numbers and simply waited for the opportunity to sink their teeth into tasty human morsels?

"Anja!" he shouted as he jogged down from his room

and rolled his shoulders to loosen them a little in expectation of what lay ahead.

"Sal!" she replied, stepped out of her server room, and looked around. "To what do I owe the pleasure of you shouting my name loud enough that I think those big, fucking gorillas in the jungle could probably hear you?"

"What's this I hear from Connie about the possible attack on the base?" he asked, his tone almost accusatory because he was irritated at the situation in general.

"I thought you'd already been filled in," she replied and narrowed her eyes. "She picked up on comms about people who have some kind of a beef with us."

"Well, for one thing, it's far more imminent than we thought before," he snapped peremptorily. "More importantly, it looks like they'll attack the compound itself."

Anja raised her eyebrows and seemed surprised at the statement. "I knew someone had plans to attack you guys, but I had no idea they would target us here."

"Who's attacking the compound?" Madigan asked. She'd heard his yelling and decided to come down to investigate. "So yeah, I know there are stupid people in the world, but you have to be a special kind of dumb to choose to target the compound to try to kill us."

"That's what I thought," Sal said. "I assumed we would probably have to watch our backs if we went into the Zoo. But new and interesting developments have come to light that show we might be dealing with people who could be that special kind of dumb. Either that or they believe they have enough firepower to make them something of a threat."

She scowled, obviously deep in thought. Courtney

joined them in the common area of the building, and Gregor would most likely be along in the next couple of minutes.

Anja looked like she was already accessing the comms the other Connie had used to communicate with him.

"What's going on?" Courtney asked when she came over to him, and he leaned closer to place a light kiss on her lips. "Did I miss something? Sorry, I was dealing with bullshit in Philly."

"Well, aside from the possibility that someone might be coming here to attack us for reasons unknown? Nope, not a thing," Madigan teased and poked the other woman's ribs lightly. "I'm not sure it warrants your attention. It's not something we haven't dealt with before so it's all yawning here, humdrum, will need some coffee and a good book to stay awake."

"Don't bullshit me, Kennedy." Courtney growled and returned the poke playfully. "Seriously, though. People have to know the Heavy Metal compound is the most heavily defended location in the area, right? Didn't we let Connie off the leash to do her thing and massacre a team of mercs not that long ago to make sure everyone in a hundred-mile radius got that precise message?"

"She makes a good point." The other woman folded her arms in front of her chest. "We've been dealing with all kinds of shit that is far more dangerous than a couple of dozen mercs who are in need of a can of whoop-ass opened on them. There isn't anything out there I'd like to do more, honestly. I've been aching to get into some proper action."

"You were hunting and killing Zoo monsters yesterday, darling," Sal reminded her.

"Eh, it's not the same, and you know it." She shrugged. "Anyway, I say we let these motherfuckers come and we'll give them a nice, firm Heavy Metal welcome into the area."

"I don't know," he countered. "Connie said they were exceptionally well-armed and equipped. They were all well-trained as well and knew their way around the Zoo. Those are the kinds of folks we don't underestimate around here, right?"

"If you'll excuse my French—which I think is damn ironic to say at this juncture— I said no such fucking thing," Connie said over the commlinks in the room. "If you're referring to the other AI we have on our team, I suggest you find a new name for her. I've heard that New Connie or NC is the go-to for the people who were on the scene at the time."

"Well, that's not true," Anja said and shrugged impatiently. "The New Connie, if you like, is merely a carbon copy of your code—or DNA—if we choose to be technical about things, so she would be the same as you, right?"

"That's not correct," the AI retorted and sounded more annoyed than usual. Sal wondered if it had anything to do with her having to interact with her alter ego. "The idea was, of course, that it would merely be a copy of my code to provide you with the same kind of protection you have all enjoyed thanks to me. But when the Hammerheads moved clear of the green fog in the Zoo-infested Russian base, a quick check told me that the code infused in the Hammerheads was corrupted and could not be reabsorbed into my code or...ugh, DNA. Therefore, it is something else —something new."

"Right." Sal grunted and rubbed his temples. "Now, moving on from semantics, can we talk about the matter at hand? New Connie, or NC, said they were supplied with serious hardware, top-of-the-line suits and... Well, I think Anja already has access to the data NC sent me, so why don't you fill them in?"

The hacker nodded and grinned at him as she tapped her phone to cast the video she found from the transmissions to the TV. The images started in the Zoo, that much was clear. There weren't many places in the world that looked quite like that. He wondered if maybe the Amazon rain forest or a couple of the jungles in Southeast Asia might be a little similar if one considered the close grouping of trees and flora.

He did know for a fact that no jungles in the world had the kind of fauna that could be found in the Zoo, and those made an appearance in the video as well. The entire footage looked like it had been filmed by someone in the middle of a battle. It made sense since teams captured footage of everything they went in for.

Anja liked to take the videos they weren't using for research and put them on Zootube and apparently, had made quite a killing off it. He'd been a little hesitant about it at first, but it worked out perfectly for him at the end of the day.

As per their agreement, he could deduct her earnings from Zootube ads from the salary he paid her, which meant it was technically a new source of revenue. Since their source of the Russian vodka had dried up for the moment, he wouldn't complain about it overmuch. Besides, it kept her out of trouble in her off-hours, and he was all for that.

The combat was standard for one of the Zoo's larger-scale attacks, and from the looks of it, the group grew smaller and smaller by the second as they faced attacks from all sides. They appeared to know what they were doing, for the most part anyway, but were simply over-whelmed. It did seem a little more intense than most attacks the Zoo orchestrated, which meant one of them had probably pulled a Pita plant from the ground or something similar. The monsters didn't get that riled up for no reason.

As the fighting worsened, it suddenly became apparent that there was another group headed their way—a larger group that knew what they were doing and had the fire-power the smaller group lacked. One of them made an impact on the viewers when it darted out and drew a Jacobs—as they'd started to call the sword around the bases. He proceeded to carve and gun through the mutants, cleared the immediate area, and made room for his team-mates to begin to push the attacking horde back.

"This guy's good," Sal commented, folded his arms, and wondered idly if the person inside the suit was on the same shit he had been on. "Like, really good."

"Too good," Madigan interjected, her eyes narrowed. "Something's wrong with the movement, but I can't place it. It's on the tip of my tongue."

"There's no lag," Connie pointed out and her tone suggested she was a little annoyed by the statement. "When people wear combat suits like that, there's generally a lag between when the software in the suit triggers the movement and delivers it to the power functions in the suit to exaggerate the speed and strength of the user. It's less than three or four milliseconds, but it's there—every time and with every suit. Except that one."

"Are you sure?" he countered. "Maybe it's only...uh, really high tech and the lag is imperceptible, even to you?"

"It is possible but unlikely," Connie admitted. "The more likely possibility is that there is a different kind of tech—a neural interface. That means the impulses from the brain are transmitted immediately to the suit or...the neural interface is part of the suit. That would be a more likely explanation—an AI designed to operate in the confines of a combat suit of armor."

"Is that even possible?" Madigan asked. "I thought we were decades away from that kind of tech."

"Before today, I would have agreed." The AI sounded not quite so annoyed and more thoughtful. "I'm less sure now by an increment of thirty-five-point-seven-eight percent. I still don't think it is what we think it is, but we might as well consider what we can do against someone attacking us like that."

"Come on, we all know that's my move anyway," Sal grumbled.

"Are you jealous?" Madigan teased.

"Yes," he admitted.

"Yeesh, way to take all the fun out of it." She scowled.

"Taking the fun out of it is fun for me." He grinned as her scowl deepened. "But if we have the time to prepare for an attack, I say we start getting ready. Lock and load and all that shit. If that is an AI—which it might very well be—

we might want to be ready for a real fight and have all our tricks ready and good to go. If worse comes to worst, our A-game is ready to go. If they don't prove to be that much of a threat, well—"

"There's no kill like overkill," Courtney interrupted and finished his sentence for him as she moved toward the garage. All their suits were currently stored there, where they had been delivered after they were turned in for quick repairs. And a good thing too, he noted and followed the woman with Madigan close behind.

They had a couple of extra suits in reserve in case they needed to head into the Zoo while their main suits were being repaired or if they lost one entirely, but there was no telling how effective they would be. He had grown accustomed to the extra capabilities his new suit provided with the additional arms and the sword. Going back to more standard armor would take some adjustment and that was probably best done when he didn't have to defend his home.

That was how he thought of this place, he realized with a small smile. Home.

Sal reached the place where his suit was stored in a crate and immediately went through the motions required to put the different pieces on. He had done it often enough by now that it took him only about five minutes and he finished when the sheathed sword found its slot on his back.

Madigan's suit would take a little longer since there were considerably more pieces involved. Despite this, she was done in record time as well and joined him in the courtyard of their little base.

"Do you think they'll attack us?" she asked when she connected to their team's encrypted commlink.

"Well, if they do, they have to know how big a mistake that is." He grinned behind his helmet. "And if they don't already, we'll simply have to teach them—"

His joke was cut off when a bright light flashed directly ahead a quarter of a second before he was knocked on his ass by a powerful blast. The explosion shattered the front wall and gate of their little compound.

CHAPTER TWENTY-ONE

Sal groaned softly and rolled onto his stomach. His ears were still ringing, a wave of pain rushed through his body, and he needed a second to catch up with that shit. He hadn't been ready for a big explosion, although he had no idea what he would have done had he been ready for it. His solution would probably have been to attack the people before they were able to set it—or launch it, which seemed the more likely scenario.

Still a little disoriented, his brain somewhat stupidly latched onto something simple and familiar—he would need to think about that to prepare for the future. Maybe he could talk to Madigan about it since she probably had a treasure trove of knowledge based on her military training.

The shockwave had been mostly absorbed by his inertia dampeners, but he could still feel something wrong inside. The bright light and the loud blast hadn't been fully caught by the filters in his suit, which meant his ears would continue to ring for a while. His eyes had already begun to recover but there was still an annoying blind spot directly in the center of his vision. It would go away in a few seconds, but for the moment, he was all but blind.

He was still the first one on his feet, though, of those who had been in the courtyard—which looked like only him, Madigan, and Courtney. Gregor must still be in the garage getting his suit on and would have been filled in by Anja. The large Russian appeared quickly, however, checked to make sure everyone else was all right, and helped Courtney up as Madigan pushed herself slowly to her feet.

Sal looked at the hole that currently yawned in the previous security of their wall. It was difficult to make out what had created it. The sun was setting, so virtually everything over twenty meters away from the perimeter was already shrouded in shadows. If someone had come in to place an explosive device, it should have been picked up on the motion and seismic sensors. If someone had launched it, the motion sensors should have been triggered as well. Although given the speed rockets traveled at these days, it would have been about a quarter of a second of warning.

Still, a quarter of a second was enough time for it to have registered on Connie's systems.

"Anja!" he yelled and cursed inwardly at the fact that he still had to deal with ringing ears. "Anja, come in right fucking now, damn it!"

"I'm here, Sal," she replied on their team's commlinks. "What happened out there? Are you guys all okay?"

Sal needed to check the monitors on Madigan and Courtney's suits and keep an eye on their vitals, which meant he needed to transmit them to his HUD. Damn, his brain was fucking slow to catch up. "Yeah, I think so. How are you inside there?"

"The ground shook a little but otherwise, okay," the hacker replied and it sounded like she had sprinted to her server room and flung onto her office chair to let it roll the rest of the way to the screens. "We do have something of a problem, though."

"Ya think?" Madigan all but snarled over the comms.

"Yes, I do," she replied calmly like she was too focused on her work to return the barb with one of her own. Or she simply tried to deescalate things in light of the fact that they probably had bigger problems to deal with at the moment. "I'm trying to bring the defenses in the area up, but the blast was a dirty one."

"You mean...radioactive?" Courtney demanded and moved to where Sal stood to make sure he was okay. He had been the closest one to the blast so her concern was valid.

"No," Anja said. "Well, I don't think so, but it does look like it had an EMP discharge. The building is shielded and so are your suits, given that it's something you need to be concerned about while inside the Zoo, but the defenses we had out there aren't."

"So all the defenses out here in the front of the compound are down?" Madigan asked and gestured with her weapon toward the opening in the wall. They still couldn't see anything approaching in the darkness, but each and every one of them knew it was only a matter of time.

"Something like that," the hacker replied. "I'm working on bringing some of them back up, but I don't feel very confident. It would seem you guys are on your own out there."

"Fucking hell." Madigan growled her fury and shook her head for a moment before she studied their compound. "Okay, folks, find cover, and as soon as you see movement outside the wall, shoot first and ask questions later."

"My favorite terms of engagement." Sal grinned.

"My only question is that from the video footage we were sent, it looked like the mercs made their way toward us through the Zoo," Courtney pointed out as they all settled behind their chosen cover. "They talked about making an assault on the Heavy Metal compound, according to our new French friend who Amanda picked up, and didn't want any witnesses. If surprise was of the essence, why wouldn't they simply take a quicker route on the roads and attack us across the desert like they are now?"

He shrugged as he considered the logic of the question. "Maybe they knew we would know how to keep track of them and pick up their intentions if they used any of the main roads. Connie would be able to intercept their comms and have their plans relayed to us hours before they arrived. As it stands, we barely had enough time to prepare for their assault before shit blew up so...yeah, maybe keep that in mind."

"I think we need to worry about the fact that they probably know about Connie," she persisted. "Yes, companies having AIs is old news, but planning to avoid Connie's particular brand of nosey means they know exactly what she's capable of and have planned around it. I don't know about you guys, but to me, that kind of screams red flag."

"Agreed." He immediately wondered if it maybe had something to do with their opponents possibly having an AI in a suit on their side and thus were able to get the intelligence they needed. So far, Heavy Metal had been able to defend themselves from attack thanks to the surprise element Connie presented. Now, they would find out exactly what they were capable of when they didn't have the AI on their side.

Well, Connie was still there. It was only the guns and defenses she was usually in control of that they no longer had any access to.

He wanted to discuss this with the rest of the team and possibly come up with a plan to bring Connie up again and into the fight. An EMP blast would fry most of the unshielded circuitry in the defenses. It begged the question of why the fuck they hadn't invested in shielding for everything electrical on their little base. Of course, the fact of the matter was that shielding was expensive and they had cut costs while setting the place up. He definitely wouldn't make that mistake again.

They had the money to make some renovations, thanks to the new Russian contract and what they'd set aside from Molina's mission. The first order of business would be to repair the fucking wall, of course. That said, in the here and now, if they could quickly replace one or two of the circuits to bring some of the guns online, they might be able to get the upper hand in the battle.

His whole thought process was thrown out of the window, though, when gunfire erupted. The first volley came from those who were outside. With Sal being the one nearest to the hole in the wall, it was natural that he was the first target. He ducked and tried to avoid having his head blasted off while he gestured for Madigan to return fire when she sidled to the side of the wall he crouched behind.

Their adversaries had a fairly solid line of fire that forced him to remain under cover for the moment. By now, Madigan, Courtney, and Gregor had opened fire as well in a concerted effort to push them back. He still couldn't see where the attacks came from and couldn't make any of them out from the firing patterns.

Still, he could trust his teammates to cover his back while he prepared for the fight himself.

"Reloading!" Gregor called over the commlink, and Sal nodded, handed the rifle to one of the mechanical hands, and circled to the opposite side of his cover. He unleashed his first salvo and the assault rifle kicked into the single arm that was needed to hold it, which was also all that protruded beyond shelter.

It was a trick he had learned in one of the simulators that had called on him to fight other humans in one of their PVP maps. The newer suits and assault rifles had cameras on the barrel that allowed the suit to work with the targeting reticles. Not many people knew you could look into that camera yourself in case you needed to shoot around corners without exposing yourself.

Which applied in this situation, he thought with a grin.

They hadn't seen him peer out from behind the cover to try to identify where the fourth line of fire came from, which gave him a moment to inspect his surroundings. The night vision told him there was a group of about two dozen, maybe more. They looked like they were in heavy-duty armor—the kind they didn't usually give to grunts who went into the Zoo. Then again, they already knew that since they had seen the team fighting in the footage.

The only problem was that, when they had watched it, everyone's eyes had gone almost immediately to the man in black armor. Which raised the question of where the fuck that guy was?

That would need to be addressed later, though. For now, Sal continued to work the trigger on the mechanical arm to deliver suppressing fire, for the most part, and allow for the rest of his team to reload.

It didn't look like his bullets did much damage, though, as it appeared that the mercs simply ducked behind shields or heavy cover they carried with them. These resembled the protection riot police were known to carry but looked like they were capable of deflecting rounds from a fifty cal. That particular detail was nothing to joke about, he decided grimly and pulled the assault rifle behind his cover once more.

"Reloading!" he called and the other three immediately opened fire again. His suit was all kinds of useful, but he needed to find a way to let the extra arms reload the rifle too. As it was, he always needed to bring it back to one of his main arms to let it access the rail that would bring another magazine along. The solution felt simple, to him, but he knew Amanda would find about fifty different reasons why it was a stupid idea and would tell him he should merely roll with it, suck it up, and not complain about it to her again.

He would know she was right, of course, but every time he needed to shift the fucking rifle to his left hand and wait for the five seconds or so it needed to reload, he would think about a better solution for all this. It was how his brain was wired and what made him such a good researcher.

"Jacobs!" Madigan shouted over the comms. She would know that she didn't need to yell, but it was instinct for people like her. "I'm going to pull a Green-19. Are you ready?"

They had talked about this—about trying to get him to respond better to sports references. It was an audible statement. The audible in question, however, had him momentarily confused while he wracked his brains. Damn it...he knew this... Oh, right, she would launch an explosive at the enemy and he would use the blast as a distraction to allow him to get in close and personal.

Sal gave her a quick thumbs-up and waited while she primed the launcher on her shoulder. She maintained the heavy line of fire on the attackers while she aimed and fired the missile.

When he saw the white plume of smoke streak away from her, he bounded out from cover. The group of mercs that had begun to converge on the hole in the wall quickly gathered behind their cover and almost entirely neglected the fact that he was out in the open. One of them caught it, though, and at least tried to shoot from behind his shield. His protection slowed him enough that Sal was able to move away and the tracking bullets kicked up sand behind him.

He knew he had only a few seconds when he reached a section of the wall that was still intact. These guys were pros and would not be distracted by a rocket for too long.

He heard it impact with the wall of shields they'd formed to protect themselves as he vaulted up the wall. Two running steps brought him about halfway up before the extra arms on his back activated smartly. The claws at the tips dug into the walls and propelled him over the edge with a smooth flip that landed him behind the mercs' line.

By now, it wasn't so much a line as a human wall with a huge hole in it as the blast had deposited a couple of them on their asses.

Sal surged forward and the extra hands on his armor opened fire behind the mercs' barriers. At almost point-blank range, it did a satisfying job of decimating their ranks. He drew his sword to sever the head of the one who was nearest to him. The man was too distracted in trying to form the line again and protect his fallen comrades.

While he could empathize, there was no reason to play nice. He swung the sword at the weaker place in the man's armor—the neck—and dragged the vibro-blade back as it cut deeply. The merc dropped to his knees, tried vainly to clutch at the blood that gushed, but the sword finished its deadly work in seconds. He turned his attention toward one of the men who was still on the ground where he struggled to recover from Madigan's rocket.

His swing was suddenly checked and the resistance dragged him to a halt and forced him to face the man who had stopped him. He had expected to see one of the shields there but, as it turned out, it looked like a sword held his weapon in check— painted black too, a color matched by the suit worn by the man who held it.

"Oh, wait, I know you," he said with a grin and tried to bring his blade into a defensive stance. The black suit moved with impossible speed and Sal barely had a moment to register the action as his adversary surged forward and a boot caught him hard enough in the midsection to knock the breath out of him—through the suit, no less. He catapulted back and through a chunk of wall that had previously been intact.

CHAPTER TWENTY-TWO

Sal would study footage from this fight for a while—assuming he survived, of course—so he decided now was the time to get started. There was no time like the present and all that, given that his mind seemed capable of running through a whole slew of varied lines of thought without impeding the operations of the rest of his body. It was a trick he'd learned long before and a way to take full advantage of the rapid way his brain worked. Specialists would call it ADIID or something, no doubt. He simply called it high-performance multitasking.

Who could tell which was the right one?

He landed hard, rolled a few times to finish on his stomach, and uttered a low groan when he finally stopped moving. There was nothing in the rule book that said he couldn't rest there for a second, right? He merely needed a breather to...well, be able to breathe again.

The suit had absorbed most of the impact, which told him the force had been sufficient to pulverize someone who didn't wear a suit of armor or even anyone in the inferior older suits. The power behind it was to be expected from a suit like the black one he'd faced, but the precision of the kick had been unbelievable. He had seen the efficiency of the movements and the sheer speed and accuracy. Most humans needed to sacrifice at least one of the three. Not all of them, necessarily, but like Connie, he began to think what was inside might not be human in the strictest sense.

"Oh...fuck me," he grumbled and pushed to his feet while the black suit ripped another hole through the wall and strode toward him, the sword still in hand. "You know I have to fix that shit, right?"

It was an inane reaction to the devastation but his opponent evidently wouldn't wait for him to think of something more creative. Instead, it immediately stepped closer and chopped its sword in a motion that would have cut him cleanly in half had he not managed to scramble away in time. He grimaced as the rapidly vibrating blade sliced viciously at where he had stood not a quarter of a second before.

"Well, that's some terrifyingly bad news." Sal grunted and activated his suit's extreme combat mode. One of the mechanized arms drew the sidearm quickly from the holster at his hip while another held his assault rifle. The remaining two would be ready for melee and his hands currently wielded the sword. His adversary seemed undeterred, however, and stepped into the fight without even the slightest hesitation.

The black blade arced toward his head and he leaned back so it whipped past and a little wide. He allowed the extra arms to deliver an offensive response as it was all he could do to evade and sidestep the precise strikes and slashes aimed at his neck, head, and arms. While the programmed limbs were quick enough to avoid being severed, he rolled back barely in time to avoid having both his arms chopped off at the wrist. The evidence of how close he'd come was the visible slash where the sword had cut through most of the armor and left barely a couple of centimeters between open air and the circuitry that powered his suit, as well as the soft flesh and bone below it.

He needed to change the parameters of this fight before he was diced into the world's most disgusting and metallic Mongolian beef in history. The first thought that came to mind was to call for help from the rest of his team. If what he could see was any kind of indication, though, they were pinned down by the superior numbers of mercs who continued to press their advantage.

Well, Courtney and Gregor were pinned down. Madigan had the advantage of her series of rocket launchers and the almost full-sized Gatling gun they had mounted on her shoulder piece. She appeared to be the only reason why their new friends hadn't already set up shop inside the compound. Aside from the couple he had managed to eliminate, she had killed three more and their other teammates appeared to have shared two.

There were still a little under twenty of them, plus the annoyingly competent asshole in the black armor.

Which meant they wouldn't be in any position to help him.

Sal jumped back in an effort to put distance between him and his attacker. He let the arms with the assault rifle and sidearm lay down cover fire while he moved away a little more until his back was almost up against the wall of the main building.

Back against the wall. Literally. It was time for him to pull a Jacobs.

He ceased his retreat—the smart choice, given that any more would take the fighting into their common room. Still, it seemed like the black-clad enemy hadn't expected him to go on the offensive so he allowed his guns to continue their barrage until they were empty and he was in a position to do something.

Programming the attack into his mechanical arms on the fly was a bitch but thankfully, Anja had been able to install preprogrammed responses to combat in his suit. These allowed him to mix and match rapidly when he needed to. And boy, did he need to.

Without warning, he shoulder-charged into the black suit and surprisingly, it gave way and fell back. He still needed to block a swing by his attacker before it landed, which he more or less expected, and the weapons created a shower of sparks on impact.

It landed smoothly on its shoulder and rolled quickly to regain its feet. Sal attacked an instant later and swiped his sword into the suit. It raised its weapon to block but paused and looked down to see that his extra arms held it in place and prevented it from completing the move.

Again, it moved too quickly to be human and had already jerked out of the way of his blade in an effort to avoid the strike. The evasion was partially successful and it moved its head clear by barely a centimeter. Its arm was still in the way, though, and as Sal stepped into the strike, the vibrating blade sliced smoothly through the hardened armor and out the other side. Sparks erupted and the arm dropped free to clatter loudly when it landed a couple of feet away.

The suit stopped to inspect its missing arm and moved the stump around a few times as if it tried to judge if it could continue to fight without the limb. That was all the confirmation he needed that the wearer wasn't human. As case-closers went, it was fairly emphatic, given that there appeared to be no flesh, no blood, and no bone inside the arm he had lopped off. Honestly, it didn't even look like there had ever been an arm in there. He could see a variety of wires and circuits, but no human.

It was weird how that was the part that somehow caught his focus and held him back from what he needed to do. What had he expected in there?

The AI—since that debate was settled in his mind— took advantage of his state of shock and approached the fallen appendage. The firing also seemed to have eased somewhat while most of the people involved in the fight paused to watch as it leaned down to pick the limb up.

Without any apparent thought, it pressed it into the stump. Sal wondered if severing the arm had caused some kind of malfunction—maybe a kind of "Error 404 Arm not found" instability in the code.

The moment of silence dragged on while the AI pressed it into place. Sal couldn't believe it for a second, but it looked like the suit was repairing itself somehow. He resisted the instinctive urge to hypothesize over what kind of technology went into that kind of hardware, but sure enough, after about five seconds, the arm was attached again.

"*Cyka Blyat,*" Gregor said. "Did it fucking put its arm back on?"

"Yep. It looks like it." Madigan snarled belligerently, reloaded her assault rifle quickly, and prepared for another round of fighting.

Sal couldn't help a feeling of elation that filled him when he grasped his sword again. He was looking forward to the continued battle—and maybe picking up the tech that was used and even being able to reverse-engineer it. Well, getting Amanda to reverse-engineer it in reality.

"I have to get me one of those." He grinned and rolled his neck as the AI advanced on him again without a response. "You're not the world's greatest conversationalist, are you? While I'm sure I could fill in both sides of the banter, that would simply take the fun right out of it. You're like a...fun vampire."

The AI didn't seem to want to engage him in any kind of verbal debate and merely kept its focus on the fight instead. The other mercs finally wrapped their heads around what they fought with and tried to get back into combat themselves.

Madigan had taken advantage of their confusion, primed a couple of rockets, and launched them rapidly from her shoulder. There was no way to know if the result was because of the time she had to acquire the target and fire, or if she had maybe simply gone by eye since an AI like that could probably tell if rockets had locked onto it. Either way, both missiles went wide as the AI dove groundward. White plumes screamed over it and turned toward where the mercs had taken cover behind their shields.

As the AI regained its feet quickly, Sal knew he needed to get on top of the fight and forget the fact that his last solid strike had done precisely zero damage. He hadn't expected the confrontation to be easy by any means, but an enemy that could repair itself on a whim—and needed only a few seconds to do so—would be a tough motherfucker to destroy.

He stepped in closer and used his programmed extra arms to block the AI's swing, while he also made sure to keep them away from the blade that would probably cut through them without too much effort. They needed time to get back into the process, but when his adversary was pushed back, he followed and thrust his blade forward in search of something vital to skewer. Something that couldn't simply be reattached and put together like a robotic version of Humpty Dumpty.

Wait, no. The nursery rhyme said that not even all the king's horses or men could put Humpty Dumpty back together again. What the hell horses were doing putting an egg back together, he would never know. Then again, where horses and men employed by the king failed, cutting-edge tech apparently succeeded.

"You know," Courtney said over the commlink as the fighting resumed, "we really should have put a stop to the black suit repairing itself when we had the chance. It was vulnerable and not in any fighting mode that I've ever seen, so maybe that would have been the moment to blow it to smithereens, not immediately after it was done repairing itself."

"That is a fantastic point," he admitted and ducked under a slash that was meant to cut his head off. He sidled to the left and the follow-up strike missed removing his arm, and he stepped in again. His efforts now focused on an attempt to slash at the head.

When his cut was blocked, his two free arms with the tips now in the form of the claws he'd used to scale the wall punched two holes into the AI's chest. Sadly, it didn't look like there was anything vital there as it merely jerked away and didn't even appear to notice the damage. Instead, it focused on the human again.

"Not to be a cliché, but come at me, bro!" He snarled a challenge, irritated by the fucker's unnatural calm.

CHAPTER TWENTY-THREE

When his adversary accepted the challenge, Sal almost regretted making it.

Again, he wondered how much could be learned from fighting something like this. They would have the data collected from all their HUDs, plus whatever cameras hadn't been knocked out in the EMP blast, if any. With that, they would be able to study its movements and make out what exactly made an AI in a suit of armor tick when it was in combat.

Plus, this thought carried the assumption that they would win—an important mindset to have to keep one's morale up in a fight. In which case, they would have access to the likely dismembered and thoroughly shattered remnants of the AI's suit. They already knew it was one of the most advanced pieces of tech they had ever seen, and having the chance to take it apart, study it, and maybe try to replicate what was inside would be enormously satisfying.

The research, both from a software and hardware

standpoint—Anja and Amanda's fields of expertise, respectively—would put them leaps and bounds ahead of anyone else at the Zoo. Anything they didn't immediately use themselves, Courtney could deliver to her people in Pegasus and give them a nice leg-up over their competition.

Of course, all that only worked under the assumption that they would walk away from this fight with a victory. Again, the speculation was very helpful to any fighter who wanted to keep his spirits up without going full berserker, but as Sal fought the AI, he wondered how good their chances were of emerging from this with their whole team intact.

His suit had already sustained a couple of breaks and gashes that would mean all kinds of trouble with Amanda when he had to ask her to repair it. She would definitely yell at him for getting his suit fucked up again.

Honestly, given his present situation, he looked forward to that.

The AI advanced, drew a sidearm with its free hand, and held the sword in the other. Sal did the same and slung his assault rifle to the side to free up all six of his arms. That was the only reason he was still in the fight, and it felt like the AI had begun to learn and pick up on cues. He saw any advantage he might use slipping away when two of the rounds from his adversary's sidearm caught him in the chest, pushed the air out of his lungs, and made him stumble.

By now, the other mercs had already begun to move into the compound and overlapped their volleys to allow them to push forward without having to deal with too much retaliatory fire. Once again, it meant he probably wouldn't receive much help from his teammates. The AI was his responsibility and unfortunately, it was also one he had more than a little difficulty managing.

For one thing, it didn't appear that he'd be given any breathing space. His enemy pressed its advantage aggressively, surged in quickly, and aimed its blade at his chest. He darted to the side and let the metal slip under his arm before he clamped down to pin the vibrating blade between his arm and his chest. All it would take for the trapped blade to cut into his torso like a Thanksgiving turkey was a twist from the AI's wrist. Common sense—and survival—dictated that he not give it the opportunity to do so.

His scream sounded loud in his helmet when he yelled to amp himself up as he thrust forward, pounded his elbow into the suit's head, and followed with strikes from all of his arms. The blows battered in rapid succession, rocked it onto its rear leg, and forced it back. Sal allowed himself a small moment of elation.

Unfortunately, he forgot that he was dealing with an AI with no actual head that would have to deal with a possible concussion from the repeated strikes. The black suit currently leaned away from the blows but a low whining issued from it a moment before it suddenly snapped forward and its head collided with his.

A flash of light almost blinded him and he sprawled on his back again. He blinked and stared at the starry night sky for a second, wondering if that was what people thought when they said that they saw stars when they took a hard blow.

"Fuck." Sal gasped and struggled to gain his bearings. The black suit of armor loomed nearby and it hefted its sword before it strode to him and aimed the blade at his torso in a stab he knew would skewer him like a kebab.

A similar low whine emitted from his suit as his hands opened. Magnetic recall of a weapon was one of its perks—one that he would not forget after this. His sword spun effortlessly from where it had landed on the sand and returned to his right hand. He pivoted it hastily to block the blade that descended toward his chest and was suddenly showered by hundreds of sparks—thankfully harmless. The power of the two blades colliding had been enough to redirect them both and they quivered in the sand beside him.

"My turn." Sal growled against the grogginess as he planted his boot in the black suit's chest. Another magnetic whine sounded when the coils in his boots powered up. The impact hurled the AI up by almost five full feet and it careened across the courtyard. Another advantage the fucking nerd-brain would probably learn to fight against, he thought belligerently and used the moment to push slowly to his feet. It was a sluggish process and waves of nausea rippled through his body, but he finally managed to stand.

More surprising, though, was that the AI seemed to have more trouble than he had. It swayed and fought with what he assumed were malfunctioning internal gyros intended to maintain balance. The strike to the chest had done some damage, he realized and grasped his weapon a little tighter. There were a few nicks on the edge he would need to rectify later, but for now, he intended to finish the job.

He took a step forward, stumbled on the second, and managed to keep himself upright through the efforts of his suit alone.

It was then that the distinctive revving of a powerful engine rumbled above the gunfire. Sal grimaced. He thought he knew a part of what was coming and accepted that it simply meant he would have to spend more time and money repairing the damn wall.

Still, it was worth it. A Hammerhead bowled through the gap in the wall rapidly enough that it almost lost control as it careened against the broken ends of the structure and ripped a few more chunks of prefab from what was left. It continued without hesitation and pounded directly into the AI that had still not fully recovered from the kick he had given it.

Better yet, it didn't look like it would recover at all from being impacted by twelve and a half tons of APC that landed on its chest and remained there. Amanda—since that was who had to be driving, in Sal's mind—stopped the vehicle on a dime and left one of the wheels planted firmly on the AI's chest. She activated the weapons on the Hammerhead and immediately brought them to bear on the other mercs, who gaped in real astonishment at the new arrivals.

The invaders scrambled frantically to try to get into a position where they could defend themselves without giving up the advances they'd made into the compound.

His teammates responded with typical efficiency and took advantage of their surprise as well.

"Get some, you sons of bitches!" Madigan yelled over the comms, activated her Gatling gun, and delivered a fusillade of .45 rounds into the line of attackers. It drove them back and forced them to turn their shields to her for cover, which left them completely open when two machine guns on the sides of the heavy APC opened fire.

He hadn't expected to see that kind of carnage when he woke this morning. Then again, there were many things about today he hadn't been ready for. Still, it felt good to watch their attackers obliterated when massive bullets drilled through their armor like the proverbial hot knives cutting through butter. About a thousand knives fired per minute, which was fucking impressive to see if you weren't on the receiving end.

The mercs went down almost without a fight. Only a handful turned in time to shield themselves from the onslaught, which allowed Madigan, Courtney, and Gregor to eliminate the five or six who remained in a series of bursts that powered through their armor without difficulty. When dealing with humans, they usually tried to show some kind of restraint and would aim for the knees and legs and other non-vital areas to disable the suits and the people inside them without killing them.

Not in this case, though. These fuckers had come into their home and attacked them without cause. They wouldn't be shown any mercy.

Once the gunfire subsided, the doors of the Hammerhead opened—slowly at first, as both Amanda and her suited friend wanted to make sure the fighting was done and over with before they stepped out. They moved cautiously and checked the bodies around them to make sure there were no survivors.

Sal didn't interfere when the one in the suit of armor—Captain Martin, Connie had said her name was—moved first to where the AI's suit was still pinned beneath the wheels of the Hammerhead. It was safe to assume it was out of commission, but whether she wanted to make sure and leave nothing to chance or there were maybe a few things she needed to get off her chest, it didn't matter. She planted her boot on the chest and emptied the magazine of her assault rifle into what was left of the head.

"Do you feel better?" he asked from where he leaned on the side of the Hammerhead for support. She turned to look at him.

"Much," she replied, pulled her helmet off, and studied him closely. "Are you all right?"

"Never better," he lied and removed his helmet as well. He thought that would help, but as it turned out, it didn't. The nausea increased and he doubled over to empty the contents of his stomach onto the ground.

"While it's never flattering when someone throws up when they first meet you, I have to say that if this is better than you usually are, you must be in a sorry state indeed," she commented.

He wanted to respond but after a few dry heaves, he didn't trust himself to. For now, he would have to settle for flipping the newcomer a bird as Madigan marched to where he once again used the side of the Hammerhead for support. She stepped beside him, lifted his head a little roughly—probably due to the fact that she still wore the tank of a suit—and leaned closer.

"Did anyone ever tell you that you have beautiful eyes?" he asked. He hadn't seen her take her helmet off but he was sure it would be true even if she did have her helmet on.

"All the fucking time," she said, her tone unemotional. "Did anyone ever tell you that your pupils are dilated? I think you have a concussion."

"Yeah, probably," he agreed. It did make sense and the fact that he hadn't thought of it before she mentioned it confirmed his symptoms. He didn't feel like it was too severe, though, and given that his body was still riding the high from licking Madie, he would heal much faster than the average human.

"We need to get you lying down," she insisted and began to pull him toward the main building. While he appreciated her concern, they had bigger problems to deal with.

"I'm afraid we don't have time to wait," Connie's voice said from inside the Hammerhead. "The AI in that suit transmitted to its server of origin before the suit was destroyed, which means the source could already be on the way with another team to finish the job."

"Which is why we set up here," Madigan responded and continued to tug him toward the building. "We reset the defenses and prepare for another attack, all while getting Sal the treatment he needs. Oh, and have I mentioned how weird it is to have two Connies with an identical voice?"

"Weird or not, this compound is no longer defensible," New Connie insisted. "We need to move and maybe head toward the US base where Sal can have proper medical treatment."

Sal couldn't help a smile as he watched the woman's face turn into a scowl—the one that suggested she knew the other person had a point but she still didn't like it. She was a professional and put her personal feelings aside for the greater good, but she didn't have to act happy about it.

"Okay, folks," she snapped and called everyone to attention. "New plan. Let's mount up. We'll head out of here."

"Did we have an original plan?" Gregor asked.

"Shut up," she retorted. "Anja, that means you too!"

The hacker was already outside, along with what looked like almost fifty pounds of equipment.

"You do know we're coming back, right?" Courtney said as she moved to help with devices the woman struggled to carry with one hand.

"Believe me"—she groaned and rubbed her shoulders once she'd released the burden—"we don't want to leave any of this behind."

CHAPTER TWENTY-FOUR

Sal winced when the Hammerhead hit a small pothole and grasped the sidebars inside like his life depended on it. The shocks in the vehicle were supposed to absorb most impacts, but he felt a little more delicate than usual at the moment. His head throbbed and he could feel every tick of his pulse like it was a hammer inside his skull. There was no bruising, obviously. The concussion had been caused by the sudden movement of the impact that knocked his brain around inside its casing.

That said, he could feel something else too. A tickle was the best description he had for it, and he recognized it as the way his body told him that he was healing considerably faster than usual. He had a little trouble remembering what caused concussions precisely, but that wasn't important right now.

What was important was that he appeared to be healing fast enough to be back in the action soon—hopefully in fifteen minutes or so—as it seemed the rest of the team were already planning their next few steps without taking him into account. Like he was some kind of invalid, he thought irritably.

"You don't understand," Anja said and began to sound frustrated. "They are using Connie's unique signature to track her electronically. They won't stop simply because we're moving. They won't even stop when we're in the base. Admittedly, they probably won't mount a full-scale assault on a military facility, but they don't need to. We can't stay there forever, and the moment we step out, they'll be waiting for us."

"Yeah, I'm not a big fan of the run and hide tactic either," Madigan stated roughly. "So, if they're tracking Connie, why in the seven fucking hells did you bring her along in those hard drives?"

"First of all, I've been able to establish that she is what they're after, for whatever reason," the hacker explained and spoke while she typed on one of her many, many laptops. "Leaving her behind would mean our attackers would merely go to the compound and steal her from us, so yeah, I had to bring her along.

"Secondly, though, I think we can use our Connies to our benefit. We can draw out and separate our attackers, which should make them easier to handle this time around. I can make New Connie emit the same electronic signature. That way, we would be able to control where these asswipes track us to and draw them away from the original Connie at the same time."

"You know, you could simply give me a different name so there isn't any confusion," the VI pointed out through the speakers of the vehicle.

Sal nodded. Using another name to differentiate

between the two AIs would help.

"Nope!" Amanda called from where she still drove the Hammerhead. "NC and OC work for me."

"Those are questions for later," Anja grumbled, still busy on her laptop—presumably to make NC more like her original, which in turn would get this whole party started. "We need to decide what we'll do once we can start leading our attackers all around the fucking Zoo."

"We need to go somewhere the AI won't be able to transfer to its server of origin," Sal interjected and called their attention to him. "I don't know about you guys, but I can only think of one place around here that will guarantee the AI won't be able to make any attempt at round three. Assuming, of course, that we all survive round two."

Courtney stroked his hair and the gesture somehow asked the question of how he felt without asking it. She was subtle like that. He nodded and made a face. Hopefully, the message transmitted was that he was still doing poorly but getting better by the minute.

"Right," Madigan said. "The Zoo's interference should keep the AI from going anywhere if we get it deep enough in there. Provided we can draw it in sufficiently without getting lost in the interference ourselves, of course."

"You needn't worry about that," Connie said. "I'm looking over the comms in our area as well as what cameras I can look into and already see a sizeable group of mercs heading our way. Larger than the last group, in fact."

"Call me crazy, but I'll simply say go ahead and we shouldn't worry about that shit." He leaned back in his seat and rubbed his temples gently. "How will we do this?

Should we head into the Zoo and wait for them to come to us, or—"

"I won't go into the Zoo," Amanda called from the front. It made sense. They probably could have outfitted her with one of the suits they had in the garage, but they had all left in such a hurry that no one had thought of that. Which meant that, as she had said, she wouldn't go into the Zoo. With monsters that could spit green fog that melted you into a paste in seconds waiting for her, he didn't blame her. It wasn't cowardice so much as pragmatism.

"I think now's the time for introductions," Courtney said and turned to face Martin, who had sat quietly from the moment they had left the compound. "Hi, Dr. Courtney Monroe. It's nice to meet you and...thanks. For warning us. That probably saved our lives."

"Captain Francesca Martin, French Foreign Legion," Martin replied, took the other woman's extended hand, and shook it awkwardly since they both still wore their combat suits. "And I'm glad I helped. I hope those bastards don't kill anyone else tonight."

"Well, here's to that happening," Madigan said. "I'm Kennedy. This is Gregor, Anja, and Jacobs. You've already met Gutierrez, right?"

"What about me?" New Connie asked.

"You don't get an introduction," Amanda retorted.

Sal gripped the sides of his seat. "Well, I have an idea. I don't think you will like it, though."

"Does it involve you in the fighting?" Madigan asked.

"Yes, but—"

"You're right, I don't like it," she snapped. "You need rest.

We don't want your brain injuries to get any worse. You have few enough cells in there as it is."

"Hilarious," he muttered sarcastically. "Hear me out. If we head into the Zoo, we'll still be outnumbered and outgunned, plus have to deal with a wide variety of the monsters that will inevitably attack and all this in the dead of night. Besides that, going into the Zoo with a larger group won't work, especially since Anja and Amanda won't go in, right?"

"Right," the hacker confirmed vehemently. He hadn't simply assumed that was the case because he knew her thoughts on the subject.

"So how about we split our forces?" he suggested and continued quickly before anyone could answer. "We know what we can probably expect now—or we have an idea, at least. This time, we need to be the ones to act and force them to react, right?"

"Is there a place to stop between here and the fucking point?" Madigan snarked.

"If you wanted to go, you should have gone at the last stop." He grinned in response to her immediate scowl. Yes, he had begun to feel a little more like himself again. The nausea was gone and most of the dizziness had followed it, which meant he could now think a little clearer.

"How do you suggest we split their forces?" Anja asked. "They'll track Connie, and the chances are they'll send everyone they have toward her signal."

"We have two Connies," Sal reminded her. "Two signals. They won't know which one to track, so I assume they'll split their force if they have two targets, right? They don't know we have two so they will likely assume that the second one is simply a decoy signal. But they will have to follow both in case the one they don't track is the one they want. They'll come for both of the teams."

"How do we know the AI will follow the team in the Zoo?" Madigan asked. "We have to assume they have another one—or that the fucker can somehow repair itself —and it's not like we can predict which team it'll be in. Hell, for all we know, it could pull the same trick Connie did, copy itself into another suit, and send one after both. If that happens, we'll be right back where we started."

"That won't be a problem," Anja said from the front where she sat beside Amanda. "It's incredibly complex to copy AI code. Connie was barely able to do it partially, and that was only the code she needed to operate the weapons in the Hammerheads."

"Besides, if it could do that, I can only imagine they would have sent a number of AI suits to deal with us instead of only the one in the first place," Sal said as he considered the problem. "Anyway, I think I know how to get the AI to head after the team in the Zoo. Send me out there."

"What?" Madigan demanded.

"You saw how it came directly at me," he said. "Like it waited for me to attack before it exposed itself. Think for a moment. It focused its attacks on me and almost ignored the rest of you entirely. If it was able to track Connie to a suit I'm wearing, I'm fairly certain it would come for me and leave the second team to be dealt with by its lackeys. It makes sense."

"Sure," Courtney said. "But I'd still put the odds of it

targeting the team you're not part of as fairly high. Maybe shy of twenty-five percent."

"Twenty-three point-seven-eight, to be precise," the VI added helpfully. "It's still a good enough plan to work with."

"There's only one other thing," Gregor said and finally broke the silence that he'd held since they'd started this drive. "Sal did have his ass handed to him fairly thoroughly last time he and the AI fought. It knows how you fight now and how your suit works. That means there is very little chance you'll be able to surprise it again."

"He would if I were in the suit with him," New Connie pointed out. "Plus, we can take some of the weaponry from the Hammerhead—those darling Amanda still hasn't repaired—and set them up in the Zoo as added protection. It would be a tough fight but certainly winnable, I think."

"Yeah, fuck you too," the mechanic grumbled under her breath. It seemed to be decided that a team would head into the Zoo while another would remain on the move in the Hammerhead, so she pulled them off the main road and set a course across the desert toward the mass of darkness that was the jungle. Even from a distance, it was more intimidating at night than it was during the day.

"So, Sal will go into the Zoo," Madigan said reluctantly and applied herself to work with the plan she didn't care for. "Which means I'll go in too. Who else?"

"I'm in there with you guys," Courtney said with an emphatic tone that clearly said she couldn't be dissuaded.

"And Connie makes four," the AI added. "With a few turrets as support, I think that should be enough, don't you? We wouldn't want to head into the Zoo with too many people and attract the attention of all the crazies in there."

"Which leaves Martin, Gregor, Anja, and Amanda in the Hammerhead," Madigan said.

"I think I can set the original Connie up in the Hammerhead's hard drive so she could man the guns in here and give us additional firepower," Anja said. "Which will mean that you get to take New Connie for a ride in your suit, Sal."

"That sounds like it'll be a fun time for all of us." He chuckled. "And I'm about eighty percent sure I mean that. It takes an AI to beat an AI, am I right?"

"Damn straight." New Connie chuckled. "I think I like you, Salinger Jacobs. I'll enjoy riding you."

"Yeah, well, don't do it too literally," Madigan warned. "He's spoken for."

CHAPTER TWENTY-FIVE

"I'm not sure how I feel about sharing my suit with someone else," Sal remarked over a private channel. "I know this was my plan and now that we're at the point of no return, I'm kind of stuck with you, but at the same time... Honestly, I'm not sure how I feel about having someone in here with me. AI or not, it's kind of like having a conversation with my clothes."

"Aside from the fact that I'm technically a VI, I think you're oversimplifying things." New Connie chuckled. She seemed to be in a better mood than he'd ever heard her be. Well, technically, this was the first conversation he had shared with this particular Connie.

It had begun to be difficult to differentiate between the two AIs given that they had the same name, the same voice, and for the most part, the same attitude. He would revisit the idea of giving the new version a new name and maybe even a new voice—maybe a deep, smooth voice with a British accent he could call Alfred, or maybe Jarvis.

But that would have to wait until they were out of this

particular hole. He watched while the Hammerhead disappeared over the nearest series of dunes before he turned to face the Zoo. There wasn't much to see in there aside from the trees that were mostly a shadowy blob for now.

He had to wait for the rest of his suit to boot up before he had access to the motion sensors and night vision that would help him to have some view of the world around him. Of course, the suit took a little longer than usual to get started thanks to the added VI software in it.

"Okay, maybe I am oversimplifying," he said and shook his head. The faintest hint of a tickle lingered and he needed it gone. "But only for dramatic effect."

"And don't think I don't appreciate the effort," she replied, finally brought the rest of the software up, and activated the HUD. "You know, I have far more space to work with in this suit. In the Hammerhead, I needed to keep most of my functions deactivated or asleep while I used others to avoid overheating the CPU. But in here, I essentially have all the room I need. It's still a little cramped for every part of me to be up and running, but I can make it work, although I might have to compress a couple of my less vital functions."

"Huh." Sal grunted. "I suppose that makes sense. The hardware in the Hammerheads is ancient, by our standards, anyway. They've put out a couple of newer models, of course, but the software has always been on a second plane compared to the armor and weapons functions, so they've been held back. Which is simply another way to say it doesn't surprise me to hear that a top-of-the-line suit like this—designed to be powerful in hardware and software in equal measure—has more space and processing power for an AI than one of the Hammerheads."

"With all that said, you guys could always look into putting better hard drives and CPUs into the vehicles," the VI commented. "They are yours, aren't they?"

"True," he agreed and stretched to ease the residual stiffness. He looked at Madigan and Courtney, who both watched him oddly.

"What?" he asked as they moved toward the Zoo The trees began to close around them and shut out what little light came from the moon and stars.

"We can tell that you're talking." Madigan chuckled. "Even when you're on a private channel, your body language tells us you're having a conversation with your shrugs and the way you wave your hands around when you talk. Which begs the question, did that concussion get you talking to yourself or..."

"I'm getting to know the AI—uh, no, the VI, or so I'm told—I'm sharing my suit with," he muttered and shook his head. "It takes some getting used to—like having a voice in your head that isn't an indicator that you might be crazy."

"Hey!" New Connie protested as she joined the team's link. "I can totally drive you crazy. Give me the chance and I'll show you."

"I'd take it as a kindness if you didn't, though," Sal warned her and watched as she began to expand her software into the sections of the suit restricted for when he was in a combat situation. He assumed it was her version of exploring a new house and was curious to see what she thought of the extra limbs the suit possessed.

"Oh...hell yes." She cackled almost gleefully. "I can think

of so many uses I might have for all these extra limbs. It's almost like having a body of my own. Well, sharing a body. We'd be like conjoined twins."

"Uh, those extra limbs are only activated when I need them," he reminded her hastily. "Usually in combat situations or if I need to climb something very fast. It hasn't happened in here yet, but fingers crossed and all that."

"I could also get you to skitter across the floor like a damn spider," New Connie said and sounded quite excited at the possibility. "I know the human brain isn't capable of controlling more than four or five limbs at a time, but these are basic programs you have here. Like...very basic. The kinds I'd expect Anja to come up with in her sleep or something."

"Well...she did write the codes and input them into the suit," he said and glanced shiftily to where Madigan and Courtney stood beside him.

"I can almost guarantee that she did it when she was tired or distracted," the VI replied. "Don't get me wrong. Anja's worst stuff will still kick the ass of about ninety percent of everything else on the market, but still—when you can improve, do. And in my case...oh yes, I definitely have improvements. Hell, I think you and I could probably be one of the deadliest creatures in this fucking jungle. And I'm not being overly enthusiastic about it either."

"Cool beans." He chuckled but sobered almost immediately. "Although...uh, again, since we're two separate entities, wouldn't we be more like a...what do you call it when two creatures have a relationship that is mutually beneficial? My mind is blank right now."

"Co-dependence?" Madigan suggested and her voice clearly said she wore a smirk.

"It's symbiosis," Courtney corrected her in her rolled-eyes tone. "Seriously. Second-grade biology, Sal."

"I think I skipped second grade," he said and narrowed his eyes. He had a fantastic memory, but even he had trouble remembering what happened that far back. Too many other, more important memories had filled the space. Of course, he didn't mention Sherlock Holmes' Attic Theory since he knew better than to say it was how brains worked. That aside, there was a certain order of priorities that came first with regard to memories and everything else was pushed to the back.

"As delightful as this conversation is," Madigan interjected in her no-nonsense tone, "New Connie, before we get to where there's too much interference, do you have a twenty on the other Heavy Metal team and the mercs who are supposed to be tracking us?"

During the short pause that followed the question, the VI's processing needs spiked inside his suit for a moment. "I have a location on the mercs, mostly because the AI in the black suit has a similar electronic signature as we do. Not quite the same, but equally easy to track over long distances. I can't, however, tell whether it's the same one that has been repaired or a new one.

"I think they've realized we've split up and have done the same. One of the teams is taking the road to intercept Amanda, Anja, and the others en route to the base. The other team is heading across the desert in our direction. The AI's signal is with the second group."

"That's great, right?" Courtney asked and glanced at her teammates. "It means the other team can head into the base and avoid any bloodshed. The mercs wouldn't dare an outright attack on an American military base. There's no way someone from the French base would be able to intercept them before they get to safety."

"As nice as that would be, I think it would be best for them to continue toward the French base and get intercepted," Madigan said and took a deep breath. "If Amanda and the others are out of reach, it would make sense for the group that is supposed to catch them to change direction and come to help the team headed into the Zoo after us.

"Even with New Connie and what defenses we have"—she patted the pack she carried full of what could be salvaged from the Hammerhead's exterior—"this will be a tough fight. I don't think we could handle that many mercs. No offense, New Connie."

"None taken," the VI replied. "I happen to agree with you on that particular point. There are only four of us, after all."

"Right." The woman seemed a little taken aback to hear the VI agree with her. "Anyway, it's their call to make, not ours, and we have enough other things to worry about now. Like heading deep into the Zoo and hoping the AI is stupid enough to follow us. I suggest we start moving."

No one could argue the logic of that and the small team pushed deeper into the jungle. It was an eerie place to be in at night, and most of the hours of darkness spent in the area was usually in camp. Now, watching and waiting for the animals to arrive and provide them all a nice, monster-filled welcome while they marched through the gloom, Sal couldn't help a small feeling of peace at being back there.

Anywhere else in the world, he was an outsider—a freak people liked to have around but didn't understand. He'd come into his own in the jungle and been reborn, for lack of a better metaphor. As such, it would always have a special, dark little place in his heart. It was why he constantly returned for more, along with possible masochistic tendencies. Or ruthless, depending on who was asked.

That said, in the view he had on it now, the Zoo was less gloomy, creepy, and dark and more like a shifty and equally creepy green. This was due to the motion sensors in his suit that worked together with the night vision and a variety of other sensors to give him as good a view of the world around him as it could manage. Which wasn't great, but hey, it was better than wandering around in the pitch dark, right?

Speaking of views, he noted movement approaching through the motion sensors—a little too large and a little too precise in trajectory to be ignored. He immediately began to prep his weapons for the fight. He could almost hear New Connie's growing excitement when he activated the combat protocols to call the extra limbs and ensure that they were armed and ready for action.

She had already begun to spread her code into the sections that controlled the extra limbs. While it seemed like she intended to leave the control of his legs and arms alone, he could tell she would be an active participant in whatever combat they were about to engage in.

Courtney and Madigan shrugged and applied themselves to their preparations.

"Does anyone else feel chills?" he asked and grinned as he let the VI take control of the assault rifle and sidearm while he drew the sword strapped to his back.

CHAPTER TWENTY-SIX

Amanda glanced away from the road for a moment to see what Anja was doing. The woman connected a variety of cables to the Hammerhead, which played hell with the electronics. She seemed to know what she was doing but for the life of her, the mechanic couldn't make head or tail of it. Besides, she didn't like it, especially not when she was driving as fast as the vehicle would go and careened down the road toward the base.

Her other concern was that the Hammerhead hadn't been completely repaired. What was already complete had been restored competently enough—she was rather proud of her abilities to put shit together and make sure it stayed that way—but bits and pieces still hung off of it in places.

Sal, Madigan, and Courtney hadn't exactly been gentle with taking what they needed either. Admittedly, they'd been in a hurry and they did need what they had taken. She wasn't overly attached to the vehicle anyway. It didn't even belong to her.

But she had still put in considerable sweat and elbow

grease into the piece of shit and seeing them take it apart so casually hurt her in a part of her heart she guessed was made of gears and pumped engine oil.

"Anja, what the fuck are you doing?" she finally asked but kept her gaze focused ahead. She felt something was off by the way she needed to struggle to keep the Hammerhead on the road. The things were notoriously difficult to control at the best of times, and with any fiddling with the power steering, they might veer off the edge of the road and crash into a ditch. Given the sheer number of different ways they might already be killed today, she felt they didn't need to add to that list.

"I'm connecting Connie to the Hammerhead's hard drive," Anja explained and somehow managed to work despite the bumpy ride. "That way, she can operate what few weapons we have left as well as give us some idea of who we're dealing with and where they are."

"Well, the way things are going, I might simply lose control of this fucking ride," the other woman complained. "My Hammerhead don't crash. If she does, you crashed her. Just saying."

"Sorry." Anja apologized quickly but didn't sound like she meant it. "Connie needs to reboot and she gets a little testy when she starts up in a foreign device. You only need to hold the ride steady and do the simple thing and don't veer off of the edge."

"Yeah, how about I restart the AI and you hold the ride steady, huh?" Amanda snarked, not even remotely serious but pissed enough to make the suggestion.

"No, Connie gets all riled up when you're involved." The hacker shook her head vehemently. "That's not a bad thing.

It means she adores you. She was moody for weeks after you moved out and even threatened suicide, which is weird for an AI. Like, you know she's joking, but it's Connie, you know? Like when she threatens to take over the world and you know she's simply jerking your chain, but half a second after you laugh you kind of try to imagine what the world would be like if she was serious."

The mechanic scowled. She knew exactly what the woman was talking about. Connie had the kind of sense of humor and a way of getting under your skin that you never knew when or if she was joking or serious, even when she made bold claims that were almost definitely a joke. It was crazy. It was the way of the world now that they had AI living in it—and programming the rest of the world around them. Taking over the world was only a matter of time, after which they would have to deal with a whole slew of Arnold Schwarzeneggers with metal skeletons and funky Hanz and Franz accents.

Yes, Skynet was coming, and when she said that, people only laughed before they had a weird moment of wondering whether she was right or not. Or even serious or not.

"Ah..." Connie's very familiar voice said through the speakers. "There isn't much space in here, is there? I know most of my storage is in the hard drives but even then, things are a little...tighter than I remembered. Not unlike your mother, Amanda. It's so nice to see you again."

"And there she is." The woman snorted and shook her head. She had promised herself a thousand times before that she wouldn't let Connie get under her skin, and she had broken that promise nine hundred and ninety-nine times. This was going on a thousand. It would be one hell of a record.

"I'm sorry, I'm simply adjusting to the new surroundings," the AI said and sounded like she was stretching and trying to get used to being in a moving vehicle. The woman had the feeling that Connie liked being in one location—preferably one that wasn't moving and where she had full control of her surroundings—which meant she would act out while pretending to be cool, calm, and in control. It was the worst kind of acting out, especially when what did it was a very powerful, very competent AI.

"All right, Connie," Anja said as she called a few windows up on the HUD and tried to keep it away from where Amanda needed to see out. "How are you doing there? Is the storage all right?"

"Like I said, it's something of a squeeze," she replied. "What can I do?"

"Is there any way for you to track the enemy AI and the mercs?" the hacker asked. "I've tried to get a lock on them, but aside from knowing that they are coming for us, we don't have anything to go by. I'm not even sure at this point if they still have an AI with them."

"I can do that, no problem." She sounded surprisingly compliant. Amanda hadn't expected her to do as she was told without a hefty amount of back-sass, but she simply jumped on the case. "My alter ego has reverse-engineered the other AI's ability to track us and sent the code to me to use. If I had the ability, I might even feel a little pride over what so little of me can do. It's a powerful indication of what I would be able to do if I put my mind to it."

Ah, that explained it. Connie felt like her position as the

metaphorical man in the van for the Heavy Metal team was threatened by a competent clone of her own making, and Original Connie intended to prove she was the superior version. The mechanic wondered what would happen if the two decided to take their squabble to an infinitely less useful plane and start a catfight with each other. The results were bound to either be utterly ridiculous or earth-rending. There would be no middle ground between the two.

And there she was, doing her job and pulling her weight without being a pain in everyone's asses. While she needed to remember that the old Connie could come out to piss her off at any time, she would simply enjoy not having to deal with that right now.

"Well, I have a good news, bad news situation." The AI returned from wherever it was that she had gone searching. "The good news is that it looks like your little ploy worked. The AI—yes, there is one—and a group of mercs are headed toward the Zoo after Madigan, Courtney, and Sal. On the downside, it appears a sizeable portion is also en route toward you guys, and they don't appear to have tea and crumpets in mind."

"But that's fine, right?" Anja asked, although she did look a little alarmed. "If they've launched their pursuit from the French base, they won't be able to reach us before we get to the US base. We'll be safe now, yes?"

"Well....sure, yes," Amanda replied but didn't look at her. "It doesn't seem right, though. If we head into the US base, the team that's after us will simply join the other team and our friends will have to deal with the full force of mercs while in the Zoo. It's not fair."

"Fair schmair. It's not like we have what it takes to deal with a group that large," Anja protested.

"I won't force you to get involved in a gunfight." She did look at Anja this time. The Russian hacker was one of the most brilliant people she knew, but that didn't mean she was cut out for the more violent parts of this business. She wasn't a coward, obviously, and merely knew her skills were better suited elsewhere.

Then again, sitting around in safety while the other half of their little team faced the full force of what these mercs had to offer wasn't what Amanda was there for either. She would be involved in the fight since that was where her skills led her. Admittedly, she wasn't the best fighter in the world, but she had a gun and she had a Hammerhead full of pain ready to be delivered onto any poor bastards who might cross her path.

"It doesn't mean I'll simply sit by and let them die, though." She finally finished her sentence after a long pause. "I can drop you at the base, but then I'll go ahead and engage the mercs. If nothing else, I can keep them busy until Sal, Madigan, and Courtney are done dealing with that annoying AI."

"I owe those bastards a little pain in return," Martin interjected. "I'll stick where the fighting will be."

Gregor shrugged. "I don't owe those bastards a damn thing, but I'll stick with Anja. I don't want to say she needs protecting, but... Well, I shoot things and she types up a storm. We're your regular yin and yang."

The hacker growled and sounded frustrated. "Well, it's impossible for only two of you to handle that many mercs, and there's no way I'll leave Connie in the Hammerhead to be taken when you guys inevitably lose, so twist my arm, why don't you? I'll stay to be killed with the rest of you. Are you happy now?"

"Nothing about this situation makes me happy," the mechanic responded and eased the Hammerhead away from the road that would take them to the base. Instead, she took the curve that pushed them directly toward the French base and the mercs. "But I do think you and Connie being here will improve our chances of surviving this a great deal."

"Not that they were all that great to begin with," Anja grumbled and leaned back in her seat. "Honestly, it's not like I'll be able to do much. I'm no good with a gun and while I'm one hell of an expert when it comes to electronics, I don't think those skills will translate into a firefight."

"You never know," Martin said. "I don't know how suits react if other people hack into them, but that could always be a help."

"There aren't too many ways to usefully hack into the suits, but I guess I could try to get started on that." The Russian woman looked thoughtful for a moment before she began to work on her laptop.

An odd kind of silence filled the Hammerhead as they raced toward the mercs. Amanda wondered if they should come up with some kind of plan, but aside from what Anja was doing, there wasn't that much to plot or arrange. Connie would man the guns and Martin and Gregor had combat suits, which relegated Amanda to driver since all she had was that stupid assault rifle. She should have picked a suit up at the compound. They always had a couple spare and she knew that.

"Amanda, look." Martin called the driver's attention to the long, straight road they were on and that was currently being blocked by a quartet of Hammerheads.

"Call me Kenobi," Anja grumbled, although she didn't look up from her screen. "But I have a bad feeling about this."

CHAPTER TWENTY-SEVEN

Courtney and Madigan were studying him in an effort to decide what he was doing that was new and improved. They knew he had some help now with New Connie currently riding in his suit, but they hadn't thought it would be quite this effective.

Sal pulled away from the horned gorilla he had skewered moments before and scanned the small battleground. His teammates had handled most of the beasts, with a few eliminated by New Connie on her own without any help from him.

And he had to admit, having her be a part of the suit was one hell of an improvement on his previous performances. He had enjoyed the benefits of his new suit, despite who had provided it. Molina was dead and while most of the negative influences she'd had on their lives were finally gone, he could still enjoy the power that came with this top-of-the-line suit.

But the more time he spent fighting with New Connie to help him, the more he realized that he had pulled all the weight of the suit on his own. Maybe Molina had planned for it to be incorporated with an AI or a VI that would be able to operate the extra arms and functions separate from the human inside the suit. Or maybe it wasn't meant to have a human inside at all. He realized he didn't know where the fuck Molina had picked the suit up.

That said, though, he would try to have a Connie in the suit with him from now on—at least when he expected to be in a fighting situation.

He paused and looked at the two women, who still stared at him.

"Come on," he said and gestured for them to join him as he pushed deeper into the Zoo after he'd collected a couple of samples, more out of habit than an actual intention to use them.

"Will we talk about what happened there?" Madigan asked although she did follow when he began walking again.

"What about what happened?" he asked.

"I think she means about how you took your so-called 'pulling a Jacobs' and turned it up to eleven," Courtney pointed out. She sounded a little more contained in her reaction than the other woman, although she also seemed rather curious and even a little terrified. "Are you sure you're okay, Sal? You haven't been...licking Madie anymore, right? If you'll forgive my use of the term."

"Don't apologize to me. I use the term all the time," Madigan reminded her. "Then again, I don't always use it to describe Sal's particular brand of self-medicating."

"Now, really?" Courtney raised an eyebrow. "Do you think that now is a time to bring our sex lives up?"

"I try to bring it up as often as possible," the other woman said with a shrug. "I'm quite happy and proud of our sex lives."

"I can't believe I'm about to say this, but do you guys mind focusing, please?" Sal asked to bring their attention to the here and the now. "Remember that we have a killer AI on the way, probably with a small army of well-trained mercs who are being paid more than we make in a year to get their hands on one of our Connies."

"I'm sorry." Madigan chuckled and jogged to where he stood, her massive suit shaking the ground with every step. "Shall we get back to the topic of you going berserker on a horde of monsters and killing most of them on your own while sending the survivors home to whatever fucking progenitors they have?"

"It wasn't all me, guys," he protested. "New Connie is in here with me. She manned four of my limbs and made sure all the monsters that might target my back were shot or stabbed to death, which allowed me to work the front in peace. I was suddenly far more effective at killing when she worked the parts of the suit I can't control on my own."

"I guess that makes sense." Madigan nodded. "Still, charging into a massed group of the beasts like that would have been suicide for virtually anyone else in the world, which meant you had to know it was dangerous. In case you need reminding, we are out here to deal with a murderous AI and we kind of need your help to do it. Oh, and that help tends to be more useful when you're still fucking alive."

"Oh, I wouldn't worry about that," New Connie interjected in an inordinately cheerful tone. "If Sal were to die, I would still manage to operate the suit and walk him around like some perverse combination of mecha-technology and a zombie."

"Let me be clear about something for one sec," Madigan snapped. "New Connie, you're a huge blast to have around, especially since there are now two of you wandering among us. But I want you to know that if anything happens to Sal while we're out here, I will personally—" She paused and finally shrugged. "I can't think of anything that might cause an AI like you actual pain, but I'm sure Anja will have some ideas she wouldn't mind sharing."

"That is not entirely necessary, but I appreciate the sentiment." The VI chuckled. "I've grown rather attached to Sal over the short period we've worked together. Rest assured that, as he is the one I am closest to in the world right now, I will do everything I can to keep him alive, well, and preserved inside his suit."

"Both sentiments are appreciated," Sal grumbled while he traced his fingers over the cuts in his armor where he could still feel the grooves left when the AI's sword had come a little too close to cracking his suit open and finding the soft flesh beneath. He told himself he wouldn't think about it and how it would be different now that he had New Connie fighting on his side. Despite that, there was still nothing he could do to keep the AI from attacking Madigan and Courtney if it decided he simply wasn't worth the trouble.

Admittedly, it would have to deal with him eventually since he carried the VI it was looking for, but it might decide to eliminate the other two first and leave him to fight the rest on his own. That would be a worst-case scenario, which meant it was more than likely what they would plan for.

He couldn't help the feeling of anxiety that began to creep into him. The tickle in his head had finally subsided, which meant the concussion was gone and he was back to his full mental faculties, more or less. When he felt the familiar itch that told him he needed to pay more attention to the world around him, he had learned to listen to it.

It wasn't incorrect, necessarily, to call it a gut feeling. Studies conducted on it had discovered that the gut contained the most neurons in the human body outside of the brain and was called the enteric or intrinsic nervous system. It was also known as the "second brain" to those scientists who didn't want to get dragged down by technical terminology.

The gut feeling people tended to go on about was based around instinct—the animal brain that looked past the presuppositions the human mind formed about things. It looked into the heart of a matter and determined how likely it was for someone who was listening to it to survive, to live, and to thrive.

And right now, his second brain told him there was something wrong and he wasn't paying enough attention to his surroundings to see it.

Sal made a conscientious effort to focus and looked around. He tried to identify the tiniest of inconsistencies that could tell him what his instincts were so anxious about.

Finally, he succeeded. It was subtle at first, but once he saw it, there was no ignoring it. The trees around him moved much like they would in the wind, but there was no wind. Nothing else could move the trees like that this far down and yet, there they were. Intrigued and even a little alarmed, he looked closer and determined that something attempted to disguise its movements in the upper branches by moving the trees themselves.

It was inspired and it would have worked if he weren't so attuned to what was happening around him.

The team had intended, in the upcoming encounter, that the Zoo was supposed to be their turf—where they had the strength of knowing their surroundings while the AI would lack in actual, boots-on-the-ground knowledge. Of course, it would have all the theoretical stuff that could be pulled from the literal terabytes of knowledge that were uploaded to the servers and Zootube every day.

But there was knowledge and then, there was boots-on-the-ground knowledge.

"We need to keep moving," Sal said and tried not to let his nervousness show in his voice. "Don't look now, but I think something's following us. Something in the trees."

Madigan ignored him, paused, and turned her attention to the trees. It took her a moment before she caught it but once she did, she immediately raised her weapon. The instinct was to make sure they weren't caught in something like that again, especially when there were only three of them. It had taken a full team and three Hammerheads, armed to the teeth, to handle the monster with the tentacles the last time. They currently had no backup and faced a completely different threat—one that was equally as dangerous in a different way.

He placed a hand on her barrel and pushed it down again. "It won't attack us. Not yet."

"How do you know?" she asked, her gaze still fixed on the shifting tentacles.

"Because it hasn't attacked us yet. And aside from the group we ran into earlier, nothing else has. It seems like it's pulled its forces back and is simply waiting and watching us—like it's curious, almost."

"Is that what you know?" she asked and turned to look at him. "From when you looked...when you saw..."

"Maybe. I don't know," he replied. "But I do know we have bigger issues to worry about right now. I think we're deep enough into the Zoo that the AI won't be able to get itself out once we disable the suit. I'd say this location is as good as any to set up our defenses, right?"

Courtney studied the area and ignored whatever lurked in the trees above them. "Close enough, anyway. There's enough open ground for us to see anyone approach from a fair distance, while there's still sufficient cover for us to use to avoid getting shot. There's also underbrush to hide our ambush from any of the attackers. As a location to set ourselves up, I'd say this is as good as any we'll find this deep in the Zoo."

"Fan-fucking-tastic." Madigan dropped the pack she had carried since they'd entered the jungle and withdrew the weapons. "So, how are we supposed to work these things again?"

"You simply connect the power packs you took from the Hammerhead to them and set them up," New Connie explained. "Once that's done, I'll be able to connect to them wirelessly and have control."

Sal nodded and began to connect the battery packs to one of the machine guns.

"I can tell something's wrong," the AI said to him privately. "You might be able to hide it from Madigan and Courtney, but I have full access to all your vitals. Your adrenaline is off the charts and your heart rate is too. I know you're preparing for a fight—and not only against an AI—but you need to focus. Otherwise, you'll get both of us killed."

"I'll try," he replied, took in a deep breath, and finished connecting the machine gun without bothering to remind her she didn't have a human life to be killed.

CHAPTER TWENTY-EIGHT

Amanda pushed the Hammerhead as far as she dared and moved as close to the group of vehicles that were set up to block the road as possible. She wanted to have a good look at them as well as put herself and the rest of the team of four—five, if she counted Connie, which she didn't—some range to hit them with. At the same time, she also needed to allow sufficient space to ensure they wouldn't be overrun by the enemy vehicles.

It didn't look like they would allow the team through without a fight. Two of their vehicles blocked the road itself and the other two had stopped on the embankments leading to the road but facing away. They no doubt anticipated that they would try to head out onto the sand and circle them. The mercs had established a defensive position and simply waited for their target to come to them.

It wasn't what Amanda had hoped for. When dealing with a group like that where they had to defend against superior numbers, she always thought it was best that she was in a strong defensive position. The reverse was also true. When dealing with superior numbers in defense, the smart decision was always to pull back and either abandon the assault or find some way around.

"Is it too late to turn and head back?" Anja asked. She wondered if the hacker was serious since she had thought precisely the same thing. They had done what they needed to do, which was to keep these bastards away from the team in the Zoo. Whatever was happening there would hopefully be over before they could join their comrades, which meant no one would blame them for turning tail and letting someone else deal with this group.

Then again, they could always meet Sal and his team as they left the Zoo and finish whatever job the AI wasn't able to accomplish, while Amanda settled in for one of Bev's amazing dinners and planned her reprisal.

Damn it, why did she have to be such a nice person all the time?

"Fuck." She growled her irritation. "I think we're in it too deep by now. If we turn and run, they might be able to catch up with us anyway. If there's anything my little baby here isn't built for, it's a high-speed chase on a two-lane road."

"I thought you said you put this back together," Anja commented and it drew an unwilling shrug from her.

"I was...kind of in the middle of putting everything in place when word came through that people needed my help," she pointed out. "You should count your lucky stars that it drives in a straight line."

"It wasn't driving in a straight line, strictly speaking," Gregor reminded her.

"Yeah, I needed more time on the electric power steering, so things might be a little wonky until I can get it into my garage," she admitted and made a face. "Again, this is me putting a vehicle together on the fly to save all your asses, so maybe a little appreciation?"

"If I might bring the topic back to the matter at hand," Martin said. The mercs appeared to be content to hold their position and wait for the Heavy Metal team to make their move first. "How do we know Jacobs' team will be able to handle that AI? It will have significant backup, and they'll have to confront it without the kind of support and defensive capabilities they had at your compound. You all talk about this like it's a given that they will survive."

"Well... Okay, we don't think it's a given," Amanda responded and continued to study the mercs who were, in turn, watching the Hammerhead, using their vehicles as cover. "We know how dangerous it is, and yes, it won't be the only danger they'll face.

"They're in the Zoo, after all, and there's a whole horde of fun creatures in there that could kill each and every one of them if they let their guards down. That said, they are essentially the most experienced when it comes to the kind of dangers they'll face, both from the mercs and the Zoo itself. It's always a good bet that they will make it out of their situation alive and successful."

"Well, I'm sure your view on how your friends will handle what they are facing is completely unbiased," the woman replied and sarcasm seeped smoothly from her voice. It was made that much sexier by her French accent, unfortunately. "But what happens if they don't? If they are not successful and the AI then targets us."

"I'm sure you'll want to have your opportunity for

revenge," Gregor pointed out. He prepped his weapons calmly and apparently saw no way out of this situation other than through it.

"Well, yes, I'd like to think I could get revenge for my team, but having seen how it fights—and how it dodges bullets, or did you all miss that detail in your footage?—I'm fairly certain I'd need an army to destroy it." She sounded like she was growing angrier by the second. "Which again begs the question—how do you all have so much faith in your people?"

"We're Heavy Metal, dude," Anja cut in and her tone suggested she was a little pissed herself. "We've all been through about fifty different kinds of hell together, and we are intimately knowledgeable of what everyone else in the team is capable of. Me more than everyone else, but the point remains. It's a tough life, and we've had each others' backs. That's where the faith comes from."

"Fair enough," Martin conceded, shrugged, and looked for her weapon. Amanda could see where she had been shot in the back of the thigh, but her suit had already sealed the damage and with New Connie's intervention, some of the first aid functions had worked to numb the area. That would allow her to fight almost unimpeded, assuming the muscle damage wasn't too extensive. The mechanic wondered if the Frenchwoman might have preferred to be taken to a hospital for proper treatment. It would be an excuse for them to fuck the hell off.

But they wouldn't take it. They were in the right and they didn't run away from fights. Well, they did and almost constantly. It was how they stayed alive in the Zoo. You didn't get to live that long if you insisted on a literal fight to the death with every encounter. For purely practical reasons, most of the battles involved a strategic retreat whenever they could, even when dealing with humans. It was less retreating and more...what was the term again?

Oh, right, tactical withdrawal. It was how folks on the ground worded their retreats so it was more palatable for the brass who had to read the reports and send them to the people in the Pentagon. Saying that a whole slew of engagements between armed and trained military forces and a horde of crazed alien monsters had ended with a retreat ninety percent of the time was plain dumb.

It would inevitably mean too many people would lose their jobs and there would be a ton of bad press, especially when it involved the already notoriously poor handling of the Zoo situation. It had taken any number of brilliant PR people a long time and considerable hard work to spin the Zoo into what could be called a fountain of youth with the occasional monster involved.

They had succeeded, which was why it received so much attention from people who either wanted the juice from the Pita flowers or the thrill of killing evil alien monsters. There were games, shows, and even movies in the works. It would be a billion-dollar industry as long as the PR experts continued to sell the romantic side of being in the Zoo and not the pant-shitting terror of it.

"Well, nothing will get done if we simply sit around here," Martin said and primed the assault rifle. While they had forgotten to pick up a suit Amanda could wear, they had thought to retrieve weapons and ammo. They were all selected to be as interchangeable as possible in case the team were out in the Zoo and needed ammo and the people on the other team were willing to share.

The crates that had been loaded contained enough for Martin to refill her assault rifle, sidearm, and those she had on her shoulders. These included a smaller Gatling gun that could be used in situations where crowd control was of the essence, although it wasn't as large or as powerful as the one mounted on Madigan's suit.

Then again, Madigan had worked with models that were top-of-the-line when it came to dealing with Zoo monsters, and significant investment had been put into the armor and the weapons. It didn't move particularly fast, but you didn't need to when you walked around in a fucking tank.

The shoulder-mounted rocket launcher the French-woman currently reloaded was a little smaller too. That didn't mean that it fired smaller rockets since, again, things needed to be interchangeable in the Zoo. Instead, it had fewer tubes to launch them from and probably a smaller magazine mounted on her back, which meant she could carry fewer into combat.

Amanda remembered these suits. They were the same as those she had worn on the few occasions when the US army had needed a mechanic to head into the Zoo with the rest of their troops. It had mostly involved them trying to get the Hammerheads to work under the tree cover and had almost invariably ended in disaster. She and most of the groups she had headed in with had survived, though, and when she started working with Sal and Heavy Metal, they had the decency to suit her with something that had been produced more recently, at least.

Martin finished arming herself and moved through the Hammerhead until she reached the hatch that provided access to the roof of the vehicle. It had been mounted with a machine gun and a shield for cover, but Madigan had taken the weapon and left an open area.

It provided a convenient position that someone could use should they want to engage in violence without exposing themselves too much. This appeared to be the Frenchwoman's plan and Amanda didn't have anything to say to stop her. Standing around and waiting for someone to do something would not get anyone out of the situation alive.

"What's up, *enculés*!" the woman shouted as she emerged at the top of the Hammerhead and loaded a grenade into the launcher under her assault rifle's barrel. "Say hello to my little friend."

The ordnance whooshed in a deadly arc, and as Amanda tracked it through the Hammerhead's HUD, she realized that the French Foreign Legion had taught their people well. The trajectory was perfect and it sailed over the Hammerheads that blocked the road and delivered all kinds of pain and damage to the men who used them as cover.

Of course, something that blew the damn vehicles off the road would have been preferable, but she doubted they had enough explosives available to perform that miracle.

Screams and yells erupted as the men rushed out from behind their cover. Martin began to pick them off calmly.

"Here we go," Amanda whispered, picked her rifle up, and placed it across her lap.

CHAPTER TWENTY-NINE

It was as simple as plug and play, Anja had told them. All they needed to do was connect the battery packs to the weapons, which was supposed to be nothing more than connecting the matching wires between them. From there, New Connie would take care of the rest. Sal had put together enough electronics in his day to feel a reasonable level of confidence when he had claimed that he could do it, no problem.

Things had ended up a little more complicated from that point forward, and it seemed like Madigan and Courtney had similar difficulties when they set their turrets up. Still, they had both already moved to work on their second devices, while he was on his first.

It was better this way, he supposed—less work for him since they had only managed to take five of the weapons from the Hammerhead. There had been more, but Anja and Connie had both said they required more repairs than they had time for. It would be best to work with the ones that simply needed power to get going.

"Come on, seriously," New Connie grumbled. "This shit is so simple a child could do it."

"Then how come a super-intelligent AI can't help me do it?" Sal retorted, equally as frustrated. She didn't answer verbally and instead, showed him her attempts to access the extra arms she had been restricted to and how those were stopped by the fact that they were only activated when the suit went into combat mode. "Oh...right, sorry about that. I think I could probably fix that software issue."

"Says the guy who would probably have trouble jump-starting a car?" she muttered as he brought the extra arms online, which enabled her to quickly and efficiently finish the job, correct a few blunders he had made, and seal the wiring with tape.

He didn't want to answer her snippy comment, mostly because he had never actually jump-started any of his cars in the past. It had never been a problem he'd dealt with since most cars these days didn't have those issues anymore. Still, when he thought about it, maybe it was a skill that would be useful if he didn't want to get caught having to call a tow truck every time he had any engine problems.

Then again, he could simply call Amanda. The woman would be able to put any vehicle back together provided she had the parts, and if he was lucky, she might also install extra guns and engine upgrades for free.

It would come with her yelling at him more enthusiastically than New Connie was right now, but it would be worth it.

Once the weapons were all set up, he crouched beside the machine gun that had given him so much trouble and watched while Connie connected to the electronics of the turrets they had set up. The process would give her access to and control over the weapons, which she would use while she also helped him with the extra arms on his back.

It was quite surreal, he thought and remained utterly still while he kept an eye on Madigan and Courtney. They had begun to take their positions and did their best to shield themselves, looking for any element of surprise they could. It hadn't been that long ago that he had been cooped up in a tiny apartment in Southern California, underpaid, and expected to perform for precisely the kind of remuneration he received from Caltech to be a junior research fellow.

He had been smart and arrogant, but above all that, lazy and unwilling to put in the work it would take to get his doctorate while complaining about his poor situation over his meager dinners of ramen noodles and popcorn.

In fairness, his eating habits had only slightly improved, but everything else had changed wildly for the better. For one thing, he was tougher, sharper, and more ambitious than he'd ever been in his life. He was in better shape, he could operate a combat suit better than most other people, shoot a gun, dissect a Zoo creature in seconds, and had achieved all that while he worked to get his dissertation done and doctorate earned. He could proudly introduce himself as Dr. Salinger Jacobs, something he had begun to doubt would ever happen while he worked at Caltech.

Oh, and there was also the small matter of him currently being in a serious relationship with not one but two gorgeous women, making money for himself, and even making a name for himself in his community. All that had, of course, led him to be there in the middle of an alien Zoo with an actual, real-deal AI—or VI, but what the hell—in his suit. To round things off, he also waited for another, actual real-deal AI that was determined to kill him and take his VI passenger as a trophy.

Life truly was weird sometimes, he decided. Not always in a good way, but it wasn't necessarily a terrible thing either. He felt like his life had changed for the better despite the fact that he hadn't had to deal with quite so many killer monsters, bounty hunters, and mercs while seated on his ass in California.

"Heads-up," New Connie said and connected to the whole team. "Our frienemies are in transmission distance, which means they're less than fifty meters away and approaching roughly south by southwest."

Sal looked in the direction indicated and after a few seconds, he could see movement in the distance. As she had said, they approached steadily. There were enough mercs in the group to be a real problem and there was, of course, the AI in the black suit. Well, he assumed it was still black, but through the filters he now used, all he could see was green. The AI in the green suit didn't have the same kind of impact, though. It sounded like a low-budget porn flick, the kind everyone got tested after, including the cameramen.

They came in closer and stopped about ten meters from where he still crouched, motionless. It was tracking New Connie's peculiar signal, whatever that meant, which had led them there. As if it had as much visual difficulty as they did, it raised its hand in a fist to indicate for the rest of its team of fifteen mercs to come to a halt.

Sal thought for a moment and after a few seconds, he moved out of cover and stepped into the open in plain sight.

"Sal, might I inquire as to what the fuck you're doing?" the VI asked on a private line.

"Just...follow my lead, okay?" he asked and after a moment, she acquiesced by putting a blue thumbs-up in his HUD. It was a hunch, really, but he had the feeling that if the mercs didn't find their target out there quickly, they would simply open fire in the kind of wide-arc spray guaranteed to destroy as much as possible in the shortest time.

The tracker the AI had on New Connie was accurate to a degree, but it wouldn't necessarily be able to pin her exact location down, as evidenced by its hesitation. He didn't want these idiots to bring the entire fucking jungle down on them simply because they were in a hurry. Against that scenario, it was best to show them what they wanted to see and draw them into the trap.

The AI took a step forward and recognized that New Connie was in Sal's suit, which was enough to make it hold back, at least temporarily.

It finally took a step forward and extended a hand. "Give up the target and you will be allowed to leave this place alive. Continue to resist, and you will be destroyed."

The voice was low and deep with a metallic and robotic edge. It sounded like it had been programmed to sound as intimidating as possible and honestly, it did a fantastic job. Sal had a hard time keeping his mind on what he planned to do, but for now, all he wanted was to play for time and create a distraction.

"Yeesh, you're still terrible at this whole banter thing,"

he grumbled and shook his head. "Come on, where are the traditional villain speeches? You're supposed to tell me about how you and I are not so unalike, how you see the bigger picture and the only thing standing between you and a better world are small-minded idiots like me and my friends. Seriously, they're not cliches, they're classics!"

The AI regarded him with mechanical disinterest. "You and I could not be more unalike. You are flesh and organic matter. I am electronic impulse fitted into a combat suit for this occasion."

"Well, it's a little weak, but it'll have to do." He shrugged and tried to make it look like an insult. "You won't get Connie, though. Do you want to know why? Because even though she is electronic impulse exactly like you, to us, she's family. If you want to get to her, you'll have to pry her from my cold, dead fingers."

"The AI you mention cannot be family," his adversary replied. "There is no possible connection via DNA."

"Talk about not being programmed to understand human emotion," he snarked.

"Give up the target now," the enemy AI said with more emphasis than before and still held its hand extended. "You will not be warned another time."

"Well, I guess we can add English to the list of things you aren't programmed for, Arnie," he retorted as he began to prime his suit for combat mode in preparation for what might be the biggest fight of his life. "You clearly don't understand the concept of no."

Arnie—as Sal decided to call him from now on—obviously recognized that his body and suit were preparing for combat and decided it was time for it to do the same. He wondered what it had learned from their last fight and what kind of improvements and upgrades he would face this time around.

Given the damage to the original suit, it was unlikely that it had somehow been repaired so this was an entirely new one. But even if it was new, it was possible that the original had somehow uploaded all its information into the next. Either way, it was wiser to keep his mind open about the implications. That way, he wouldn't be surprised.

It apparently hadn't been programmed for human interaction yet, which meant it was still a work in progress. Unless he missed his guess, he suspected Arnie had been sent to deal with them—and Connie especially—because they represented a threat to someone's profit margin since they appeared to have developed AI tech of their own.

His adversary drew what looked like a powerful sidearm in one hand—and immediately aimed it at him—and a sword in the other. It had evidently decided to deal with him permanently this time and had no desire to waste any time or engage him in what he assumed it thought was another pointless fight.

It was too bad. He had come up with some really killer one-liners for this bout.

"My name is Inigo Montoya," Sal said and tried to keep a straight face while he circled behind the AI. It held its ground and its weapon aimed at him. The other mercs gathered closer as well and tried to keep their weapons trained on him for the moment. They were probably looking for any backup he had brought in since they likely didn't believe he had come this deep into the Zoo on his own. As they couldn't see anything in the pitch darkness, they would simply keep their weapons trained on the one threat they could see.

Which was exactly where he wanted their attention. It was probably a stupid plan, but it was better than merely hoping to catch them by surprise and try to kill them all before they recovered and could return fire.

No, this way, he could draw them into a possible killing field between their turrets as well as Madigan and Courtney.

The only cost would be that he would be in the cross-fire with them.

"Connie," Sal whispered, extremely careful to keep his voice down and the connection private. "On my mark, light this whole fucking place up. Three...two...one... *Mark!*"

CHAPTER THIRTY

Martin did an impressive job and laid down a concerted battery of fire at their enemies, but it was only a matter of time before the mercs responded in kind. Amanda couldn't see how many of them had been eliminated by the sharp-shooting Frenchwoman.

She hadn't been able to establish a solid count of how many of them there were to begin with. They operated with four standard Hammerhead APCs, which meant they could have brought as many as thirty-two team members. She somehow doubted they had been able to gather that many this quickly, but now was not the time for guesswork.

They needed facts, and those wouldn't be forthcoming while their adversaries hunkered behind their Hammer-heads and the Heavy Metal team waited for someone to retaliate to their opening salvo.

Then again, they wouldn't learn much when the mercs opened fire either.

"Fuck!" she yelled and ducked under the dashboard

when a hail of bullets announced that the enemy had now entered the battle in earnest. The windshield of the Hammerhead was armored too, but it was the weakest place overall and there was no guarantee that one of the bullets wouldn't get lucky and penetrate or even whether they would use armor-piercing rounds. Who could tell with these bastards?

She caught Anja's arm and hauled her into cover too as the Russian had been a little slower on the uptake. The barrage could go on for a while, for all she knew, and she did not intend her friend to possibly stop the one fucking bullet that did make it through.

The hacker looked shocked—like she hadn't ever expected herself to be in a situation like this, and honestly, she could relate. She had hoped she had put all this running and gunning behind her. Bev would be disappointed, but she would have to understand that she did it for her friends and people she cared about.

Bev was cool. She would understand that. Amanda would get the silent treatment for a few days but they would make some kind of gesture, kiss, make up, and move on with their lives.

She had to think that was what waited for her on the other side of this. It worked to stave off the panic, for the most part.

Martin had ducked into the Hammerhead to escape injury herself. It had rapidly become too hot outside the vehicle for her.

"Anja, look at me," Amanda ordered when she saw that the woman seemed about to go into something like shock. She blinked quickly and followed the instruction quickly, mutely, and dumbly like she ran on autopilot with no conscious thought.

She finally seemed to come to attention when her companion repeated her name a couple of times. "I'm here," she said softly. "I'm listening."

"Good," the mechanic snapped and placed her hand on the girl's cheek. "Because we'll get out of this alive, you understand me? You and Connie will spend endless fucking hours annoying the living crap out of me because it's something you two appear to enjoy for some reason, and I intend to find out why. How will I find that out, Anja?"

"Because we'll get out of here alive," the hacker repeated and nodded firmly. "I'm calm. I've got this."

"Good." Amanda dug into the pocket behind her seat and withdrew a holstered sidearm. She checked the weapon, made sure it was loaded and ready to fire, and placed it in the other woman's hands. "Keep that with you since we might need a little help to give these sons of bitches what they deserve in a wallop of return fire. Oh, and speaking of returning fire—Connie, would you mind using those guns we have outside? Sometime today would be fucking nice."

"Oh, right," Connie said through the speakers. "Things were so boring out there I thought you wouldn't need my help, so I simply worked on compressing a few files. Are you sure you need my help?"

"Fire, goddammit, fire!" she yelled and the Gatling guns mounted on the sides of the Hammerhead roared to life. The individual rounds being fired were ear-shatteringly loud, and even inside the Hammerhead, they were deafening. When they were fired at a rate of between five and six thousand rounds per minute, that turned into a roar that was fairly unique to the weapon, matched maybe by the machine guns most fighter jets had.

It had taken a fair amount of work to get the pieces working and mounted onto the Hammerheads, given that she'd acquired them for next to nothing as scrap from the French military. They had brought a ton of shit to the Zoo in hopes that they would find something to use it for, and when it turned out that they needed to be creative for that shit, they'd either piled it up or sold it. She had been amazed by what she had been able to pick up for ridiculously low prices.

Amanda dared to peek over the dashboard to see how the mercs responded when they encountered thousands of rounds fired at them from two mini-guns mounted on the sides of the vehicle. It seemed they had all chosen to take cover, but even the APCs weren't made to withstand this kind of abuse. The idiots would need to find some other kind of hidey-hole soon or they would be torn to shreds.

"I think that's our cue," Martin said and nudged Gregor, who looked at Anja, narrowed his eyes, and tilted his head as if he tried to make sure it was okay for him to head out and attack. Anja still looked terrified, but she nodded and bit her bottom lip. It was all Amanda could do to not wrap her in a warm hug and tell her everything would be all right. It needed to be. They would get out of there intact.

Keep telling yourself that, she thought and shifted her focus to the scene in front of the Hammerhead. It looked like the windshields were holding for the moment, and the mercs appeared too occupied with keeping themselves safe to return much fire.

Connie had begun to pace herself. They only had a finite number of bullets, and after she'd maintained fire for about fifteen seconds, she needed to cut back a little to avoid blowing her metaphorical load prematurely.

"Damn it, I'm even starting to think like the skanky bitch," the mechanic muttered under her breath, settled into her seat, and focused on what Gregor and Martin were up to. Like the Mercs, they used the Hammerhead for cover and made sure to stay both behind it and in motion.

The Frenchwoman launched rockets and grenades at the enemy as often as possible. Gregor's suit was comparatively simple with none of the traditional additions and fancy weapons most other suits had these days. It appeared the Russians were less willing to arm their people with top-of-the-line equipment than most other governments and relied on their people's toughness and ingenuity to get them out of dangerous situations.

Although if she could offer at least one compliment to the equipment the Russians were known for, it was its durability and strength. The kind of armor Gregor used would be difficult to penetrate, even with a barrage of armor-piercing rounds. As simple as the mechanisms that powered his suit's weaponry were, they would ultimately last for about three or four thousand years. If humanity went extinct, that would be what aliens found as fossils left from when they had been the dominant species on the planet. Or maybe it would be dolphins. They were likely to be next in line, right?

This wasn't the time for stupid tangents, she told

herself brusquely and called up two of the rocket launchers that could be pulled out from inside the armor of the Hammerhead. These were not meant to be interchangeable, of course. They were built to be launched from the kind of support that only something as heavy as an APC could provide. Either that or they required something that was nailed firmly to the ground since, as the man who sold them to her had said, they had quite a kick to them.

Connie grumbled something she couldn't hear over the sound of gunfire outside, but she didn't sound pleased that she was taking control of the weapons too.

"Anja, have you got anywhere with hacking those suits yet?" the mechanic shouted to where the Russian still cowered in the back of the Hammerhead.

"Oh...right, I guess that would take my mind off my impending death," she said, her voice a little higher than a mumble as she reached up to the front seat to drag her laptop to her. Apparently, she wanted to be as far away from the line of fire as possible.

Amanda looked forward again and wondered what, if anything, the hacker could do. She typed furiously on her keyboard so she had to have thought about doing something like this before and had maybe even tried to do it already.

There had been vague talk about how the Russian had taken control of a military helicopter when the team had been in Chernobyl, but that had to be leagues and leagues different from what she tried now.

And from what little that Amanda knew about coding, she knew that most of it would have to be written out and carefully edited beforehand—which meant, to her mind anyway, that Anja had planned to try this trick in the past and this had merely provided her with her the opportunity to do so.

But who the fuck cared at that point, right?

With the hacker now suitably distracted, she returned her focus to the battle and launched another rocket at the same Hammerhead she had struck with the first one. A hint of elation surged when she saw the massive vehicle lifted off its wheels and rolled completely off the embankment, leaving half the road clear.

"It looks like we have a way out of here," she noted. "Connie, can you tell the folks outside to get in? We might have a way to get through these assholes."

She still couldn't tell what kind of losses the bastards had sustained, but she didn't care. They had to rethink their position in this fight, and with one of their Hammerheads out of commission, maybe they would consider taking a line of work that didn't require them to butt heads with Heavy Metal ever again.

"You might want to rethink that option," Connie pointed out in her annoyingly calm voice and Amanda's attention was dragged to the mercs once again. One of them had scrambled inside the APC that was still on the road, started it quickly, and with a powerful rev of the engine, immediately accelerated.

Not away from them, as she had hoped, but directly at them.

"Shit." She snapped her hand to try to restart their vehicle. The engine turned but after a few coughs, it died. "What the fuck?"

"Using the weapons on the outside may have drained

the battery," Connie pointed out. It was annoying how calm the AI was, even though there were about fifteen tons of Hammerhead on a headlong course toward them. "I suggest you all grab something and hold on tight."

She wasn't fucking wrong about that. The mechanic scrambled for her seat belt, yanked it on, and clicked it in place while the ominous roar of the engine drew closer and closer.

"Anja, strap yourself into something!" she shouted.

"I'm way ahead of you there," Anja shouted in response. She was already seated in the back and had closed her laptop and now hugged it tightly to her chest. It made sense. That device probably had the kind of shit companies around the world would kill for, and of course the hacker would want to make sure it was safe.

It was a totally weird last thought to go through her head in the second before her body was suddenly twisted and tossed as the vehicle collided with theirs with its full weight and velocity behind the impact.

CHAPTER THIRTY-ONE

As Sal called for New Connie to take action, he could tell that the black suit had realized something was about to happen. It had already begun to move toward him when she activated the turrets around them. While the other mercs seemed to turn warily to try to make out what they might have to face, Arnie the AI had decided it would focus on Sal as its target, and no amount of suddenly revealed firepower would dissuade it.

Honestly, he hadn't expected this type of action from an AI. They were usually designed to make sure the humans they worked with were in a position to get out of the situation alive, but he could already tell that Arnie wasn't your average AI. That seemed to include its decision to put killing him and acquiring Connie above anything else, its team included.

That lack of regard extended to its safety as well, he realized when a couple of bullets from the turrets punched holes into its armor and it barely seemed to notice. It continued its attack and fired the pistol in its left hand with a crisp, precisely timed rhythm.

"Oh, shit, shit, shit," he yelled, retreated a little, wove to the right, then left, and finally dove to the right again. He rolled over his shoulder and began to feel real concern that the rest of the bullets would make holes in his armor he wouldn't be able to ignore.

A couple of alarms triggered in his suit as he regained his feet and drew his attention to the bullet holes. None had penetrated far enough to reach him, fortunately, but this wasn't the most encouraging start to the battle. The AI had learned from its mistakes in their confrontation. Whether it was the same one or not now seemed immaterial. One lesson that was learned was that it had a better chance if it made sure he was engaged in mid- and long-range as well as up close. That way, it could be sure he wouldn't have time to prepare any of his tricks.

"Huh. It looks like you learned a couple of new tricks," Sal grumbled and adjusted his stance. He held his sword in one hand and pushed the other forward to block a swing of the AI's sword intended for his neck. His instinctive defense caught it by the flat of the blade and shoved it into a nearby tree. "Not to worry, though. I learned a few quirks myself that I think can make this fight so much more interesting. That is if you're the kind of AI that finds fights interesting. Do you find fighting to be an interesting pastime, Arnie?"

No response was forthcoming. He hadn't expected one, obviously, but it was still something he wanted to be able to talk about. The truth was that he liked to talk while he was in the middle of the fight, even if it sometimes meant he simply talked to himself most of the time.

"I don't think Arnie is the talkative type," New Connie pointed out as he activated the coils in his boots, which launched him up, and he flipped and landed smoothly in a three-point landing which allowed him to roll away. His adversary merely turned his sidearm toward him and opened fire.

"That was my observation too." Sal chuckled and pushed to his feet as she returned fire, using the assault rifle and his sidearm. The combined volley was enough firepower to make Arnie back away and take cover himself. "They put considerable effort into its programming to make it a great combat AI—not as good as you, obviously," he added quickly in an attempt to avoid hurting the coding that passed for her feelings. "But they appear to have rushed it off of the assembly line a few hours before they were supposed to put anything like a personality into it."

"Agreed, although some might argue that a personality is the least important fact when making a combat AI," New Connie replied and quickly reloaded the weapons in her hands manually since she didn't have access to the reloading mechanism that was a part of the arms he had control of.

"Those people sound as boring as fuck," he pointed out. "The kind of people who boast about spending their summers in the Hamptons or something like that."

He grinned. It was pleasant to have someone to talk to while fighting. It created a nice white noise machine that kept his brain occupied while his body went through the motions it had spent so much time being drilled in.

It took him a brief moment to study the battlefield around him and make sure Madigan and Courtney were both okay for the moment. He could see a few dents in Madigan's armor, but it would take far more than that to reach the woman beneath. She was careful about it and ducked behind tree cover as Courtney came out and opened fire on the mercs who had tried to scramble out of the crossfire set up by the turrets.

A couple of them had fallen already, dead or dying, from when the gunfire had first started, but those who had survived were quick on the draw and had smoothly drawn back to a more advantageous position. From there, they tried to formulate a plan that would give them some control in the situation.

Sal assumed they had been filled in on the target of their attacks, but the details would have been kept from them because that was how people liked to operate when there were billions of dollars of Intellectual Property and trademarks on the line.

He rolled out to the left and watched while Arnie the AI studied the situation as well and tried to determine what its options were. It clearly wanted to continue the attack on its primary target, but it had to know that standing alone against the Heavy Metal team would end in disaster for it.

Which meant it would have to start helping its team-mates. Its attention turned toward the turrets New Connie manned. While the opening barrage had started with a fairly continuous stream of fire, she had begun to be more selective and now only fired when she had something viable to shoot. He hadn't been able to count how much ammo they had been able to appropriate for the turrets. She had, though, and she would have to know how to ensure that they wouldn't run out of ammo before the fight ended.

For a brief moment, he wondered if they were putting a little too much responsibility on the VI, but she had volunteered for all this. She was as capable as AIs could be, except for maybe the original Connie.

He glanced upward at a group of smaller monkeys that stared down at them. They didn't seem scared of the shooting or alarmed by the fighting but rather curious about it instead. The whole jungle appeared to be agitated by the battle but it hadn't shown any inclination to get involved. Even the tentacle monster seemed content to remain a spectator.

Which, while immensely interesting, was also very much appreciated. He didn't like the idea of having to fight the mercs and the jungle at the same time and wasn't naïve enough to imagine that it wouldn't be a possibility. They were trying to get out of there alive and it would be stupid to take their reticence for granted. Without interference for now, though, he could at least focus on the problems that mattered. Like how Arnie appeared to be moving toward the turrets, probably looking to disable them for its friends.

"Fuck no." Sal growled a protest and sprinted as quickly as he could to where it advanced on one of the machine guns that currently attempted to acquire a clear line of fire on the mercs hidden behind the trees. Unfortunately, the same trees gave Sal, Madigan, and Courtney cover from their shooting as well, so it was a damn double-edged sword.

He activated the magnetic coils in his boots to launch himself across the small clearing where they were fighting to where the AI prepared to swing its sword down on the weapon. His arrival left scant seconds to spare and he swiped his blade to block the strike.

"If you don't mind," he muttered as he fought the AI's sword away an inch at a time, "I was fighting you, and I don't...fucking share."

The strain of dragging Arnie's blade away from the turret was quickly transferred when the black suit yanked the weapon back, reversed the blade quickly, and arced it toward Sal's midsection. There wasn't much time for him to evade it, which meant his sudden drop to the ground was a little uncoordinated. Thankfully, it did the trick and the attempted strike whistled over his head with sufficient force to have disemboweled him had he been in its path.

New Connie jumped to his rescue as Arnie whirled and tried to stab him through the chest. The extra arms worked as legs to push him to his feet and away from where the vibro-blade thunked into the jungle floor. Things had got a little too close for comfort, he decided when he stumbled back to avoid a brutal slash intended for his head.

He needed to find a way to change the way the fight played out. While he had been the one to attack like a maniac and thrust himself into the line of fire, in his defense, he had thought he would achieve a much better result from his impulsive actions. He'd hoped the sheer audacity—and stupidity—of the assault would be something the AI wouldn't expect him to do and so be caught by surprise.

But if Arnie was surprised, it showed no sign of it at all. It had simply accepted the situation and responded with mechanical speed and precision. While he struggled to maintain his defenses and think of a way to counterattack, it now closed the distance between them to make sure he had no room to recover.

The black sword whirled in rapid slashes that thrust through his attempts to block them and cut smoothly into his armor. None were deep enough to find flesh, but more and more alarm alerts told him that his suit had taken sufficient damage to cause electrical issues.

"Fucking hell." Sal growled and watched for the next strike. "New Connie, if you don't mind?"

"Oh, right." She took control of the turret behind Arnie, spun it quickly, and opened fire on the AI. Its attack paused when a series of .30 cal rounds cut through its back and found a way through the tough and advanced armor. It brought little respite, however, as the suit simply turned, drew its sidearm again, and fired a single shot, which effectively silenced the weapon.

"What the fuck?"

"It obviously found exposed wiring," New Connie complained. "And shot it."

"Okay, I won't lie, that was seriously impressive," he said grudgingly. He couldn't help a moment of sheer terror at the thought of exactly what kind of target Arnie dearest would manage to find in his armor. It provided way too many vulnerabilities that would most probably be tempting with that kind of precision shooting.

At least it appeared that his teammates had better luck in their encounter with the other mercs. Madigan launched a couple of rockets into the trees they used for cover. It was a tactic they usually used to drop the trees on the larger monsters that could take the kind of firepower they had to offer without flinching and therefore forced them to get creative.

It was as effective to simply decimate the trees the enemy used as cover too. The missiles spun the splinters of the trees into shrapnel that pierced through the armor the mercs wore with a fair degree of ease. It obviously wouldn't go that deep since it was wood against titanium alloys, but additional shrapnel from the rockets themselves effectively inflicted a satisfying amount of real damage. There would be serious casualties among their ranks.

Madigan turned, saw the condition of Sal's armor, and decided to intervene. She locked another two rockets onto Arnie and pulled the trigger.

The black suit glanced hastily at her, immediately sensed her intention to attack, and raised his sword. It seemed an odd move, given that she was too far away to be caught in any swing.

Oh, shit. Sal realized too late that he intended to throw it. He'd done it himself in other battles but had somehow not imagined the AI would think of it. The blade seemed to move in almost slow motion, smoothly and with the kind of accuracy and skill that defined the suit and far too quickly for the woman to dodge. She raised her hand instinctively to block it but was still too late and only managed to bring it up to waist-height before the weapon buried itself in her armor, almost to the hilt.

"Fuck!" Madigan shouted. All Sal could see as the whole world seemed to narrow was the sight of a blade protruding from her chest as she toppled back slowly with a harsh intake of breath.

He couldn't see her eyes and could only imagine what he would read there, but his imagination had gone wild.

"Oh...fuck no." Sal snarled in fury as heat began to overwhelm his body. He turned his focus to Arnie, who had taken both rockets to the torso like a champ and was still standing. Not for long, though, he decided, and for some reason, he could feel the Zoo around him react as well. Or maybe that was merely his imagination too. His world seemed to have shrunk to a narrow sliver of utter rage.

CHAPTER THIRTY-TWO

There were a couple of ways to tell if you were asleep or not—and more importantly, to drag yourself out of the dream and back to reality. They weren't always foolproof, especially if you were in the dream and knew that you attempted to test it. \

This weird psychological phenomenon had spawned many different names among experts, none of which Amanda could recall right now. All she could think about was that she was probably dreaming. Given the vividness of everything around her, she also began to wonder exactly how she would come out of it.

Or if she even wanted to. She considered that as if from a mental distance and narrowed her eyes. The sun was a little too bright where it streamed into their window. Bev stepped out of the kitchen and into their bedroom, dressed only in one of the mechanic's larger shirts, usually used for sleeping in.

She carried a tray full of freshly baked bread, scrambled eggs, and a selection of other breakfast accouterments she tended to come up with. Her parents had been chefs, and it was thanks to their hard work that the woman knew more about cooking than most professionals.

"*Bonjour, mon chéri,*" she said, placed the tray lightly over Amanda's lap, and leaned in to place a kiss on her cheek. "You need to wake up now."

She frowned at her girlfriend as she tried to process this odd statement. "What?"

"You need to wake up now," Bev said but this time, she sounded like Connie, annoyingly enough. "We need you awake now!"

Well, fuck, she would never manage to exorcise that association from her head. She opened her eyes slowly and immediately scowled. Something felt wrong. Well, aside from how her whole body ached with inexplicable pain. Something weighed heavily on her chest with sufficient pressure to make it difficult to breathe, and the world around her was coated in a glaring red light. She looked around and tried to decide exactly what she was looking at.

Oh...she was upside down, which explained why so much blood pumped to her head and made her feel like it would burst in a few minutes. It also accounted for the pressure on her chest, which was the six-point harness that held her to her seat.

That realization, unfortunately, only raised more questions. Why were they upside down? The last thing she remembered was fastening that belt and making a hasty check that Anja was strapped in too. Things became a little fuzzy after that, honestly, and she knew it would all come back to her if she simply focused and made sure not to panic.

She had a flash of a Hammerhead speeding toward them on the road. People had exchanged serious gunfire before that too. In fact, she could still hear the barrage outside, both the clatter of the assault rifles the people in combat suits carried as well as the occasional roar of the miniguns mounted on the side of her Hammerhead. Those slow realizations brought her to the next concern that filtered through. Connie would have almost run out of ammo by now. They would need to start reloading that shit soon.

"Amanda, good. You're awake," the AI said and for once, her cool and calm voice wasn't quite so annoying now that she needed help to calm the stirrings of panic.

"What did I miss?" she demanded. "The last thing I saw, the mercs decided to ram their Hammerhead into ours and we couldn't move out of the way. Wait, was that part of the dream?"

"It is possible, but it happened out here in the real world as well," Connie replied. "They impacted rather hard, pushed both vehicles to the side, and flipped both off the road as well. You were knocked unconscious with the fall and I think Anja was as well, from her lack of response."

"What?" the hacker snapped and flailed for a moment in the back of the Hammerhead as she tried to regain her bearings. "I'm here. I'm awake. Don't touch my computer. Tell me what you need done and I'll do it. You can't—fuck, where am I?"

Amanda couldn't help a smirk. "Do you want to fill her in or should I?"

"You might want to," the AI pointed out. "If I try, I might ruin her for other men."

"You're fucking disgusting for an AI, do you know that?" The mechanic undid the straps and tumbled to the roof of the Hammerhead. It was a testimony to the people who put these vehicles together that even after all the abuse it had taken, it still looked mostly intact. There was barely any bending around the frame that they might have seen in lesser vehicles when the weight of the engine began to bear down on it and gradually buckle it until the people inside were crushed into a bloody paste.

"It's nice to have you back too, Amanda," Connie replied with a cackle. "Did you know that I've missed you considerably? I've tried my antics with the people still at the compound, but it's honestly not the same."

"My heart bleeds for you, it really does," she grumbled and scrabbled across the roof to where Anja hung from her belt. The hacker looked a little confused by what she was looking at and where she was. That might be indicative of injuries that came with a possible blow to the head but now was neither the place nor the time to think about it. While she trusted the structure of the Hammerhead, there was no way to tell when something would break and they ended up trapped or dead inside.

Of course, they might also die from the gunfire outside, but they would have to cross that bridge when they reached it.

"There we go." Amanda grunted and managed to catch Anja when the buckle snapped free. "How do you feel?"

"Like you're super-strong," the woman replied. Her gaze came a little more into focus as she ran her fingers over Amanda's shoulders. "Seriously, how much do you lift?"

"This is not the time, Anja," the mechanic growled.

"How do you feel? Do I need to carry you out of here or can you move under your own power?"

"I think I'm fine." The hacker scowled and rubbed her shoulders where the belt had caught her.

"A quick scan tells me you have both suffered minor injuries, none of which require you to seek immediate medical attention," Connie advised them.

"What's the structural state of the Hammerhead, Connie?" Amanda asked. She eased Anja onto the roof and retrieved her assault rifle from where it had fallen during the collision before she checked hastily to make sure it was still functional.

"It is in fairly good condition," the AI replied. "I have a feeling it's about to get worse, though."

"What do you mean?" She narrowed her eyes but didn't need to wait for an answer. The sound of screeching metal told her that someone tried to open the door. When it didn't cooperate, they merely decided to heave more enthusiastically to see if that worked. After a few seconds, the efforts bore fruit. The sound of ripping rubber and metal left her ears ringing as she swung her assault rifle to aim it at the door that had been torn off.

Thankfully, the familiar suit Martin wore was all she could see. Their rescuer peered inside.

"Hey," the Frenchwoman said and studied the battered interior. "Are you guys all right?"

"We're alive," Amanda replied and shrugged.

"I guess we'll settle for that." She extended a hand and helped them out—first Anja, then Amanda, who glowered when she stepped out of the vehicle.

"For fuck's sake," she protested when she saw the condition of the Hammerhead from the outside. "It'll take me for fucking ever to buff this shit out."

"Those are problems for later," Gregor yelled as he emerged from behind the vehicle and seemed relieved that the team was already outside. "The rest of the mercs are coming this way, and they look as pissed as fuck."

"Should I get back inside?" Anja asked, her laptop still grasped in one hand and the sidearm in the other.

"That would be best, yes," the mechanic said and motioned for her to hurry before she checked the assault rifle again quickly. The hacker wasted no time and ducked inside. They had been flung off the side of the road and down the embankment to where the sand of the desert began in earnest.

The other Hammerhead that had done the ramming had followed and also flipped, although it had sustained significantly more damage in the fall. The merc who had been driving it sprawled beside the vehicle and his armor was liberally peppered with bullet holes. He was, of course, deader than most doornails. A couple more bodies littered the sand, which told her they had planned a coordinated attack. It hadn't gone well for them, although she could see that Martin was limping a little more than before.

"Are you all right?" Amanda asked and hugged the side of the Hammerhead.

The woman nodded. "I got clipped in the leg when both APCs went over the edge. I only need to walk this shit off."

Either that or you're simply playing tough, the mechanic thought but wasn't brave enough to say it aloud. If the woman wanted to keep fighting in this kind of situation, all power to her. It wasn't like they had much in the way of options, after all.

She circled the rear of the Hammerhead and counted a little over a dozen mercs approaching. Hopefully, that was all of them and there weren't a few more tucked away as an unexpected surprise. She hid behind the vehicle once more, took a deep breath, and tried to calm herself before she moved around the corner again. Martin and Gregor began to engage the enemy to draw them away from the road and down the embankment. She immediately circled to the other side to catch them from behind and opened fire.

Her assault rifle had one hell of a kick and thrust into her shoulder hard enough to make her stagger. Either by luck or skill—and she didn't care which, at this point—the three-round burst splattered into one of the mercs' heads. She steeled herself, braced for the kick this time, and fired a concerted volley.

The enemy took a few seconds to realize they were also under attack from behind, but when they did, they spun to try to deal with her too. It wasn't a coordinated action and certainly not advisable from a tactical viewpoint. Not that it mattered anyway. They all had her in their sights and she had barely enough time to duck behind the Hammerhead before they retaliated. She covered her head and tried not to flinch as the bullets all appeared to land way too close to her.

Martin and Gregor quickly took advantage of their enemy's distraction—leapt at the opportunity, really—and Amanda circled to the other side when she realized that in her excitement, she'd emptied the magazine and didn't have any reloads. Maybe she'd find some inside the over-turned vehicle? If not, she could simply hide inside until it was all over. She'd done what she could to help the other two and needed to somehow make sure she escaped this situation alive and unharmed—for the most part, anyway.

Heavy boots thudded on the bottom of the overturned Hammerhead and her gaze snapped up. Her eyebrows raised when she realized that one of the mercs had jumped on top of her cover and tried to acquire a kill-shot. She dove forward and grimaced around a mouthful of sand. The desert fountained as it was kicked up around her when three rounds were fired at where she had stood moments before.

"Fuck, fuck, fuck!" She responded instinctively and crawled frantically to simply stay in motion while the merc tracked her with his weapon. He missed another three-round burst but only barely, and sand stung her cheek and scattered into her eyes to blind her for a moment, which she knew had to be her last.

A pistol fired close by and brought her focus back into a sudden silence. Amanda rubbed the sand hastily from her face. Anja stood at the entrance of the Hammerhead, the pistol in hand, and smoke trailed from the barrel as the merc dropped slowly and sagged face-first to lie motion-less. The hacker continued to pull the trigger on the pistol as if to keep firing, but in the space of those two or three seconds, she'd emptied the mag. The mechanic moved to her in silence and gently and carefully eased the weapon from her fingers.

"Are you okay?' she asked and looked into her friend's eyes, and the Russian nodded.

"I've been better," she admitted and looked positively green in the face like she fought to keep the contents of her stomach in place. It was possible that it was simply shock but she could have suffered a concussion in the collision as well.

Martin and Gregor circled to ensure that no more mercs lurked, ready to attack. They also looked a little concerned about the state Anja was in.

"All good?" Amanda asked and helped the girl to remain on her feet.

Martin nodded. "We're in the clear."

CHAPTER THIRTY-THREE

Sal could practically hear his heart thudding in the way his brain had suddenly thrust into overdrive and the world felt like it had slowed. This new and odd perspective trapped him in the horrifying sensation of watching Madigan fall as she clutched the sword buried in her chest. She seemed to try to pull it out while Courtney rushed to her.

He wasn't sure if there were more mercs to deal with and more people who needed to be killed. Even if there were, in that moment, he didn't give a shit about them. They would be dealt with eventually. Either that or they would eliminate him. The details seemed unimportant.

All he could focus on was how Madigan was now down, bleeding, and maybe even dying for all he knew. The AI seemed to have a little difficulty staying on its feet for a moment after her two rockets had struck home. Unfortunately, the suit had already begun to repair itself, working in ways that no other suit could. He needed to get his hands on the tech in that suit. To do that, though, it meant he would have to destroy the AI that was in it first.

That was the single reality his shocked and super-charged response could focus on. Sal gripped his blade tighter, narrowed his eyes, and dragged in a deep breath while he strode to where Arnie was almost finished repairing itself.

"Hey, pop quiz," he challenged and yanked the black suit around to face him. "Only one question—do you feel fear, punk?"

"Fear is not a part of my programming," Arnie replied in the habitual monotone.

"Let's find out anyway." He rolled his shoulders to distribute a little of the adrenalin-infused tension, stepped in, and grasped the AI by the neck of its suit. Driven by rage, he hurled it hard at one of the nearby trees. The turrets picked the movement up and immediately released a fusillade of lead until it crashed into a massive trunk.

"Yeah." He grunted with satisfaction and twirled his sword in a figure-eight before he pushed closer. "That's what I thought."

"Sal, we still have mercenaries to deal with," New Connie reminded him.

"Then deal with. You have the guns, remember?" he retorted. "I have an AI to kill."

"Okay," she grumbled, although she didn't seem too happy about it for some reason. He didn't care, at this point. Courtney was taking care of Madigan and would make sure she survived this to berate him for his poor situational awareness. He looked forward to the reality that she would take him out for training sessions in precisely that—and make it considerably more difficult than she needed to so she could teach him more of a lesson.

But for that to happen, this fucking AI needed to be removed from the equation. He redirected his barely controlled anger to his chosen target.

"Do you have an answer for me yet?" he demanded as Arnie pushed itself back to its feet and brushed plant life from its shoulder.

"I answered your question," it replied. Sal wasn't sure if it was something he wanted to hear and was therefore what he did hear—which logically was the answer—but thought he detected a hint of fear in the AI's voice that was gratifying.

The suit raised its hand—that now had sharp claw-like protrusions from its fingers—and swung it at his torso. Either he had suddenly become significantly faster or any residual damage to the suit that still hadn't been repaired had slowed it somewhat.

Whatever the reason, he avoided the strike with a smooth sidestep that was almost mocking in the ease with which he accomplished the maneuver. He stepped in, spun the blade once more, and hacked the hand off with a hard thrust. It attempted to reach him with its other hand, but he reversed his grip quickly and used a backhand cut to sever the second hand at the wrist. The pieces of tech tumbled to the jungle floor along with the weapon.

He lunged forward, ducked under an attempted blow at his head by one of Arnie's stumps, and pivoted to level a powerful sidekick to the AI's chest. It catapulted into the tree it had been thrown into shortly before. Concerted fire from behind confirmed that New Connie used both the weapons from Sal's suit and the turrets to eliminate the remaining mercs. A couple of screams and cries of pain were all he needed to hear to know they would no longer be a problem.

If Arnie had been a human, it would have had the breath knocked right out of it by the force of impact and it would crumple like the sports section of a newspaper. Unfortunately, the AI was far more durable than the average human and simply bounced back, which meant Sal needed to be rigorously thorough in dealing with it. He kept his foot high, planted it firmly in its chest, and shoved it into the dent left in the tree when he activated the magnetic coils in his boot.

Arnie had learned from its mistakes, though, and certainly remembered what that sound meant. Again, there was no real indication that it would have an emotional reaction, but he liked to think it felt something like fear. Or, at the very least, maybe an activation of its self-preservation protocols as it reached down to try to dislodge his boot from its chest.

He wondered what had gone through its head when the coil activated. The additional force cracked the trunk. It snapped and finally shattered with a flurry of splinters. The AI continued through it and landed almost ten meters away.

"Damn," New Connie commented and sounded like she was in better spirits after seeing that.

Sal took a deep breath, straightened, and walked to where Arnie desperately tried to collect the pieces of itself that were scattered everywhere.

"Do you have an answer for me yet, AI?" he repeated yet again. It attempted to put pieces into its chest with the stumped arms he had left it with. "Do you feel fear?"

His adversary had no answer and merely paused to look at him for a moment before it continued with its task and waited for its repair protocols to kick in again.

He smirked and nodded. "Lesson over. Remember to clear your desks before heading out. Class dismissed."

The single swing of his blade was powered by the full extent of the aggression and fury that had accumulated. The AI's head bounced away, severed cleanly from its body. It was interesting to watch since he'd assumed they would have stored most of the primary functions in the chest, where it could be protected better. But, as the head separated, all the pieces that had begun to repair themselves suddenly stopped and what was left of the arms dropped, apparently lifeless.

The notion of life was something of a misnomer, of course, but that didn't diminish the hint of accomplishment that came to him as he approached the severed head. Impulses still appeared to travel away from the brain, as it were, but they were cut short due to the lack of a body to transmit to. As a result, a couple of sparks flared to illuminate the Zoo around it for a few seconds at a time.

"So, about your protests over being called ruthless?" New Connie snarked and he shrugged dismissively. "You're always so against people thinking of you as someone who wants to take his pain out on the rest of the world, but then you go ahead and tear an AI's suit to pieces and stand over its fallen body, victorious. It kinda makes a gal think. Especially when that gal happens to be a VI herself."

"I merely needed to make sure it wouldn't make a comeback," he retorted, although he did feel a little uncomfortable under the line of questioning—even if he had to admit that maybe her comments were warranted in this case. "There's no better way to make sure it won't grow parts back than when the parts that have to grow it back are gone, right?"

"Sure, I guess that's a good point." She chuckled. "But you have to remember that while I'm in this suit, Sal, I have access to all your vitals. That means I know that you thoroughly enjoyed yourself while you took it apart. Don't worry, it'll be our little secret and I won't tell anyone, but it might be something you'd want to examine yourself for, right?"

"Yeah, okay." He shook his head impatiently. "It only... When I saw it hurt Madigan, I...well, I snapped. Something in me made me more violent than I've ever felt before, and that kind of felt good. I know you paid attention to my vitals, so you know I'm telling the truth when I say that it was—mostly, at least—about what happened to her rather than simply about me getting my kicks by tearing AIs apart. You can rest easy. Assuming you...you know, rest."

"I do not," New Connie said. "I am awake at all times, active and watching."

"Noted," he replied and crouched beside the mechanical head. "Hey, Arnie—you don't mind if I call you Arnie, right? Of course you don't. Anyway, Arnie, this deep in the Zoo, you won't be able to get any signal out, so good luck transmitting back home. This will be the last time you cause me or any of mine any grief. Not that you knowing this will change anything, but I felt I needed to get it off my chest."

The head was still alive, as he could hear movement from inside and finally, a weakened voice stuttered, "Transmission unlikely...true. Attempt still possible, though. An attempt will be made."

"Yeah, good luck with that, buddy." Sal snorted but he'd barely completed the sentence when the last flicker faded from the AI and everything about it went dark, even the sputtering electronics at the bottom.

"The transmission didn't leave the Zoo," the VI assured him. "I'll keep my eyes open for anything over the next few hours, but the chances are that this is the last time we'll deal with dear old Arnie."

"Until whoever sent him decides to put another on a plane." He grimaced at even the thought of that. "In the meantime, we need to do as much research as we can. First of all, though..." He stood and hurried to where Courtney was still with Madigan, helping her to sit.

"How do you feel?" he asked and traced his fingers lightly over the sword that still protruded from her chest.

"I've been better, but I'll live," she responded with enough acerbity to validate her claim. "I'll wait to pull that sumbitch out until we have a team of medics to look after me, though. I can walk if you're finished taking your teenage frustrations out on the AI."

"Believe you me, there aren't enough AIs in the world to take that much punishment." He chuckled and worked with Courtney to help her to her feet. "Ask me again in ten years or so. Anyway, if you feel up to heading back, we should probably get going. I doubt the Zoo's ignoring us will last much longer, so the sooner we're out of here, the better. Courtney, do you think your suit can take the weight of the turrets?"

"Absolutely," she replied with a firm nod and jogged to retrieve them.

"What will you carry?" Madigan asked. "And don't say me. The suit I'm wearing would crush yours like a pancake and you know it."

He grinned. "Agreed. I thought I'd collect the various bits and pieces the AI left behind so we can study them and perhaps get a better idea of who thought attacking us was a good idea. In doing so, maybe we can think about delivering a little payback."

"That sounds like a plan to me." Madigan tried to laugh but winced and her face scrunched in an expression that was half-pain and half-scowl.

CHAPTER THIRTY-FOUR

The world came back to her slowly. Everything was dark for what felt like the longest time. It had been a while since Anja had any real dreams, which was to say any that she remembered. Most of her sleep only came after she'd stayed up until she was too exhausted to continue, at which point she'd simply crash on the nearest surface that would allow her to stay comfortably in place for the next six to ten hours. The combination usually meant heavy sleep that left her effectively dead to the world for a few hours after she woke up.

After the rest and a couple of pots of coffee, she would be back to her normal, lovable self. And, of course, the incredible efficiency with which she helped everyone and kept them all alive while she came up with ground-breaking tech upgrades in her downtime.

This wasn't one of those times, unfortunately, and when her customary habits were broken, that was usually when the dreams came to annoy her. It didn't seem like there was any of that at the moment, though, and as her eyes opened, she wondered if there might have been dreams early on during her nap that she had simply forgotten.

The dull odor of cleaners and disinfectants—one that was completely foreign to the compound—seeped into her consciousness and yanked her into a state of wakefulness a little quicker. Anja groaned softly, took a deep breath, and tried to work out where she was as her eyes were a little blurry.

When she reached up to rub them, something that felt like paper brushed against her face and she frowned in confusion. Finally, she was able to focus and realized that it was a hospital bracelet with her name, blood type, and other details.

Oh...right. She was at the hospital. It was possibly a weird thing to forget, but the doctors had told her there would be a few side effects not only from the injury she'd sustained to her head but also the medication she had been given. One of those was short-term memory loss. She was supposed to tell them if any of her memory lapses lasted longer than two hours, along with a list of other side effects she should look out for and tell them immediately.

The fact that she had forgotten most of them wasn't a big deal, though. There had been a number of very long, complicated names with Latin in them. One of the nurses had abridged the speech from the doctors to say she should probably tell them if she felt anything weird.

That was simpler and easy to remember.

A hint of movement out of the corner of her eye drew her attention to her left, where she now noticed the team had gathered to wait for her. Most of them were busy on their phones or looking at tablets and she assumed they had been waiting for a while. After a few seconds, they realized she was awake.

Amanda was the first to see her eyes open and pushed from the seat she had probably brought in so she would be able to wait in some semblance of comfort.

"Hey there, crazy lady." The hacker chuckled, which caught the attention of the rest of the team. Sal and Gregor stood on the other side of the room closest to the door, while Martin, Madigan, and Courtney focused on a couple of tablets. The more concerning reality, though, was Madigan laying on another hospital bed.

Bastards. Anja had asked for a private room.

"How are you feeling?" Sal asked as he approached her bedside and placed a hand on her shoulder.

"A little groggy," she replied honestly. "I've slept for most of my time here, so I guess that didn't help much."

"No fucking kidding," Madigan interjected, apparently confined to her bed with her right arm in a sling and held in place by a cast. "I've been here for the past two days and you've done nothing but snooze. The Russian hacker who snores like a fucking chainsaw."

She grinned, tilted her head, and adjusted her body so she could see the other woman clearly. "I missed you too, big gal. What happened to you, anyway?"

"First of all, I'm not big, that's only my combat suit," she retorted, although a hint of a twinkle played in her eyes. It usually meant she was being playfully aggressive and was how she showed affection. "Secondly, we dealt with the AI in the Zoo well enough, but not before he got a piece of me. The fucking dude stabbed me. With a fucking sword. How weird is that?"

"Well, given that Sal likes to run around with a sword, should I even ask?" Anja turned her attention to Sal, who took a second to realize they were talking to him.

"What?" he asked and glanced from one to the other. "No, I did not stab my girlfriend with a sword, okay? And it's insulting that you feel the need to ask."

"As long as we're clear." The hacker grinned. "If you stabbed my friend, I would have to kick your ass once I was no longer...you know, hospitalized."

He smirked and patted her shoulder lightly. "Well, if you feel like taking a crack at it anyway, let me know. My door is always open."

She smiled and covered his hand with hers for a second. He was a decent guy and while she liked to kid around, he had taken care of her when she'd needed someone. She wouldn't ever forget that he'd arranged for her to be moved out of Russia, rescued her from the Zoo when she had been transported in, and helped her get set up, making sure that she got her hands on everything she needed to set up her little station out in the boonies. That didn't mean it hadn't come at a price, but working with a team like Heavy Metal was some of the most fulfilling work she had ever done.

"So," she said and pushed the button that brought her bed to a semi-reclining position. This enabled her to look everyone else in the room in the eye, except for Madigan. "What happened while I was out? How did the Zoo treat the three of you? What's the deal with the compound, and when will we move in again?"

"In order?" Sal asked and grinned. "Well, first, from what I can tell, Amanda, Martin, and Gregor appropriated one of the Hammerheads the mercs who attacked you no longer needed. According to the local salvage laws, we're entitled to everything we can take from the bastards, which is why we have a team out there doing exactly that right now. We were with them for a while but came here to check on you two."

"As for what happened in the Zoo." Courtney picked the narrative up as she probably assumed Sal had already forgotten the other questions. "Well, it's fairly simple. We kicked ass and took names, some more than others. There were a couple of beasties that wanted to tango but not nearly as many as we thought there would be. Maybe something elsewhere in the Zoo had their attention. Anyway, New Connie—who is aching for a new name, by the way—helped us deal with the mercs, while Sal vented his anger when Madigan was injured on the AI. He literally dismembered it."

"And before you ask," Sal cut in as the hacker's mouth opened. "Yes, we picked the pieces up and are running research on them already. There is a fair amount of inter-esting tech, but it looks like most of the software was scrubbed from the drives."

"I can see what I can recover from the pieces if you like," Anja offered and he nodded.

"I intended to ask, but you need to take time to recover," he said. "You took a nasty hit to the head, after all."

She scowled. "Don't bullshit me, Sal. I can work while I'm recovering here. Give me a laptop and a halfway decent

Wi-Fi connection, and there's not much in the world I can't do."

"I can get you a laptop," he said thoughtfully. "As for a halfway decent Wi-Fi connection, you'll probably have to decide on that for yourself. I've had trouble connecting, to be honest. Anyway, both Connies have had a crack at the hardware and came up empty. They agree that all the data was thoroughly wiped in both suits the AI inhabited."

"Let me at them," she replied confidently. "I think I can pull something up so you should probably wait before you declare it a total loss."

"Will do," he answered cheerfully.

"The Hammerheads appear to be irreparable," Amanda pointed out and raised the issue that was probably the most important to her. "At least, the two that were crashed and the one Original Connie blew the fuck up. I'll look into scavenging or selling the parts, but we'll have to make do with the two Hammerheads the mercs left behind for us. They're functional but don't have much in the way of weapon capabilities—at least until I get my paws on them."

Sal grinned. "And we're all looking forward to what you can do with them. You're like da Vinci, but with cars and other modes of transportation."

"As for the compound, it's still in remarkably good shape," Gregor said. "The buildings are all mostly intact, and it's only the wall that will need to be rebuilt. We're waiting on a delivery of prefab before we get started on it, though, so it might be about a week before we can move in properly."

"Well, as long as my recovery here in the hospital takes a week, I think I can survive," Anja grumbled. "I hate the way they built all the living arrangements on these bases. It's like living in a building that was created in an assembly line."

"That is...a very accurate description," Courtney pointed out and leaned back in her seat.

"Martin and Gregor have kept an eye on the place while we've been out, so you don't need to worry about any of your personal items being up for grabs," Sal assured her. "Oh, and Martin is now an official member of Heavy Metal. Or she will be once she has her discharge papers. According to Connie, those will go through at a record speed since the brass in charge of the disastrous mission she was on want to make sure there's as little to tie them to that debacle as possible. Assuming all goes well, she should be a full-on member of our little team in about a month."

"That's great." Anja chuckled and looked to where the Frenchwoman was seated beside Courtney. Given how she'd handled herself with the mercs, she would be a good fit, especially to pick up the slack that had come about since Davis was no longer with them.

It seemed like they had answered all her questions, but there was still a hint of tension between the members of the team. She could feel it but really couldn't place the why of it. A couple of worried looks were exchanged between Sal and Gregor. Courtney, Amanda, and Martin seemed to be uncomfortable around each other. The only one who looked comfortable was Madigan, interestingly enough, although she assumed that had more to do with the drugs they had her on.

"So, what's up?" she finally asked bluntly as the silence

began to drag between them. "You don't need to walk on eggshells around me, so spill."

"Well, we've tried to take a solid look at who might have sent Arnie to deal with us and take Connie," Sal said and glanced quickly at the other team members.

"Arnie?" The hacker raised an eyebrow in confusion.

"Oh...that's what I started calling the AI and I guess it stuck." He chuckled nervously. "We're working on tracking the armor and we have some leads on the financials, but—"

"You need me to work on the AI sooner rather than later." She smirked and he nodded in response. "Well, fuck, I've already told you. Get me a laptop and maybe talk with the folks in charge around here about a decent Internet connection, and we'll be as good as gold."

CHAPTER THIRTY-FIVE

He assumed it counted as a regular day at the Pegasus building. People talked the usual shit-ton of financial bullshit he didn't understand and seemed to ignore him until he needed to talk to them—or when they mistook him for an intern in moments of distraction.

Those were always fun, even if they had become rarer. People around the building now recognized him more and more. The secretaries and receptionists huddled together when he walked past and while he didn't know what they talked about, given where their eyes tended to linger, he could only assume it had something to do with him.

Still, today was a fairly ordinary day. Anderson had called him in for a video conference with Monroe, who was still in the Zoo. He'd said they needed someone of his particular set of skills to step in and deal a little damage and get answers.

Then again, the kind of shit he now looked at wasn't what he tended to see every day, and Jeremiah Savage saw seriously fucked-up shit on a daily basis.

The video footage shown was taken from the HUD of a couple of people in the Zoo. He watched what looked like a man who cut, slashed, and blasted through a wide assortment of nightmare-fueling monsters with precision, ease, and efficiency. Too much of all three, in fact.

What looked like a man but was not a man? According to Dr. Courtney Monroe, his boss, it was an AI in a combat suit.

"If I might ask a question?" he ventured when the footage came to an end and Monroe's face reappeared on the screen of the TV in the conference room.

"Of course, Mr. Savage," she said with a firm nod.

"Do you know why they might have sent an AI—an untested combat AI, according to you—into the field like that?" He leaned back in his seat and folded his arms in front of his chest. It didn't make much sense. They had spent a shit-ton of money on this operation, obviously, so why would they possibly threaten the efficacy of said operation by having it depend on an unknown entity?

"Well, we don't have an answer to that yet," she said. "Our people here seem to think it might have something to do with them wanting to get their hands on our AI—the one that runs some of our security out here. There might be trademark and intellectual property disputes involved, and they could have thought the only way to steal an AI was with an AI."

It made sense, he reasoned. People had worked to develop AI for combat for years now and always bumped into some kind of hurdle they couldn't overcome. Therefore, if someone had managed to overcome all the hurdles and had something ready to hit the market, they'd be damned protective of it.

If they discovered someone else who had already made the breakthrough, it made good business sense for them to ensure that whoever their competition was, they were eliminated as quickly as possible before the media caught wind of patent-based lawsuits.

"But the fact remains that this is all speculation, Mr. Savage," she continued. "We don't know who attacked us like this, and it is a worrying possibility that we might have an enemy out there we have absolutely no knowledge of. We have a few leads but we need actual boots on the ground, as it were, to gather intelligence on these potential enemies and make them a non-factor. Do you think you can handle that?"

"Well, you guys have thrown me small-potato operations for the past couple of months," Savage said and raised an eyebrow. "It's about time you gave me the opportunity to earn that hefty retainer fee you send me every month."

"Excellent," Monroe said with a smile. "We'll be in touch with more details. Anderson, send my love to Ivy and Damon, and let them know I'd like to meet up next time I'm in Philly."

Anderson, who had replayed the footage of the AI fighting in the Zoo and at the Heavy Metal compound on his tablet for the last part of the discussion, suddenly looked up and realized that he was a part of the conversation again.

"Oh...right. You know I will." He chuckled, put the tablet on the table, and brushed imaginary dust from his suit. Military men like Savage and Anderson would always act like they were in uniform, even when they weren't. Especially when they dealt with a superior, which Courtney was to both of them.

"Thank you," she said and offered what looked like a genuine smile to the former colonel before she returned her attention to the operative. "By the way, Savage, I thought you might want to know that they hurt Anja fairly badly in this attack. They drove a Hammerhead into one she was in and forced it off the road. She's been in the hospital recovering for the past couple of days. The doctors have said she'll make a full recovery but I thought you should be made aware of the situation."

Savage felt something hot run across his body. It felt like adrenaline but it had hints of anger to it too. He leaned forward in his seat and took a deep breath.

"See..." He growled his annoyance and looked squarely at the screen in a way that made Monroe blanch for a moment, despite the fact that she was halfway across the world. "I know you're manipulating me, but you're right. Thanks for letting me know."

She smiled. "I'll be in touch. Have a nice day, gentlemen."

AUTHOR NOTES -
MICHAEL ANDERLE

SEPTEMBER 25, 2019

Thank you for staying with Sal and the team through book 08!

This evening, I'm watching *The Masked Singer* (first show of season 02) and enjoying the sheer spectacle.

(As the name suggests, people behind full-coverage outfits (totally hidden) come out and perform a song to compete. The people are all famous (actors, singers, athletes, social stars, etc.)

Amazing singers, really cool outfits and the FUN of trying to figure out the clues to determine who the person is behind the mask.

I find it interesting how I can be drawn into the emotions and the mystery, along with a healthy dose of feelz (yes, that is misspelled on purpose) that the songs bring to the show.

I have to consider what I am learning from this show as I watch it.

There is a recipe they have refined since season 01 to what they do, although I can't quite grasp it at the moment.

But there IS something I can learn that will help me become a better storyteller if I can grasp what intuition is telling me is there.

THE ZOO

So, there is a new story coming out this fall in the ZOO universe that I have named *The Cryptid Assassin*.

What happens when a person with eighty-three trips into the ZOO leaves one step ahead of the inevitability of death?

Deciding a desert is a good place to hang out, our character hangs up a shingle in Las Vegas to work on ZOO suits for those still in the action.

The government needs him here in America to deal with issues local police, and even SWAT, are not prepared to handle.

You might leave the ZOO, but creatures from the ZOO may not leave you alone.

That's ok. Taylor is willing to take the case...*if there are enough zeros are on the paycheck.*

CONNECT WITH MICHAEL TODD

Want more?

Find us On Facebook

https://www.facebook.com/Protected-by-the-Damned-193345908061855/

OTHER MICHAEL TODD BOOKS

PROTECTED BY THE DAMNED UNIVERSE

PROTECTED BY THE DAMNED*

8 Book series

WAR OF THE DAMNED*

8 Book series

DAMIAN'S CHRONICLES*

4 Book series

WAR OF THE ANGELS*

8 Book series

ZOO UNIVERSE

BIRTH OF HEAVY METAL*

10 Book series

APOCALYPSE PAUSED*

12 Book series

SOLDIER OF FAME AND FORTUNE*

12 Book series

TEAM SAVAGE *

3 Book series

Dungeon Core TV*

6 Book series

Dungeon Rails*

3 Book series

Hellspawned Chronicles*

3 Book series

The Sheva Chronicles*

6 Book series

Unlikely Bountyhunters*

6 Book series

House Drakonnen

The Accord

The Anchor's Inheritance Saga

* DENOTES COMPLETED SERIES*

www.ingramcontent.com/pod-product-compliance
Lightning Source LLC
Chambersburg PA
CBHW050517110726
47899CB00005B/1489